Fool Me Once

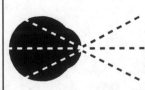

This Large Print Book carries the
Seal of Approval of N.A.V.H.

A TAROT MYSTERY

FOOL ME ONCE

STEVE HOCKENSMITH
WITH LISA FALCO

THORNDIKE PRESS
A part of Gale, Cengage Learning

GALE
CENGAGE Learning·

Farmington Hills, Mich • San Francisco • New York • Waterville, Maine
Meriden, Conn • Mason, Ohio • Chicago

Copyright © 2015 by Steve Hockensmith with Lisa Falco.
Tarot images from Roberto de Angelis's Universal Tarot; used by
permission of Lo Scarabeo; further reproduction is prohibited
Thorndike Press, a part of Gale, Cengage Learning.

LIBRARY OF CONGRESS CATALOGING-IN-PUBLICATION DATA
Hockensmith, Steve.
Fool me once / by Steve Hockensmith with Lisa Falco. — Large print edition.
pages cm. — (Thorndike Press large print mystery) (A tarot mystery)
ISBN 978-1-4104-8424-6 (hardcover) — ISBN 1-4104-8424-6 (hardcover)
1. Large type books. I. Falco, Lisa, 1970- II. Title.
PS3608.O29F66 2016
813'.6—dc23   2015031725

Published in 2016 by arrangement with Midnight Ink, an imprint of
Llewellyn Publications Woodbury, MN 55125-2989 USA

Printed in Mexico
1 2 3 4 5 6 7 20 19 18 17 16

A12006 668392

Fool Me Once

■ ■ ■ ■

PART 1
READINGS

■ ■ ■ ■

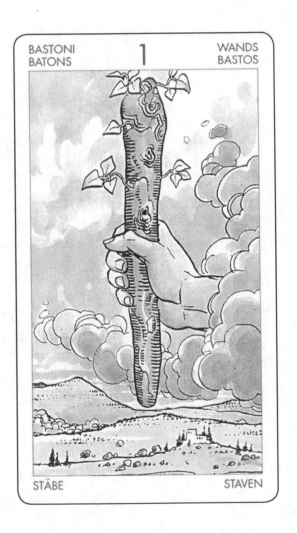

Behold: the magic cucumber! Also known as the Ace of Wands, card of bold beginnings, vitality, and adventure. The hand of Fate offers you either a walking stick for a new journey or a club for beating the stuffing out of an old problem — or it could be the kindling you've needed to start a new fire in your life. Go ahead — light that sucker up! Just be careful not to get burned.

Miss Chance, *Infinite Roads to Knowing*

Anyone who says "I'm going to kill you," Biddle used to tell me, *isn't* going to kill you. Why would they be talking to somebody who's practically dead already? The ones who really mean it just say it with their eyes, and then they do it. *Learn to recognize that look,* Biddle would say, *and you'll have the edge you need to save yourself — or at least you won't die surprised.*

So I learned the Look. The Looks, really. One white-hot with hatred, the other ice-cold and calculated.

It was the first Look I saw on Bill Riggs's face. He'd followed his wife into the White Magic Five and Dime and was reaching for her, trying to clamp onto a wrist and drag her outside again.

"You're coming home," he said to her.

And what his scowl-twisted mouth and flushed face and widened eyes said to *me* was, "I'm going to kill her. Maybe not today.

11

Maybe not tomorrow. But eventually. And I'll say I'm sorry but I won't really mean it because in my heart I'll know *it was my right.*"

So I moved one quick step to the left, and that was all it took to change everything.

I'd been walking toward the fish tank in the shop's waiting area, where customers I didn't have could flip through the latest *People Weekly* while I gave readings to other customers I didn't have. So I was near the door when Marsha Riggs burst in, with her husband — the controlling, abusive one I'd helped her walk out on two weeks before — two steps behind her.

I'd already come between Marsha and Bill figuratively. Now suddenly I was between them literally.

"Keep going, Marsha," I said as Bill came to a halt practically standing on my toes. "Don't stop. Up the hall and up the stairs. Tell Clarice that Bill's here."

Marsha didn't say anything, but I could hear her footsteps as she hurried past the store's counter and fled up the hallway beyond.

"Get back here this instant!" Bill called after her. "Don't you run away from me!"

He took a step to the left.

I blocked him.

He took a step to the right.

I blocked him again.

"I can do this dance all day, Bill," I said. "You're not getting past me."

And that's when he turned the Look on me.

"You scheming [female sexual organ]," he said. "I oughta break your neck."

"[Female sexual organs] don't have necks, Bill," I said.

"You know what I mean."

I did.

Maybe I should have felt relieved. He was saying he wanted to kill me, which meant he wouldn't — if Biddle was right.

Then again, the last time I'd seen Biddle, he was being led off into a cornfield to get a bullet in the back of the head. Perhaps he wasn't the expert on survival he thought he was.

"I knew Marsha would show up here sooner or later," Riggs said. "First your mother brainwashed her with those stupid cards, and now you're taking over."

"I don't know what you're talking about," I said, though I did.

"That's why you're trying to get rid of me."

"No, I'm not," I said, though I was.

13

"Bullshit! It was you who set me up with the cops."

"That's crazy," I said, though I had.

Riggs crossed his arms over his chest and gave me a spiteful smile.

"It's not gonna work. Know that. The problems you've caused for me — they're going away, this little temporary problem with Marsha included. And after they *do* go away . . . *you're* going away, too. I'm gonna make sure of it."

"*You* need to go away, Bill. Now. Out of my store."

Riggs waved a hand at the shop's stock in trade: pewter charms and quartz-gravel crystals and cutesy-poo mass-produced voodoo dolls. The stuff dreams are made of — most of it made in Taiwan.

"Or what?" Riggs said. "You'll put a hex on me?"

I took two slow, deliberate steps backward, my gaze never wavering from Riggs.

"I don't need a hex."

I reached out, picked up the phone by the cash register, and punched in numbers with my thumb, all while still looking hard into Riggs's eyes. I knew if he was going to make a move, now was when he'd do it.

Riggs glowered back at me, the muscles in his neck so tense it looked like his head

14

might pop off like the cork shooting from a champagne bottle. Riggs wasn't a big man, but he was young and in decent shape. And he'd had training once upon a time. According to Marsha, he was in the army all of five months before being thrown out for insubordination, disorderly conduct, and general belligerence.

The guy was too violent *for the army.* Think about that.

I had. A lot.

That's how I'd set him up. I'd upgraded his Camaro with a few new features: drugs, an unregistered gun, a busted taillight, and a new bumper sticker — BAD COP. NO DONUT — that was bound to get him noticed by the surliest of state troopers. His bad temper had done the rest.

And apparently it hadn't stopped there.

The flesh around his left eye was pink and puffy, and there were scabs and scrapes on his chin and cheeks.

He'd been in a fight.

"Who you calling? The cops?" he sneered at me. "I was just trying to talk to my wife. There's no law against that."

"Well, yes and no," I said.

Riggs cocked his head slightly to the side like a confused dog.

Maybe a pit bull.

A rabid one.

"Hi, Deputy," I said into the phone. "It's Alanis McLachlan. I'm about to make your job a lot easier. He's here, standing right in front of me in my shop. Followed his wife in. No, don't worry; he's not causing any trouble. But you might want to hurry over with that court order. I don't know how much longer he's going to be here. Great. No problem . . . my pleasure . . . see you soon. Oh, and thank you for the flowers. They're lovely."

I hung up.

"Court order?" Riggs said.

Suddenly the confused pit bull looked scared.

He was out on bail. "Court order" could mean a quick trip back to the pound.

"Marsha got an order of protection," I said. "A restraining order. It'll take effect as soon as you're served with it, which should be in about four minutes. If you're still here, that is."

Riggs chewed on that a moment. I could see his fear and confusion fade — to be replaced by fury. He lurched forward.

I reflexively jumped back. But it wasn't me Riggs was moving toward. It was the hallway.

He leaned to the side to shout past me.

"Marsha! I love you, honey! You know that! You're being manipulated! These people are not your friends! Come home! It's not too late!"

Riggs paused, listening for a response. When he realized he wasn't going to get one, he glared at me again.

"This is all your fault. You've brainwashed her with your mumbo jumbo and those stupid cards."

"Oh, so you're sticking around to chat?" I said. "Lovely. You'll get to meet Deputy Ferguson. Fascinating guy. Arizona's number-one caber tosser."

"You're gonna regret messing with me."

"I didn't even know Arizona *had* a number-one caber tosser until he told me that," I said. "I didn't know Arizona had caber tossers. Or cabers."

"Bitch."

Because Riggs was finally leaving, I let him have the last word.

As soon as the door closed behind him, I picked up the phone and dialed the same number I had a minute before.

"Jesus, Alanis — are you all right?" said Eugene Wheeler, my lawyer. "I've been standing here wondering if I should call the police."

"Everything's fine now. Sorry — I didn't

expect you to pick up on a Sunday. Look out your window."

Like the White Magic Five and Dime, Eugene's office was on Furnier Avenue, the closest thing little Berdache, Arizona, has to a main drag. I peered out the big picture window at the front of my shop, past the zodiac signs and tarot cards and black-and-white yin-yang painted on the glass, and saw Bill Riggs stomping off to his Camaro.

In the distance I could make out a big pear-shaped shadow — Eugene — looming behind the words WHEELER & ASSOCIATES on another storefront window.

Together we watched a scowling, muttering Riggs jerk open the door and throw himself in behind the wheel.

"Five'll get you ten he Starsky-and-Hutches it," I said.

Eugene didn't take the bet, maybe because he didn't know what I meant but probably because he knew I was right.

Riggs peeled out fast, engine roaring, tires squealing, a cloud of gray exhaust fumes and scorched rubber swirling in his wake.

"He's going to be even more pissed when he figures out there's no order of protection," Eugene said.

"By then I'll have finally talked Marsha into getting one."

"Don't hold your breath. Last time I spoke to her, she was even waffling on the divorce."

I sighed.

Two days before, while doing a tarot reading for Marsha, I'd turned over a Three of Swords in the near-future position and a Nine of Swords in the outcome slot.

One shows a heart pierced by three blades hovering over an agonized man, the other a weeping woman writhing in her bed. *You want a side of emotional torment with your betrayal and upheaval?* the cards seemed to be saying.

I'd tried to dance around that with a little no-pain-no-gain, stay-the-course spin. But Marsha knew the cards well enough to see the obvious interpretation herself.

It didn't take much to discourage her. Those two cards would have been enough, and I should have known it.

"I've never met a more passive person in my entire life," Eugene went on. "The woman makes a doormat look hyperactive."

"Someone else has been controlling her life for nine years, Eugene. Bill moved her away from her family and friends and then barely let her out of the house. The only thing she ever got to decide for herself was what to clean first when he went to work.

Give her more time. She's coming along."

"Thanks to you. I still don't understand why you're doing so much for her. Picking up my tab. Paying for a motel room. *Buying her a car.*"

"A $300 clunker, Eugene."

"You've known her less than a month."

"I've known *you* less than a month, and just look at how close we've grown."

There was an uncomfortable silence while Eugene tried to figure out if I was being sarcastic and, if not, what he should say in response.

Eugene's about as emotionally intuitive and available as you'd expect a fiftyish American male named Eugene to be. Maybe if he'd had hippie parents who had christened him Moonbeam Starchild he'd be offering hugs to strangers with flowers in his hair. But no — he was a Eugene, there were no hugs, and the only thing you'd find in his hair was perhaps, on a particularly humid day when even the most manly man of commerce could justify it, a light coating of Aquanet.

"Right . . . well . . . anyway," Eugene said.

He stopped there. "Right . . . well . . . anyway" really just meant "Could we talk about something else, please?"

I obliged him.

"Have you heard any scuttlebutt about the charges against Riggs?" I asked.

"Just that the county attorney thinks the drug possession is fishy, but that's nothing new. As far as I know, the state still wants to prosecute for resisting arrest and aggravated assault on an officer. Why do you ask? Did Riggs say something about it?"

There were footsteps behind me, and I turned to find a willowy, dark-skinned girl moving up the hallway, clutching a gun.

"Sorry, Eugene — can't gossip now," I said. "Give my best to everyone at the Rotary Club."

"Uhhh . . . okay."

Eugene hung up.

I don't know if Berdache even has a Rotary Club. But if it does, Eugene's the president emeritus.

"Bill's gone?" said the girl with the gun — my half sister, Clarice.

She was leading a procession now. About ten yards behind her, halfway down the hall, was a girl with short, bright blue hair and clothes as black as her lipstick: Clarice's gothy girlfriend, Ceecee.

Ten yards beyond *her,* at the bottom of the steps leading up to the living space on the second floor, was Marsha Riggs. From so far away, you almost couldn't see the faded yellow bruise under her left eye and the contusion high up on her forehead.

"Yeah. He's gone," I said.

Ceecee sighed with relief. But Marsha just stared at me wide-eyed, looking like a wary rabbit about to turn fuzzy tail and jump for the nearest hole. I almost expected her nose to twitch.

Clarice lowered the gun — a BB pistol with all the stopping power of a spitball.

"Thanks for coming up to tell us," she grumbled.

"Sorry. Got distracted. But it's definitely over now. You and Ceecee can go back to doing your homework or smoking crack or whatever it is you two do up there in the afternoon."

" 'Smoking crack.' That is so '90s, Alanis," Clarice snorted. "We're sniffing crank."

"Oh. Right. Well, carry on."

Clarice and Ceecee headed back upstairs while Marsha gaped at me more wide-eyed than ever.

"We're just kidding around," I said. And then, because I couldn't resist: "We're all on meth."

Marsha managed to curl one corner of her mouth ever so slightly upward to indicate that she got the joke — or realized that it was supposed to be a joke, anyway.

I reminded myself to tone it down around her. Marsha was earnest, gentle, guileless. Exactly the kind of person I'd been raised to avoid.

An honest man is hard to find, Biddle had told me. *And thank god for that!*

Because you can't con an honest man, they used to say. And it was true enough of most of the old scams. But my mother, Barbra, had found a new one for herself — one where honesty was fine so long as there was a heaping helping of gullibility to go along with it.

Fortunetelling.

Marsha had been one of Barbra's best customers. Mom had milked her for hundreds if not thousands before she died.

I was paying Marsha back. I wanted to pay everyone back — all the people my mother had manipulated and cheated — with my help, until I'd finally run from her. And what better way to make amends than through one of Mom's own cons?

Of course, there was no way I could ever find all of my mother's victims. So I'd hunkered down in the White Magic Five and Dime and made do with the ones who found their way to me.

"You okay?" I asked Marsha.

She came up the hall, passing the little

curtained nook where I did readings, and joined me in the store's front room.

"I guess," she said.

"Bill must have been waiting for you to come here — staking the place out. I'm glad you didn't go with him. You know what would have come of that."

Marsha nodded tentatively.

"I feel guilty, though," she said. "About him going to jail, maybe to prison. Isn't that when a wife's supposed to stand by her husband?"

"Not if he's an abusive, controlling prick, Marsha. Then it's an opportunity."

Marsha winced at the word *prick*.

Bill might have treated her like a slave, a prisoner, property, and sometimes even a punching bag, but she still wanted to believe he wasn't all bad, and I suppose he wasn't. But he sure was bad enough.

"Wanna help me feed the fish?" I said.

Marsha nodded again, enthusiastically this time, grateful for the change of subject.

I led her to the fish tank by the waiting area. It was the one and only change I'd made to the White Magic Five and Dime since moving in. The rest — the crucifixes and African masks and tarot symbols on the walls, the New Age baubles and bric-a-brac in the display cases, the general air of faux-mystical seediness — I'd left the same.

If you want to attract mice, you don't put caviar in the trap. Leave the cheese.

The little canister of fish food was beside the tank. I handed it to Marsha.

"Just a little," I said.

Marsha gave me a small sad smile. She'd never given me a big happy one.

"Don't worry," she said, flipping up the lid on top of the tank. "I had fish once."

She took out a pinch of fish food and crushed the red and green and purple flakes as she sprinkled them over the water.

Most of the fish were hanging out at the bottom of the tank near a big porcelain pirate ship with a jagged hole in its hull. But the second the flecks of food hit the water, the fish — about a dozen silvery angelfish and electric blue tetras — were wriggling wildly upward, racing to suck in as much as they could before it was gone. There was no such thing as "enough" to them. They'd mindlessly take and take till they destroyed themselves.

My mother had no use for animals — they're not known for their bank accounts — but I think she would've appreciated the fish.

Look past the gills and the fins and the pretty colors, I could hear her or Biddle say, *and they aren't that different from people.*

Despite the feeding frenzy, the fish missed a few colorful flakes, which drifted slowly, like a rainbow of snow, toward the bottom of the tank. The algae eaters would take care of them. I squatted down to look at one as it swam lazily past the pirate ship.

Through the hole in the ship's side I could see the dark outline of a box. A treasure chest — if you have a really sick definition of "treasure."

Inside it were my mother's ashes.

Clarice and I had given Mom a mini burial at sea, leaving her to rest where she'd spent so much of her life: with the bottom feeders.

It was a reminder for us never to sink so low ourselves.

"Bon appétit," I said.

You've got the whole world in your hands — or at least a bowling ball that looks kind of like the world. You're gazing out at the horizon, taking in your domain while searching for unexplored territory and unconquered foes. Don't worry; you'll find both. It's a big world out there, and you're not the only one looking for a fight.

Miss Chance, *Infinite Roads to Knowing*

After Marsha fed the fish, I offered to go make us some tea.

"Thanks," Marsha said. "That'd be nice."

For some reason, people find it comforting when a woman makes them tea. It's the only reason to make it, really. I'd rather drink Coke myself. Or liquid soap.

I find my comforts elsewhere.

While a mug of water heated up in the microwave in the back room, I hurried up to the building's second floor.

"Quick," Clarice said when she heard me coming. "Get rid of the heroin."

She and Ceecee were sitting on the floor by the couch in the living room — "the living room" in the little upstairs apartment being merely the couch and the floor and the TV nearby. Textbooks and papers and pencils were scattered around them.

The BB gun was on the kitchen counter. It had been left at the White Magic Five and Dime a couple weeks before by a mark who'd come looking for jewelry Barbra had conned out of him.

Another satisfied customer.

"Don't flush your stash on my account," I said as I picked up the gun. "I just came for this."

"You'll shoot your eye out," Clarice said.

"That's all right. I only need one to aim."

I was back downstairs in front of the microwave before it even beeped.

Soon I was walking up the hall, a mug of steaming tea in one hand, a mug of cola masquerading as tea in the other, with the gun jammed into the back of my jeans. I put the cups down on the store's main display case, then pretended to be excited by the sight of a tour bus passing by outside.

"Please stop please stop please stop," I said.

When Marsha turned to look out the window, I slipped the gun under the counter beneath the cash register.

Men like Bill Riggs couldn't even be trusted to act in their own best interest. If he changed his mind and came back, I wanted to be ready. A soothing cup of tea wasn't going to do the trick with him.

"Dang. Sorry, Alanis," Marsha said as the bus kept cruising past. It was black, with the words *MAGICAL MYSTERY TOUR* painted on the side in big, swirly, acid flashback–inducing paisley. It drove through town four times a day, headed back and forth between Sedona and the (supposedly) mystic energy–soaked spot called Devil's Ridge.

It never stopped.

"Oh, well," I sighed. "Maybe next time."

"Business still slow?"

"Only if you define *business* as providing services and goods to paying customers."

"Uhhh . . . ," Marsha said, furrowing her brow.

"Joke," I told her.

"Oh. Right. Well, at least you've got one paying customer here."

I knew where she was headed with that, but I pretended I didn't.

"You're not a customer," I said, swiping a hand at her.

She opened her mouth to reply.

"Your tea's getting cold," I said.

While Marsha dutifully picked up her mug and took a sip, I plotted my next distraction.

She'd come for a tarot reading. And I wasn't going to give her one.

I'd learned to respect the tarot since inheriting the White Magic Five and Dime. I wouldn't call it supernatural or magic, but I also wasn't thinking of it as I had the first thirty-something years of my life: as just another con. The cards really were a gateway to . . . something.

Still, that didn't mean I thought they'd be good for Marsha just then. The tarot offers implications, insights, suggestions, but she tended to take them as commands. And she'd had enough of that from her husband and my mother and maybe even me. She didn't need another master. She needed a reason to live.

"What did you do before you married Bill?" I asked her when she started leafing through one of the books we had in stock — a self-published guide to the tarot called *Infinite Roads to Knowing*. I didn't want her asking to try some new tarot spread she saw in it.

"Not much," she said. "I was a cashier at a pharmacy, going to community college. I thought I might become a veterinary assistant."

"Why not a veterinarian?"

Marsha smiled shyly, her eyes still on the book. She was a short, slight woman — so much so that from behind you might think she was one of Clarice and Ceecee's friends from high school. You'd know better as soon as you saw her face, though. She was thirty, but her sallow skin and haunted eyes made her look decades older.

"Oh, I couldn't be a vet," she said.

"Why not?"

Marsha shrugged her bony shoulders. "I don't know. I just can't think of myself like that. I always see myself as the assistant."

"Perhaps it's time you found a new way of thinking."

Somehow I managed not to wince at my own words. What I really wanted to say was "grow a pair, lady." Instead I'd trotted out a line from every self-help book ever written.

Talking like Dr. Phil. Taking tarot cards seriously.

Being in Berdache was doing weird things to me.

The front door swung open, and a couple walked in out of the blinding-bright Arizona afternoon.

Skills that had been drilled into me from the time I could talk kicked in automatically. I noted their clothes, their complexions, the way they walked, the looks on their faces. In an instant I knew who they were and what they wanted and how I could turn that to my advantage if I chose to.

Cold reading, Mom and Biddle called it.

Cops call it sizing up suckers.

"We saw the sign in your window," the woman said — as I knew she would. She was fortyish, dressed in shorts and a T-shirt, and flushed slightly pink on her right-hand side.

The man hung back a step, looking sheepish. He was dressed the same, aged the same, and with the same pink glow to his skin, only on the left-hand side.

"Which one?" I said, though I knew the woman hadn't meant OPEN. I wanted her to say the words herself.

" 'Under new management,' " she said. " 'First reading free for returning customers.' "

I smiled.

"And you're returning customers?"

The woman nodded. The man didn't.

"We used to be in here all the time," the woman said.

I kept smiling.

"Well, welcome back, folks," I said. "Who used to do your readings? Claire Voyant or Cy Kickmann?"

"Oh, Claire," the woman said. "She was amazing. The predictions she used to make! So accurate!"

I stopped smiling.

"Come on, Amy," the man said, taking a step toward the door.

"What?" the woman said. "Is something wrong?"

I just stared at her.

Suddenly, it wasn't just half her face that was flushed red.

Without a word, she turned and walked out of the shop. The man followed her.

"I told you this was a dumb idea," I could imagine the man saying as they returned to their car and he slipped once again behind the steering wheel. (Drivers get more sun on the left.) " 'Claire Voyant.' Geez, Amy."

"It was worth a try," the woman would say. And off they'd go, continuing their tour of central Arizona and its spiritual vortexes and towering red-rock formations and traditional Native American casinos.

"Uhhh . . . what just happened?" Marsha asked.

"Just a little misunderstanding."

I'd put the magic word — FREE — in the window to lure Barbra's old customers/ victims. I wanted to make amends, help.

Despite what my mother and Biddle would have said about that, it didn't make me a sucker. I wasn't going to let anyone make a fool of me except me.

"So," I said, "how does somebody become a vet, anyway?"

I couldn't talk Marsha into veterinary school.

I couldn't talk her into going back to college.

I couldn't talk her into getting a degree online.

I couldn't talk her into squat.

She didn't have any money, she said. She didn't have any experience. She didn't have any prospects.

What she really didn't have was any *oomph.*

Outside, meanwhile, the sun sank into the hills and the day ended and the night began.

"Come on! There's got to be something you're passionate about," I said. "Something that lights a fire in you."

Marsha gave me one of the languid, passive shrugs I was beginning to know so well.

"I guess I'm not a fiery person."

She suddenly brightened, shoulders unslumping and eyes widening in a way that told me exactly what she was about to do: change the subject.

"What about you, Alanis?" she said. "What are you passionate about?"

I mulled it over a moment.

"Grilled cheese with barbecue potato chips and a kosher dill," I said.

"What?"

I walked to the window and turned off the neon *OPEN* sign. Then I locked the door.

"Closing time," I said. "I'm hungry."

Marsha re-slumped.

"Oh."

"Fortunately for you," I said, "I share my passions."

Marsha blinked at me.

"Come on up. I'll make you a sandwich," I explained.

Marsha grinned with obvious relief.

It wasn't just a reading she'd come to the store for. She'd come so she wouldn't have to be alone.

She followed me down the hall and up the stairs. I'd stayed in Berdache to put things right and had ended up picking up a stray.

Maybe I was a sucker after all.

"Good night, Ceecee," I said when the credits rolled on the movie she and Clarice had been watching.

"Oh, come on, Alanis," Clarice said. "Let her stay a little longer. Please."

She and Ceecee gave me sad puppy-dog eyes from the couch.

"Sleep tight," I said to Ceecee with a little

buh-bye flap of the hand. "Bedbugs, etc."

Ceecee turned to Clarice, kissed her chastely (grownups were watching), then got up and shuffled toward the stairs.

"Good luck with your date tomorrow," she muttered at me.

"Date?" said Marsha from the apartment's dinky little dining-room table. She'd eaten her grilled cheese there, half-watched the movie there, chatted with me there about anything other than her future, and generally gave the impression that she was glued there like a barnacle.

Ceecee whirled toward her, suddenly bright-eyed and smiling.

"Yeah! She's gonna have dinner with —"

"Out," I said, pointing at the stairs.

Ceecee turned and started trudging toward the steps again.

"You're mean," she mock-pouted.

"And don't you forget it," I said.

I didn't let myself feel badly about kicking her out. I'd already picked up two strays: Marsha and a sister I hadn't even known I had a month before. I didn't need a whole pack.

"So . . . a date?" Marsha said to me.

I shrugged dismissively.

"I'm helping a guy take his eighty-five-year-old mother to Olive Garden. It's not exactly *Fifty Shades of Grey.*"

Clarice snorted.

"You. School night. Bed," I said to her. Not because I was worried about her getting enough sleep. I just didn't want her bringing up who I was going out with.

"Mom never cared if I stayed up late on a school night," Clarice said, not moving from the couch.

"Mom wouldn't have cared if you knocked over Fort Knox as long as you split the take with her."

"True," Clarice said.

She finally got up and headed for the bathroom.

"You guys," Marsha said, grinning and shaking her head.

She thought we were joking again. She was wrong.

Clarice paused to look at her in an almost pitying kind of way, then threw me a quizzical look.

I knew what the glance was asking.

(A) Can you believe this square (or whatever it is kids call squares these days)?

(B) Is she sleeping here?

I'd known the answer to (B) since we'd come upstairs.

"I think I'll turn in, too," I said. "Marsha — do you want my bed or the couch?"

"What? Oh, no! You don't have to do that! I've already taken up too much of your time today."

"This isn't going to take up any of my time at all. I'll be asleep. I don't care if it's on a couch or a bed."

"But — !"

"Marsha. That was a freaky scene with Bill today. If you don't feel like going back to your motel alone — and who would after that? — you can stay here tonight. It's no trouble at all. Right, Clarice?"

I looked at my half sister.

"Of course," she said.

But there was that look pointed at me again. Eyebrow slightly cocked, lips curled into the slightest hint of a smirk.

Clarice and I shared a trait we must have inherited from our respective fathers, whoever they were. Something we sure as hell hadn't gotten from Barbra.

We each had a conscience.

Yet although Clarice had told me she understood my little crusade to make up for Mom's crimes, she hadn't fully stepped out from Barbra's shadow.

She wasn't fleecing patsies with my mother anymore. But she still thought of them as patsies.

"Well . . . okay, then. I guess I will stay,"

41

Marsha said. "Thank you. I'll take the couch."

"Great," I said.

I turned to see if that smirk was still on Clarice's face. If it was, I was going to wipe it off with a stare. All I saw was the bathroom door as it swung closed, though.

A second later I heard Clarice lock the door.

Once Marsha was settled with pillows and blankets on the couch, she opened a book she'd found on the coffee table and started reading. It was the same book she'd been looking at downstairs earlier that day: *Infinite Roads to Knowing* by one "Miss Chance."

This was a different copy, though: it was *my* copy. Which was why it was filled with underlined passages and scribbled notes in the margins.

Infinite Roads to Knowing was my Cliffs-Notes for the tarot. I had it to thank for half of what I knew (or pretended to know) about the cards. Another 25 percent or so I'd gleaned/stolen from Josette Berg, the New Age Earth Mother who ran a rival bullshit emporium across the street. The rest I just pulled out of my butt.

Strangely, though, when I checked my out-of-the-butt stuff later, it usually turned out to be right in line with *Infinite Roads to Knowing*. Maybe Miss Chance and I shared a psychic bond. We definitely shared some genes.

Infinite Roads to Knowing had been written by Barbra and Clarice. Mom had printed up copies herself so she could sell them in the shop without having to share any of the profits with real publishers or real writers or real tarot readers. Real slick.

"Hey — what do you think of the book?" Clarice said when she finally came out of the bathroom two days (or so it seemed) after going in.

"I've read other tarot guides, but I think this one's my favorite," Marsha said. "Whoever wrote it is really deep but fun, too."

Clarice shot me a Look again. I couldn't blame her for it this time.

There was a round of good nights, then Clarice went into her bedroom and closed the door.

"Bathroom's all yours," I said to Marsha. "There's an unopened toothbrush in the medicine cabinet."

Marsha sat up straight to stare at me over the back of the couch.

"Where are you going?" she asked.

I was starting toward the stairs to the first floor.

"Oh, I'll be back in a minute. I just have to prep the store for tomorrow."

"Prep the store?"

"You know. Rev up the psychic vibrations, feed the spirit animals, warm up the karma. Back in a jiff!"

I flashed Marsha a smile as I went down the stairs. It lasted about four steps.

As soon as Marsha couldn't see me, the smile was gone.

I slowed down, too. I was descending into near-total darkness, and I didn't intend to turn on the lights.

Lights help you see where you're going, sure.

They also help other people see *you*.

When I reached the first floor, I felt my way along the wall until I saw a dim gray glow up ahead: moonlight streaming through the windows in the office. I headed toward it.

Ceecee had unlocked the office's back door when she'd let herself out. I relocked it, then looked out at the small parking lot behind the White Magic Five and Dime. All I saw was the ancient, sputtering Honda Civic I'd bought Marsha and the boxy black Cadillac my mother had left me. To Barbra, the Caddy had probably looked classy. To me, it always looked like it was waiting for a funeral procession.

Who knows? Maybe it was.

I stepped back into the blackness and made my way to the front of the store. When I reached it, I double-checked the lock on the door, then peered out at metropolitan Berdache, Arizona.

Times Square it was not. Hell, Sedona it was not, though it tried. The little town's tourist traps — a sprinkling of vortex-themed tchotchke shops and restaurants and motels along Furnier Avenue — were all lightless, lifeless. Every so often a car or pickup truck would cruise past, but that was it for nightlife.

I scanned the quiet streets. It wasn't just Bill Riggs's Camaro I was looking for.

From my late, unlamented mother I had inherited $45,000 and a store and a Cadillac and a sister and a *lot* of enemies.

Customers who'd been scammed. Partners who'd been cheated. Con artists who didn't like the competition. I could expect any of them to drop in anytime.

In fact, some already had. A family of con artists/grifters called the Grandis had taken me and Clarice for a little ride not that long ago. It was only by a miracle that we'd managed to ride back. It was not a ride I wanted to repeat.

A block away, at the entrance to an alley, I spotted an orange pinprick. A tiny light that fell and faded, then rose and brightened, fell and faded, then rose and brightened.

The glowing tip of a cigarette.

I watched it until it finally flew in an arc like a shooting star and disappeared. Whoever was out there smoking had flicked it away.

I waited to see if there would be a little flicker from a lighter, then another pinprick.

All I saw were shadows.

I went upstairs. I said good night to Marsha. I waited for her to fall asleep. Then I gathered up my blankets and pillow and went back downstairs.

Here's what staying in Berdache had got me: a night lying on a hardwood floor listening for a break-in, cell phone on one side of me, BB gun on the other, while my sister and a hapless, helpless friend I hardly knew slept soundly and safely upstairs.

For this, I thought, *I gave up a telemarketing job I could do in my sleep and a one-bedroom apartment in the Chicago suburbs and every night quiet and safe and alone?*

I smiled to myself.

"You bet," I said.

BASTONI
BATONS

3

WANDS
BASTOS

STÄBE

STAVEN

There you are again, gazing off at the horizon with your giant carrots by your side. You've sent your ships to sea, and soon they'll be returning with exotic treasures from distant lands. You've done well so far. Poor people don't get to go around with orange juicers on their heads and bed sheets wrapped around their waists. But there's no guarantee your efforts will pay off so well every time. All the wiles in the world won't do much good against a typhoon.

Miss Chance, *Infinite Roads to Knowing*

I woke up alive, which is always my preference. No one had broken in to kill us in the night. I hate mornings, so it's always nice to have *something* to be grateful for come 7 AM.

It was the sound of Clarice stomping down the stairs that had awakened me. Or at least I assumed it was Clarice. It could have been a Clydesdale.

"You awake?" the Clydesdale asked when it reached the bottom of the staircase.

"Suhh," I said.

"How was the floor? Comfy?"

"Guhh."

"Maybe it's time we finally got an alarm system."

"Luhh."

"Barbra always said they're a scam, but I don't know. Seems like it'd be worth the money."

"Juhh."

"Well, nice talking to you. Ceecee and I are going down to Sedona after school, so I probably won't be home till late."

"Puhh."

"Oh, and tell Mr. Castellanos I said hi when you get together for your hot date at the Olive Garden tonight."

"Grrrrruh."

"Bye!"

"Buhh."

Clarice clomped off, unlocked the back door, and left.

I lay there a moment, listening for more footsteps upstairs. I didn't hear any.

Somehow Marsha had managed to sleep through the Clydesdale's departure. Or she was lying on the couch just like I was lying on the floor — awake but hating it.

"Cuhh-fuhh," my brain said.

Coffee.

I started to push myself up. It wasn't easy. My legs were aching, my back sore, my neck stiff.

An alarm system, huh? I thought as I hobbled off toward the coffee maker in the office. *Maybe that's not such a bad idea . . .*

Once I'd caffeinated myself, I went upstairs to get dressed.

For the last fifteen years I'd rocked the I

Don't Give a Crap look: T-shirts and jeans and Chuck Taylors and short fifteen-dollar haircuts. But that wouldn't do for the proprietor of the White Magic Five and Dime.

I put on a purple dress with a floor-sweeping skirt, black boots, hoop earrings, and a necklace with a silver pendant shaped like a rose. I topped it all off with rings on every other finger and a touch of actual, honest-to-god makeup just to show that I *did* give a crap — though there was a bit of misdirection as to what I gave it about.

Put it all in a plastic bag and the label you could slap on it would be Fortuneteller.

For me, every day was Halloween.

Marsha slept through my trick-or-treating prep. She'd been lonely and scared out at the remote motel I'd been putting her up at while she (hopefully) made her separation from Bill permanent. This was probably the deepest, most restful sleep she'd had in two weeks.

Infinite Roads to Knowing lay splayed out on the floor beside the couch, as if Marsha had put it down intending to pick it right back up again the second her eyes were open. I was tempted to snag it and take it with me.

The clothes and jewelry and makeup were

only part of my costume; knowledge of the tarot was the rest. I was getting better at faking it. In fact, there were times I couldn't tell if I was faking at all. But I needed to know more . . . and to my surprise, I *wanted* to know more.

Still, I left the book where it was. There were other tarot guides downstairs in the store — ones not written by con women and their teenage apprentices. Why was I reading *Infinite Roads to Knowing* over and over anyway?

I headed down to the White Magic Five and Dime, unlocked the front door, turned on the OPEN sign, and positioned myself behind the display case.

Then I took out a fresh copy of *Infinite Roads to Knowing* and started reading.

Would-be customers came and went.

A tourist with a French accent bought a package of incense sticks. A tourist with a Southern accent took a picture of *Infinite Roads to Knowing* with her phone, presumably so she could order it from Amazon later. A teenage tourist tried to steal a bag of rune stones. ("I think something just fell into one of your pockets," I whispered to her after her parents announced it was time to leave. "Why don't you make sure they're empty before you go.")

Then the door opened, and a woman marched in with such steely determination and distrust on her face there was but one thing for me to think.

Bingo.

"I've come for my freebie," she announced.

"You're a returning customer?"

She nodded brusquely.

I believed her.

It was obvious what kind of customer she'd been. The kind that had seen through my mother's BS.

"Welcome back," I said. I stretched an arm out toward the hallway behind me. "You remember where to go?"

"I remember," the woman said.

While she went striding toward the dark little nook where I did readings, I went to the front door, locked it, and flipped around the sign that said BACK IN 15 MINUTES. When Clarice was there I didn't have to close up while I read, but most days I was on my own. I knew I was losing business because of that, but I didn't particularly care. The people I really wanted to see would come back.

Like the woman I found sitting across from me at the reading table. She was sixtyish, stout-ish, swarthy-ish. There was nothing-ish about her expression, though.

She already hated me, which wasn't fair. Get to know me, *then* hate me — that's the way it ought to work.

"I'm Alanis."

I held out my hand. The woman took it by the fingers and shook it limply for all of second.

She didn't introduce herself.

"Your mom used to run this place, am I right?" she said instead.

"That's right."

The woman looked like she regretted even the flaccid, unfriendly handshake she'd given me.

I nodded at the tarot deck sitting on the table.

"Why don't you shuffle," I said, "while thinking about what you'd like to ask the cards."

"I know how it works. And I know what I want to ask."

The woman snatched up the cards and shuffled them roughly.

"Here's the question," she said. She never looked down at the cards in her hands; her eyes were locked on mine. "Am I looking at a con artist?"

She slapped the cards back on the table.

For a second I wondered if I should act shocked. Look hurt. Feign taking offense.

I decided against it. The woman suspected I was a phony. Play-acting would simply confirm it.

And it wasn't an unreasonable question. I'd asked it myself a thousand times — sometimes even while staring in the mirror.

"Okay," I said. "Let's see what the cards say."

I took three cards and placed them face-down in a row between us.

"Just three cards?" the woman said.

"It's a straightforward question, so we don't need a lot of input," I said. "And anyway — this reading's a freebie, right?"

I smiled.

The woman scoffed.

I tapped the card in the middle of the row of three.

"The present."

I moved my hand to the left and tapped again.

"The past."

I moved my hand to the right and tapped the card on the opposite end of the row.

"The future."

I went back to the other end and turned the card over.

"The Two of Wands."

"I know what it is," the woman said.

"Good. Then maybe you know what it means?"

"Sure. Wands is the suit of fire. It's all about . . . well . . ."

For the first time, the woman looked unsure of herself.

"Doing things," she said. "Taking action and . . . stuff. That guy's looking for something to do — or waiting to see how something he tried is gonna pan out."

"But this is the past," I reminded her. "This is something that *was* tried. A risk was taken that may or may not have paid off."

"What does that have to do with whether or not you're a crook?"

I shrugged, keeping my expression pleasant.

"Your question is about me, but the cards are about you. What experience do you think this one might reflect?"

The woman looked blank for a moment, then smiled for the first time.

It wasn't a friendly smile. It was a *gotcha*!

"I've been to this store in the past," the woman said. "And I know what I think based on *that.*"

"All right. But that was then. This is now."

I turned over the middle card.

I was hoping the cards would have my back — that I'd flip over something that was obviously positive: the High Priestess or the Empress or the Two of Cups or the Ace of Trust-Us-She's-Really-Not-Going-to-Screw-You.

No such luck.

As far as I was concerned, the Moon was

the shrug of the tarot deck. The "go figure." The "what were they smoking when they came up with that one?"

Not that I was about to admit it.

"Ahhh, the Moon," I said. "A card of deep emotions and unforeseen opportunities. You see the road there? The path between two towers? Look how far it goes — all the way to the horizon. That's a rewarding journey one could go on, but you have to be unafraid to take the first steps away from the past. You have to trust."

I thought it was a pretty good spiel . . . until I looked up from the card into the woman's eyes.

There was no gloating triumph in them now. There was fury.

"You're a liar," she spat. "Madame Jezebel has told me all about that card. It's not about trusting people, it's about fooling them."

"Yes, that's true. The Moon card can be about deception. But —"

"But nothing! What was gonna happen next? You were gonna tell me someone put a curse on me? That you could lift it if I only trusted you . . . and gave you all my money?"

"No. I wasn't going to say anything like that."

"Yes, you were. You're a fraud, just like your mother."

The woman snatched up the last card and threw it faceup on the table.

"Ha!" she barked.

This is what she saw:

"You're a liar, but the cards aren't," the woman said. "There I am giving you my

61

money — if only I was dumb enough to believe you."

"That's not you giving me money. That's success. That's things working out as they should."

She spat out another bitter "ha!" before pushing her chair back and standing up.

"Madame Jezebel was right about you," she said. "I don't know why I even gave you a chance."

She turned to go.

I said the only thing that I thought would stop her.

The truth.

"I *am* a fraud," I said. "And my mother *was* a con artist. But that doesn't mean I won't help you."

It worked.

The woman turned to face me again, her expression both puzzled and distrustful.

"Obviously, she swindled you somehow," I went on. "She swindled a lot of people — one scheme after another across the country. I don't know how she got into tarot reading, but I sure as hell know why: it was her last scam. But I'm not here to keep it going. I'm here to wrap it up. Tell me what she took from you, and I'll give it back."

"Why would you do that?" the woman asked. She didn't look convinced, but she looked — maybe, by some miracle — open to convincing.

Then I blew it.

"Why?" I said. "Because it's the right thing to do."

I knew it wasn't as simple as that, and she did, too.

"Well, isn't that sweet?" she sneered. "What do you need to send me the money? The routing code for my bank account? My PayPal password? My social security number?"

"Give me a day, and I'll hand it to you in cash."

"Yeah, right. Nice try."

The woman turned away and stepped out into the hall. Something she saw off to her left stopped her again.

"I hope *you* haven't given these crooks any money," she said. "Because — news flash — we're not getting it back."

Then she spun to her right and stalked off toward the front door.

I jumped up to see who she'd been speaking to, though I already knew. There was a knot in my stomach so big it felt like I'd swallowed a bowling ball.

Marsha was sitting on the stairs. I didn't know how long she'd been there eavesdropping on the reading. It was clear it had been long enough, though.

Her eyes were wide, her face pale.

"Listen," I said.

But she didn't. Before I could say another word, she jumped up and scrambled up the steps. By the time I was halfway up the stairs after her, she was already coming back down, with her purse and her keys in her hands.

"I was going to tell you eventually," I said as she squeezed past, refusing to look at me. "It just didn't seem like the right time. Maybe once everything with Bill was sorted out —"

Marsha stopped when she reached the bottom of the stairs.

"So you just let me keep believing lies?"

She still wouldn't look at me.

"Yes," I told her. "I'm sorry."

Tears began to stream down her gaunt cheeks.

"Now I don't know what to believe," she said. "I don't know who to trust."

"Marsha —"

I took a step down the stairs toward her.

She bolted down the hallway toward the back door. A moment later, I was watching her speed off in her rusty old Civic.

She'd let me explain later, after the shock wore off. I hoped.

In the meantime, I had to hope something else, too: that she didn't cross paths with her husband.

She was vulnerable — and that was just how he'd want her.

BASTONI
BATONS

4

WANDS
BASTOS

STÄBE

STAVEN

For some people, "domestic bliss" is an oxymoron. The only bliss they get around the house is when no one else is there. But the Four of Wands reminds us that a home sweet home isn't an impossible dream. Family life can be harmonious and rewarding; appreciate it while you can. In the moment it might feel like domestic bliss, but in hindsight you might realize it was just the calm before the storm.

Miss Chance, *Infinite Roads to Knowing*

It was a twofer. I'd blown it twice with one conversation.

I hadn't been able to convince Former Customer X that I wasn't a lying scumbag, and I'd convinced Marsha that I was one. All because I ran out of options and tried being honest.

Whoever said the truth shall set you free was full of crap.

To top it all off, I was having a Scooby-Doo moment. Quoth Fred: "Looks like we've got a mystery on our hands."

Who was Madame Jezebel, and why was she bad-mouthing me and Barbra? Not that my mother didn't deserve it. But it had ruined my chances with one of Mom's marks.

"Let's split up and look for clues," Fred would have said.

There was only one of me, so I couldn't split up. But I could split.

I left the White Magic Five and Dime and walked across the street to visit the competition.

When I was growing up, we didn't have neighbors. We had "the guy in the room next door" or "the people above us" or "the assholes down the hall," and we never had any of them long. Sometimes we'd switch motels five times in a week just to stay ahead of one unhappy camper or another.

I think the longest we ever stayed anywhere was the time Biddle moved us into a foreclosed McMansion outside Nashville and convinced the neighbors Mom was a loaded divorcée and he was her butler/chauffeur. It was probably a bogus investment scheme or a high-end variation on the badger game or the Spanish prisoner. Whatever the play was, it didn't involve me, so for three whole days I was free to drift around the neighborhood doing whatever I wanted.

I played freeze tag with other kids. I swam in their backyard swimming pools. I ate popsicles and ice-cream sandwiches on their porches.

I was almost normal. Then Mom noticed.

"Stay in the house," she told me one morning.

"Why?"

"You'll blab."

"I won't."

"You'll let something slip."

"I won't."

"You'll blow the setup."

"I *won't.*"

"I know you won't — because you're not going out. Biddle, get her a TV."

And that had been that. "Neighbors" went back to being hazy, distant figures to be distrusted and avoided. Even after I ran away from Barbra, I never let my guard down. But maybe finally, twenty-plus years later, I was willing to try.

"Howdy, neighbor," I said as I walked into the House of Arcana.

The store was a mirror image of the White Magic Five and Dime: the same but opposite. Packed with supposedly mystical bric-a-brac yet bright, cheery, airy.

Josette Berg, the owner, looked up from the small cauldrons and potion kits she was arranging just-so on a display table. She was a tall and willowy woman with long, frizzy gray hair and a shapeless beige frock that wouldn't have looked out of place on Obi-Wan Kenobi.

She grinned at me with effortless, beaming sincerity.

In some ways, she was *my* opposite.

"Good morning, Alanis," she said. "What brings you in today?"

"I need to borrow a cup of good vibes."

"Oh, I'm afraid we're all out."

"You? I don't believe it."

The shop's only customers — a pair of cashiers from the local grocery store who'd sometimes spend their breaks poking around the White Magic Five and Dime before leaving without buying anything — finished poking around and left without buying anything.

"Actually, I have a question for you," I said to Josette. "Have you ever heard of somebody called Madame Jezebel?"

The look of near-beatific positivity on Josette's face sagged in a way I'd come to recognize, and I knew what she was going to say before she said it.

"She's a fortuneteller. Psychic Vibes on Route 179 — that's her place. She's —"

"One of the Grandis," I said.

Josette nodded grimly.

She didn't approve of the Grandis. I didn't approve of the Grandis. No one would approve of the Grandis unless they approved of manipulative bloodsuckers.

So the woman I'd just read for had run from my mother straight into the welcoming arms of the most dangerous con artists in the county. Out of the frying pan and into the pits of hell.

The cards had been clear, too. The woman had trusted, been burned, but needed to trust again — trust *me* — for amends to be made. Amazing. Yet I hadn't been able to get the message across.

Time for another lesson.

Josette wasn't just my neighbor. When it came to reading the tarot for a customer, she really was my Obi-Wan.

"Got time for a reading?" I asked her.

She gestured at her customer-free store. "What do you think?" she said, her smile returning.

"Great. Why don't we use a Celtic Cross this time?"

"A classic," Josette said. "And what is it you want to ask the cards today?"

I thought it over. "Have I lost my freakin' mind?" seemed a bit too blunt.

"Was I right to stay in Berdache?" I said instead.

Josette led me back to her reading nook and had me shuffle the cards there and think about my question. Then she took the deck and laid out ten cards, like so:

Then Josette slipped the bottom card from the cross in the middle and flipped it over. The reading began.

"We start with your current situation," Josette said.

"Wands: the suit of fire, creation, new endeavors. But here, in the Ten of Wands, we see the downside of that. You can take on too much, be too ambitious, and load yourself with burdens that might not be yours to bear. So you're excited to be committing yourself to something new, but maybe you've bitten off more than you can chew. And affecting that situation is . . ."

She turned over the other card at the center of the spread.

"The King of Wands! Well, well! This is an important man in your life . . . or one who'll be important soon. He's powerful, energetic, restless, unpredictable. Be ready, Alanis. I'd say he's going to shake things up.

"But back to your problem — the first card. Your burden. Where's that coming from?"

She moved to the card just below the first two.

"Hmm. Here we have a journey you've been on . . . perhaps a sad one. Yet you're carrying something with you that you'll need in the future: those swords. They could be skills you've accrued or wisdom you've gained.

"Now — the recent past."

She turned over the card to the left of the center cross.

"More swords! And another man. Swords can mean conflict, of course. But not always.

And not necessarily with the king here. He's an authority figure. A defender of the status quo. A no-nonsense type. A good man to have in your corner, I'd think. Let's see what you two are up against. A possible outcome . . ."

She flipped the card above the center cross.

"Wands. Again. And more conflict — a lot of it. You're surrounded, on the defensive. You've got the high ground and a way to fight back, but the odds aren't necessarily in your favor.

"Hmm. Maybe the near future will look a little brighter."

She went to the card to the right of the center cross.

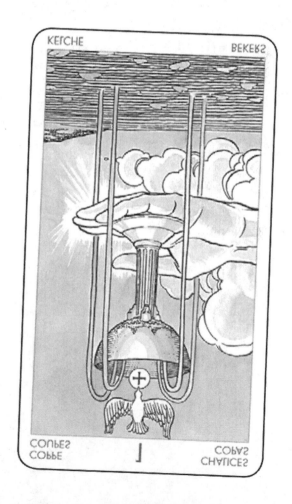

"Oh. Our first reversal.

"You know how it is, Alanis. Not everyone puts any stock in reversals, but I do.

"Usually the Ace of Cups is a wonderful card to get. It signifies love, abundance, a gift of happiness, and spiritual fulfillment. Good stuff!

"Reversed, we get the opposite. The love pours away. We get conflict again — disruption, chaos — and the gift turns into a curse. Not so good.

"Let's see where you're coming from — the self."

She moved her hand to the four cards to the right of the cross and turned over the one at the bottom of the line.

"Well, there's an old friend: the Fool! He always seems to pop up in your readings. I think that's you coming to Berdache, Alanis. The wanderer beginning a new journey with a heart full of hope. But he's reversed today. Maybe there's reason not to be so optimistic. Maybe it's time for a little caution. Maybe the Fool needs to slow down a little. Think things through more.

Look before leaping.

"Moving up, we see what's around you — your environment."

She flipped the card above the Fool.

"Look at that: another reversal. A lot's being turned on its head.

"The Magician shows us power and skill used well — for creativity and transformation and new beginnings. Reversed, that power and skill might still be there, but they're being thwarted or misused.

"I think this might be another yellow light. You have abilities and insights, but are you in too much of a hurry to use them? What are your true goals — and are there better ways to achieve them?

"Moving up again, we come to what some readers call your hopes and fears. I look at it more as the spread's last chance to get in a word before the grand finale — just something you ought to know. In this case —"

She turned over the third card in the line of four.

9

"We're back to wands. That guy looks a little tired, doesn't he? He's been through a lot of battles, you can tell. And he's ready for more, no matter how weary he might be. Look at his face, though. See the suspicion there? The distrust? He's got reason to be cautious, but he should be open to help, too. He just needs to make sure he accepts it from the right people.

"All right. Finally. The bottom line. The outcome.

"Drum roll, please."

Josette let her hand hover a moment over the final unturned card, then picked it up and put it back down faceup.

"Ah. Oh. Okay. Hmm.

"Sometimes the cards look . . . um . . . a little more dramatic than they really are. This isn't necessarily an act of violence we're looking at. It just means things are going to get a bit . . . intense. But I know you've been through intense times before. The key thing is not to overreact. Stay focused and calm and confident and everything will work out fine. Probably.

"There are a lot of wands in this spread. That's your passion, your enthusiasm, your fire: keep that alive in you. I think it's what's drawing trouble to you, but it's what's going to see you through, too.

"That'll be thirty dollars, please. Cash or credit card?"

Josette was smiling when she asked for the thirty bucks. She'd stopped charging me for readings a week before.

"Professional courtesy," she'd said.

The smile she wore now was small, tentative. A "sorry — just kidding" kind of smile. The kind you give someone you're trying to cheer up.

I gave her a big, bright smile back. What did I have to be gloomy about? I'd accepted that the tarot had some value as a sort of psychedelic Rorschach test, but that didn't mean it could predict the future. The only reason I'd gotten a reading at all was to pick up tips and improve my tarot patter . . . right?

Still, I glanced back down at that last card — the Ten of Swords, looking like an out-take from *Gladiator* — and I knew what I'd do the second I was back in the White Magic Five and Dime.

I was going to check on Marsha Riggs.

Marsha didn't answer when I called her motel room, and I gave her plenty of chances. I must have called ten times that afternoon. The phone just rang and rang.

I'd thought about setting Marsha up with a cell phone, but I hadn't gotten around to it. I kicked myself for that now.

I tried Eugene's office, too, but Marsha wasn't there and he hadn't heard from her.

"I have the scoop on Bill Riggs, though, if you're interested," he said.

"I'm interested."

"I got curious when you asked about the charges against him this morning, so I called a buddy of mine in the state at-torney's office. He said Riggs somehow landed *Charles Dischler* as his attorney, and now the possession and assault and resist-ing arrest charges — the whole smear — it's

87

all going bye-bye."

"You say 'Charles Dischler' like I should know that name."

"You should if you ever need a better lawyer than me — and you win the lottery. He's probably the most famous criminal defense attorney in Arizona, and he doesn't come cheap."

"Riggs is a twenty-nine-year-old hothead shmoe who sells condos and timeshares. How'd he come up with the money for someone like that?"

"Beats me. But however he got it, it's the best investment he ever made. A week ago he was looking at jail time. Now the state's just praying he doesn't sue."

"Great."

There was a long silence I felt too glum to fill with more talk.

Finally Eugene said, "Are we done? Another minute of this and I'll have to start billing you."

"We're done. Thanks for the gossip."

"My pleasure. And, Alanis — don't worry. I'm sure Marsha's fine."

"Me, too," I lied.

I hung up and headed for the door.

I drove to the drab, dark little house at 1703 O'Hara Drive. The Riggs's home.

I was afraid that I would find Marsha's ancient, dent-dimpled Civic in the driveway. That she'd run back to what she knew — as smothering and sometimes brutal as it was — when she discovered that she didn't really know me at all.

The Civic wasn't there, which didn't necessarily mean Marsha wasn't there. But her husband's red Camaro was parked out front, so peeking in the windows didn't seem like a good idea.

I sat in my car, watching the house. It wasn't long before I noticed that I wasn't the only one.

Half a block away, on the opposite side of the street from me, was a white and blue Arizona Highway Patrol cruiser — with (I had to assume) an Arizona Highway Patrol Officer behind the wheel. I was too far away to make out any details other than (A) he was a human being and (B) he was a big one.

And (C) he didn't like me watching him.

His cruiser was pointed toward me, but when he drove off — which he did about half a minute after I laid eyes on him — he backed into the nearest driveway behind him and pulled out headed in the opposite direction, all so he wouldn't have to drive past me.

So somehow Bill Riggs suddenly comes up with the money to get the charges against him dropped — some of which were because he Hulked out on the state trooper who had found the goodies I'd stashed in his glove compartment — and the next thing you know the highway patrol's wandering into his neighborhood . . . which happens to be a good mile from any highway they could be patrolling?

And here I'd thought Riggs was just an abusive asshole. Now it turned out he was an *interesting* abusive asshole, which was not an improvement.

I drove the twenty miles to the motel Marsha had been staying at. She didn't answer when I went to her room and knocked on the door. The fact that her car wasn't in the parking lot gave me no comfort.

There was plenty of desert around to ditch a dinky old rust bucket like that — along with whatever might be in the trunk.

I'd barely gotten started at this do-gooding thing and already I had to wonder if I'd done very, very bad by Marsha Riggs.

I went back to the White Magic Five and Dime and spent the rest of the day going through the motions. Every half hour or so

I'd notice that Marsha still hadn't called, so I'd call her.

She never picked up.

A tall, dark, handsome man appeared before me.

I didn't notice.

I was standing behind the counter at the White Magic Five and Dime, staring at the pirate ship at the bottom of the fish tank and still thinking about Marsha Riggs and Bill Riggs and that human pincushion on the Ten of Swords.

The tall, dark, handsome man cleared his throat.

"Sorry," I said. "How can I help — ? Oh."

The tall, dark, handsome man gave me a small, almost wary smile.

He was Victor Castellanos.

My date.

"Hi," Victor said. "Ready to go get Mom at the home?"

Quite the Casanova, huh? "Ready to go get Mom at the home?" What red-blooded American woman could resist a pick-up line like that?

I could've, actually, though I'd spent the previous two weeks browbeating the man into asking me out. His mother had been one of Barbra's most loyal — and gullible

— customers, and at first he hadn't believed me when I'd said I was trying to pay her back. His penance — because he was indeed so tall, dark, and handsome — was an evening on the town.

Bringing Mom along had been his idea — because "you two seem to have hit it off," he'd said.

I knew better.

Victor Castellanos was six feet tall and weighed two hundred pounds and coached the high school wrestling squad. And he was afraid of me.

For a split second I considered backing out. It was the thought of short, dark, and wrinkled that made up my mind — Victor's mother, Lucia Castellanos.

Lucia always seemed so glad to see me. It was an experience I hadn't had much with mothers, and I liked it.

"Let me just close up the shop," I said, coming around the counter.

Victor took a big step back to maintain the four-foot safety zone he always seemed to keep between us. The handsomest man in town, and he treated me like I had cooties. Oh, well.

At least I could look forward to all the breadsticks I could eat.

■ ■ ■ ■

"Forget Olive Garden," Lucia said when we picked her up from the Verde River Vista Senior Residences. "Mr. Ranalli down the hall from me finally died — in his sleep, the lucky bum — and it's put me off Italian."

"Sure, Mom," Victor said. "Where do you want to go instead?"

Lucia wrapped her little wizened claws around my arm and pulled me closer.

"Let's let beautiful decide."

I didn't let the compliment go to my head. Lucia wore glasses so thick the lenses practically looked like ice cubes. I could've been a Wookiee and she still would've called me beautiful. I was a single female going out to dinner with her unmarried pushing-forty son. For women like Lucia, that's about as beautiful as it gets.

"Do you guys like El Zorro Azul?" I asked.

"Not really," said Victor.

"We love it," said Lucia.

"But Mom — the last time I took you there, you said the salsa made you —"

"You're thinking of someplace else," Lucia declared firmly. "If gorgeous here wants to go to El Zorro Azul, we'll go to El Zorro Azul."

■ ■ ■ ■

So we went to El Zorro Azul, where Lucia refused to touch so much as a single tortilla chip, let alone the salsa. She even seemed wary of the water. When it came time to order, she refused to pick anything out for herself, saying she'd "just nibble off Vic's plate."

"Has Vic told you he was the third-ranked wrestler in the state his senior year?" Lucia asked me.

"Thirteenth, Mom," Victor said. "And that was twenty years ago."

"Has Vic told you he was the highest-scoring player on the Berdache basketball team?" Lucia asked a little later.

"Second-highest, Mom," Victor said. "And I'm sure Alanis doesn't care."

"Has Vic told you he was the captain of the debate team when they won the state championships two years in a row?" Lucia asked a little later.

"Co-captain, Mom," Victor said. "And we came in second both —"

"Victor," I cut in. "Your mother's proud of you. You don't have to nitpick the details."

Victor blushed.

Lucia beamed.

The food arrived.

Lucia never even picked up a fork.

"Has Vic told you he made the dean's list three times at Arizona State?" she said.

She's too young, Biddle had said from time to time when my mother was cooking up some new scheme that involved me.

She can handle it, Barbra would say.

That was the highest praise I ever got from her.

So a mother making her son miserable by reciting every halfway impressive thing he'd ever accomplished, including learning to tie his shoes when he was four? I thought it was goddamn heartwarming.

And my heart needed some warming just then. It was the only way to ignore the cold dread growing in my gut.

Victor insisted on dropping me off before taking his mother home. It would be more convenient, he said.

And I knew it was true — both because the White Magic Five and Dime was just a few blocks away and dumping me there first meant we wouldn't be spending any more time alone together.

Lucia thwarted that plan.

"You're going to escort her to the door,

aren't you?" she said to Victor as I started to step from the car.

"Well, I . . ."

I couldn't see the look Lucia gave her son, but it must have been a doozy.

"Of course I am," Victor said.

He hopped out and joined me for the eleven steps to the White Magic Five and Dime.

I unlocked the front door and stepped inside, then turned to face Victor.

"Thank you for a lovely evening," I said.

I wasn't being sarcastic, yet still he winced. Subjecting someone to ninety minutes of nonstop maternal bragging hardly constitutes "a lovely evening," and he knew it.

"Thank *you* for making my mother happy," he said. "She really likes you."

We both stole a look back at Victor's car.

Lucia was watching us expectantly from the back seat. (Both Victor and I had tried to get her to sit in the front passenger seat, but she'd insisted that "the view was better" from behind us.)

"And what about you, Victor?" I said. "Why do I make you so nervous?"

"You don't make me nervous," Victor protested nervously.

"Yes, I do. Is it because my mom was a con artist? Or are you just intimidated by strong women?"

"I'm not intimidated by strong women!"

"Oh? Good."

I grabbed him by the lapels of his blue blazer and pulled him in for a kiss.

"Mmf mmf!" Victor said.

I let him go.

"That was for taking your mother out for a night on the town and letting her embarrass you in front of a stranger," I said. "You're a nice man."

I turned to look at Lucia again.

"Good night!" I called to her.

She gave me a thumbs up and a wink.

I stepped back and started to close the door.

"Alanis!" Victor blurted out.

I froze.

"Yes?"

Victor's angular, olive-toned face had a strained yet determined look on it.

I am not intimidated by strong women, I could practically hear him thinking. *I am not intimidated by strong women. I am not, I am not, I am not.*

"Maybe we could go out again sometime," Victor said. "Just you and me, I mean."

"I'd like that. Good night."

As I closed the door on him, I could see the look on his face change.

First came satisfaction. He was *not* intimidated by strong women.

Then came a wave of "why did I do that?" dismay.

I didn't really know how he felt about strong women. But he obviously was still intimidated by *me.*

I went upstairs. I called Marsha. She didn't answer. I went to bed.

Eventually, I fell asleep.

The Knock woke me up the next morning.

Three firm raps: not too slow, not too quick.

My eyes instantly opened wide, and I sat up and looked around for the back window my mother would already be scrambling through, Biddle lingering just a little behind her, beckoning to me silently.

Come on come on come on come on come on!

Cops!

But there was no back window, no Barbra, no Biddle.

It had been a dream.

Except the Knock came again — as it always did after a short pause.

Rap. Rap. Rap.

Open. The. Door.

I'm. The. Law.

Not a dream. Maybe a nightmare. I rushed out of my bedroom in the T-shirt and shorts I sleep in.

Clarice poked her head out of her room as I headed for the stairs.

"Wha izzit?" she said.

"I don't know," I told her.

Though I did.

It was 5:44 on a Tuesday morning. The police were at our door. They had news.

Bad news.

About Marsha.

I hurried down the stairs and up the hall to the front of the store. When I opened the door, I found a reedy young man standing there. He looked just barely old enough to shave — if his parents would even trust him with a razor. But his Men's Warehouse suit and scuffed shoes and dour expression all confirmed what the Knock had already told me.

"Yes, Officer?" I said, though I wanted to get right to the heart of it and ask "Is she in a hospital or the morgue?" — that's what I needed to know.

The young man blinked at me in surprise for a moment, thrown that I'd known what he was before he'd even spoken.

"Alanis McLachlan?" he said once he had

99

his grim, stony Cop Face firmly in place again.

"Yes. What is it?"

"I'm Detective Burby of the Berdache Police Department. I'm here to ask you a few questions about William Riggs."

My stomach felt as though it was plummeting like an elevator with a snapped cable.

Here it comes, I thought.

"What has he done?" I asked, already knowing the answer — or so I thought.

"Done?" said Detective Burby. "Had his brains bashed out by a baseball bat, that's what. William Riggs has been murdered."

We're *all* members of Fight Club, so we may as well talk about it. Like it or not, we're going to face battles large and small each and every day. "Why don't *you* ever cook dinner?" "What do I have to do to get that raise?" "Hey — that biatch is about to take the last doughnut!" Of course, some of us relish the conflict more than others. And some — like the wannabe warriors on the Five of Wands — just want to wave their big sticks around (paging Dr. Freud!) while striking poses. Learn to spot the difference between a real threat and wand waggling, and you might save yourself the extra energy you need to snag that last doughnut.

Miss Chance, *Infinite Roads to Knowing*

I let myself panic the way Biddle had taught me.

Quietly.

You can think "ohhh, shit!" Biddle would tell me. *But you never say it — unless it's the right thing to say.*

So my *ohhh, shit!* echoed silently in my skull while I stared into Detective Burby's young, smooth, deadpan face.

He stared back at me. Hard.

He wanted to see how I'd react. That was why he was throwing Bill Riggs's death at me like a slap.

I gave him the appropriate response.

I took the dampers off — just a bit. Enough to let my shock show through.

My jaw went slack, my eyes wide. I let my left hand go to my throat, and a quick gasp escaped my lips. I started to slump into the door jamb.

I stopped myself.

(*Don't overdo it, kid,* I could hear Biddle say. *You wanna Meryl Streep it, not go Joan Crawford.*)

"Ohhh, shit," I whispered.

Because sometimes it *is* the right thing to say. And the one thing I didn't want Burby saying just then was "why don't you seem surprised?"

"What happened?" I said.

"That's what I'm trying to find out." Burby held a hand out toward the store behind me. "Mind if I come in? I'd rather not have this conversation on your front step."

"Oh. Of course. I'm sorry. Come in, Detective."

I moved back, and Burby gave me a brusque nod as he stepped inside.

His gaze swept over the shop, taking in the hodgepodge of totems and talismans my mother had thrown together — Buddhas beside dreamcatchers by crucifixes next to pentagrams. He snorted to let me know what he thought of it all.

The kid looked like he'd gone to the Police Academy straight from a Boy Scout Jamboree, yet he felt comfortable showing his disdain for me ten seconds after telling me someone I knew was dead.

Classy.

Then again, the last Berdache PD detective I'd welcomed into the five and dime would soon be on trial for the murder of my mother — and I was the star witness against him. So what could I expect, a hug and a plate of fresh-baked cookies?

"Can I offer you something?" I said. "Coffee? Tea?"

Burby shook his head and pulled out a notebook and pen.

"I'm good," he said.

He looked like he believed it, too. He thought he was good. Very good.

I actually hoped he was right. Because if he wasn't good — if he was dim-witted or corrupt or lazy — I knew who he'd try to pin Bill Riggs's murder on. He had a prime suspect gift-wrapped under the Christmas tree: the victim's wife.

A chilling thought popped into my head.

Bashing Bill's brains out with a baseball bat didn't seem like Marsha's style, but sometimes people will do surprising things when they're being pushed around by a violent a-hole.

What if she actually did it?

Ohhh, shit indeed.

I used some of this new panic in my performance. It's what Meryl Streep would have done.

"My god . . . I can't believe it," I said, voice trembling. "Bill Riggs murdered. I'm just glad Marsha wasn't around him anymore. If she'd been there, she might have been killed, too."

Burby's eyes narrowed.

"If she'd been where?"

I shrugged. "Wherever Bill was killed."

"How do you know she *wasn't* there?"

How adorable. The kid was trying to trip me up already. This was probably his first murder investigation without training wheels, and he was eager to show off, the little prick.

I decided to show him what can happen when you get too cute with people too fast.

"Are you saying Marsha *was* there?" I cried. "Oh, no! Is she all right? Oh god! Who could possibly do a thing like that to such a sweet, harmless woman?"

I began sobbing.

I'd been able to turn the waterworks on at will since I was three. It was a move I owed my mom. There always seemed to be tears waiting for me whenever I needed them.

Burby's stony Cop Face quickly cracked.

"What? No — you've got the wrong idea. Just calm down, would you?" he spluttered, looking horrified by what he'd wrought. "Your friend wasn't there, all right? At least, we don't think so."

"You don't *think so*? So she's *missing*?"

"Well . . . we can't find her."

I began sobbing again.

Burby stretched out a gangly arm and gave me an awkward pat on the shoulder.

"Please . . . there's no need for that. We don't have any reason to believe Mrs. Riggs has been harmed. Yes, we haven't found her, but we haven't been looking long. That's why I'm here, actually."

I looked at Burby, stopped my sobs, and nodded as I wiped away my tears.

Of course, I'd known Marsha hadn't been with Bill when he was killed — not as another victim, anyway. Burby wouldn't have been acting so coy if she had. I was just teaching the kid a little lesson about jerking around people in shock.

"Maybe you'd better tell me what happened, Detective," I said.

"Yeah. Right. Maybe I'd better."

Burby took in a deep breath before going on. He looked relieved not to have a hysterical woman on his hands anymore — so relieved that he put his Cop Face right back on and went back to eyeing me like he half suspected I was Jane the Ripper.

"William Riggs's body was found early this morning by a former co-worker. The former co-worker said he'd called Riggs a few times to check on him after he got out of jail. Riggs had a rough time in there, and he was . . . agitated when he got out. Riggs wasn't answering his phone, so the former co-worker decided —"

"Does this former co-worker have a name?" I asked.

"Of course," said Burby. "So as I was saying: *the former co-worker* decided to drop by Riggs's house. Riggs's car was in the driveway, but he didn't come to the door when the former co-worker knocked. The door was unlocked, so the former co-worker opened it. William Riggs was lying in the living room, just a few steps inside the house."

" 'Brains bashed out by a baseball bat,' " I said.

Burby almost managed not to wince at his own words. Almost, but not quite. Maybe there was some hope for the kid.

"Well," he mumbled, "brains bashed out by *something.* A baseball bat's just our best guess at the moment."

"It's horrible. Horrible," I said, shaking my head. "But I guess we shouldn't be surprised."

"Oh?"

"Well, you said Bill had a rough time in

jail, and the last time I saw him he did look a little beat up. He must've made some enemies when he was locked up."

I paused to give Burby a chance to fill in the facts.

He didn't take it.

"And Bill had gotten mixed up with a bad crowd recently, hadn't he?" I eventually continued. "His death must have something to do with the drugs and gun the state police found in his car."

I paused again.

"We're exploring all possibilities," Burby said blandly.

I nodded as if that actually told me something.

"I bet the killer was looking for more drugs," I said. "Was there any sign the house had been searched?"

"Do you have any idea what someone might have been looking for other than drugs?" Burby asked instead of answering — though his question told me what I wanted to know anyway.

Yes, the place had been searched.

I shrugged. "Bill and Marsha weren't rich, and they kept things in their house really simple. They didn't own anything fancy or valuable that I know of."

"What did you think of William Riggs?

Did he seem like a meth head to you?"

"Well, he did seem angry all the time. Is that a meth head thing?"

"How about his wife?"

"Does *she* seem like a meth head?"

"No. What do you think of her?"

"I think she's sweet and harmless, like I said a minute ago. Bill wasn't much of a husband — wasn't much of a human being, from what I could tell — but this is still going to be a huge shock to her."

"When was the last time you spoke to her?"

"Yesterday morning."

"Where?"

"Here. In the shop."

"What was she doing here?"

"Waking up."

Burby cocked an eyebrow at me.

"I live upstairs, and Marsha stayed with me Sunday night," I explained.

Burby's eyebrow went up another half an inch.

I suppressed a roll of the eyes.

"She slept on the couch," I said.

Burby tried to hide his disappointment.

"Could she have left in the night without you noticing?" he asked.

"No."

"No?"

"No."

"How can you be so sure?"

"Because I slept right there in the hallway, near the bottom of the stairs."

Burby's eyebrow went up higher than ever. It was really getting a workout.

"Bill's friend. The former co-worker," I said. "He must have told you Marsha had left Bill — and Bill wasn't taking it well."

"Yes. He told me."

"Well, Marsha was scared," I said. "And so was I. Bill knew she was here. He came in and made a scene that day, so I wasn't taking any chances."

"Whose idea was it for her to spend the night?"

"Mine."

"Are you sure about that?"

"Of course I am," I said. Though I wasn't.

Marsha had hung around so long and so late I *had* to ask her to stay. She hadn't given me any real choice.

But why would that matter to Burby, unless . . . ?

Ohhh, shit. Again.

"How long had Bill been dead when TFCW found him?" I asked.

Burby blinked at me.

"The Former Co-Worker," I said.

"Oh." Burby's eyes narrowed slightly, and

he watched me closely as he went on. "We estimate that Riggs had been dead between thirty and thirty-four hours."

I Streeped up a blank face even as I worked out the math — and didn't like the answer.

Bill had been killed Sunday night. The night Marsha had slept over.

I was Marsha's alibi.

"So how did you know to come talk to *me*?" I said to change the subject. "TFCW again?"

"That's right. Riggs had mentioned you a few times. He thought you were manipulating his wife — trying to steal her from him."

I scoffed. "If he was worried about someone stealing her, he should've tried treating her decently."

I heard soft, shushing footsteps behind me, and I turned to find Clarice shuffling up the hall in sweatpants, T-shirt, and fuzzy bunny slippers.

"What's going on?" she asked me sleepily.

She looked a lot less sleepy when she got close enough to see Burby. The man might have looked like a skinny high school senior trying on one of his dad's suits, but Clarice would know a cop when she saw one.

"William Riggs has been murdered," Burby told her.

He was still trying the shock tactics. This time, though, he didn't get any shock at all.

"Well, I certainly hope you find the culprit, Officer," Clarice said. "He deserves a medal."

Burby glared at her. "That's pretty harsh."

Clarice shrugged. "Riggs was harsh. Just ask his wife."

I widened my eyes ever so slightly, trying to send Clarice a silent message.

Shut.

Up.

She didn't get it.

"Hey, now Marsha doesn't have to bother divorcing him," she said. "Bonus!"

Burby jotted something in his notebook, then turned to me and jerked a thumb at Clarice.

"Who is this?"

"My little sister," I said.

Burby glanced back at Clarice — willowy, tall, *black* Clarice — then shook his head and scowled.

"I'm not being a wiseass," I said. "She's my half sister."

Burby turned to Clarice again. "So you live here?"

Clarice waved a hand at her bunny slippers. "What does it look like?"

"And when was the last time you saw

Marsha Riggs?"

"Yesterday morning. She'd spent the night on our couch."

"And whose idea was that?"

"Whose idea was it?" Clarice looked surprised by the question. It was finally dawning on her that Marsha was actually a suspect.

Too bad Biddle was long dead by the time she'd been born. She could've used some of his acting lessons.

"It was Alanis's idea," she said.

"Just like I told you two minutes ago," I said to Burby.

If someone's going to try to catch me in a lie, I at least want them to be subtle about it.

Burby ignored me.

"Did you notice Mrs. Riggs going out anytime in the night?" he asked Clarice. "Or talking to anyone on the phone?"

"No. I didn't notice anything. I was asleep."

Burby finally turned back to me again. "How about you? Did you see Mrs. Riggs talking to anyone on the phone?"

"No. And I didn't see her handing anyone a baseball bat or a briefcase full of small unmarked bills either."

The left corner of Burby's thin lips curled

ever so slightly upward.

He wasn't appreciating my wit. I was finally losing my patience with him, and he was enjoying it.

"All right. I think that's all for now." He pulled out a business card and handed it to me. "If Marsha Riggs contacts you, call me immediately. And don't try to contact her. Understood?"

I took the card but didn't say anything.

Burby's lip curled up even more.

He turned toward the door, then immediately spun around again.

"Oh — and one more thing."

I'd have thought he was doing a Columbo imitation if he'd been old enough to know who Columbo was. I think he was really just trying to annoy me some more.

"Do you have contact information for Mrs. Riggs? An address or a cell phone number?"

"She's staying at the Desert Breeze Motel in Sedona. Room 254. She doesn't have a cell phone."

Burby scribbled in his notebook, then turned to go again.

"Detective," I said. "Marsha Riggs is an extremely sensitive and vulnerable person. Please . . . go easy. This could tear her apart."

Burby didn't bother looking back at me till he was halfway through the door.

"Is that a psychic insight?" he said.

"No. Just common sense. And common decency."

Burby looked amused to hear the words "common decency" coming out of my mouth.

He gave me the verbal equivalent of wadding up my words and dropping them into a trash can.

"I'll take it under advisement."

Then he left.

The second the door was closed, Clarice gave me her one-word evaluation of the man. It rhymed with *glass mole.*

"Yeah. A big one," I said.

"So . . . who do you think did it?"

"I have no idea."

Which wasn't entirely true. I didn't know who had brained Bill Riggs with a baseball bat, but I did know who had probably set him up for it.

Me.

BASTONI
BATONS

6

WANDS
BASTOS

STÄBE

STAVEN

And so the crusade begins. The conquering hero rides to war atop a mighty steed who is undercover as Batman. But what's that hanging at the top of our hero's trusty battle baguette — victory laurels? When nothing's actually happened yet? It looks like someone's galloping off with a little too much confidence in himself . . . and I don't mean the horse.

Miss Chance, *Infinite Roads to Knowing*

I'd engineered the bust that put Bill Riggs in jail. If he'd pissed off the wrong person there and got himself killed for it, it was my fault.

I'd framed Bill Riggs for drug possession. If he'd been murdered by some addict who'd come sniffing around for meth the man didn't have, that would be my fault, too.

And if Marsha had actually killed the SOB . . . well, I don't know if that would be my fault, but I sure as hell needed to do something about it.

I stepped to the window of the White Magic Five and Dime and watched Burby getting into an Impala that was so boxy, plain, and gray, all it needed was a neon sign on the roof flashing *UNMARKED POLICE CAR.*

My mouth was speaking before my brain even knew it had a plan.

"I'm going for a little drive," the mouth said.

"No, you're not," said Clarice.

I glanced back at her.

She was giving me a don't-kid-a-kidder look.

I didn't want to kid her either. Didn't want to lie or dismiss her. Didn't want to be my mother. Yet there was only so much I could tell her.

So I told her.

"Allow me to rephrase," I said. "I am going to get in Mom's Caddy and drive away quickly and do things that would make me a spectacularly bad role model, which is why I'm going to refuse to take you along. That better?"

Clarice nodded approvingly.

"Much," she said.

I got in Mom's Caddy and drove away quickly. Quickly enough, in fact, that I caught up to Burby's gray Impala within a minute. I followed it until it hit State Route 89 and turned south.

Burby was heading toward Sedona — and the Desert Breeze Motel. For at least the next hour, I could be sure he wouldn't be in Berdache.

That was all I needed to see.

I swung the Cadillac around and sped back to town.

I found Clarice and Ceecee upstairs eating cereal out of giant mixing bowls. Ceecee wasn't quite as goth as usual — she had on her usual combat boots and black-on-black-on-black clothes, but she hadn't bothered with any black eyeliner or lipstick. There was no need to get so fancy just for an appointment with Cap'n Crunch, and obviously she'd been in a hurry to get to our place.

I'd been gone less than fifteen minutes.

"That was fast," I said to Clarice, with a jerk of the head at her girlfriend.

"I was about to say the same thing to you," Clarice said.

"I'm just passing through. I've still got plenty of bad role modeling to do."

I headed into my bedroom and opened the closet.

"We have a theory!" Ceecee called out as I picked out an outfit — sleek gray pantsuit, white blouse, clunky but comfortable shoes.

It was the shoes that would be the subliminal clue.

The pantsuit would say "real estate agent" or "attorney." The shoes would say "cop."

Just in case people didn't get the hint, I

grabbed a notebook and a pen and jammed them into a bulky shoulder bag.

"Hey! Don't you want to hear our idea?" Clarice said.

I started getting undressed.

"Hit me," I said.

"Suicide," said Ceecee.

"We think Riggs was trying to frame Marsha," said Clarice.

That stopped me mid-zip.

"Suicide?" I said. "By baseball bat?"

"Oh," Clarice and Ceecee said together.

"Is that how he was killed?" said Clarice.

"So it seems. His head was bashed in."

There was a moment of silence.

I went back to getting undressed.

"It still could have been suicide," Clarice eventually announced. "Riggs was a psycho. If anyone could bash in his own head, it'd be him."

"Maybe," I said. "But was he psycho enough to bash in his own head and then hide the murder weapon afterward?"

There was another silence.

This one went on for a long, long time.

When I came out of the bedroom, I found Clarice and Ceecee pensively eating their now-crunchless Cap'n Crunch.

Clarice looked me up and down.

The down brought her to my shoes.

"And where are you off to, Officer?" she said to me.

"Do you really need to ask?"

Clarice thought it over, then nodded and went back to her cereal.

"Let me know if you come up with any more theories. I like yours better than mine," I said as I headed down the stairs. "And you two had better be in school when I get back."

"Wait. What? I don't get it," I heard Cee-cee say as I left. "Where is she going?"

"Thuh thene uh thuh thime," Clarice said through a mouthful of soggy cereal.

The scene of the crime.

1703 O'Hara Drive.

The Riggs's home.

I parked the Caddy across the street and watched the house for a few minutes. There were no police cars or vans out front. The cops and evidence techs had wrapped up and left, leaving no sign they'd been there except for a big X of yellow crime scene tape over the front door.

I got out of the car and marched crisply toward the house. When I reached the driveway, I began circling around Bill Riggs's Camaro.

I pulled out my notebook, flipped over a

page, and began writing.

I'm looking at a car, I wrote. *I'm trying to seem official. Sooner or later, a neighborhood busybody is going to approach me. He or she will have questions. He or she will also have answers. La la la. Da da da. Scribble scribble scribble. You are out of Coke, soy dogs, and mustard. Swing by the grocery store when you have a chance. My hand is starting to cramp. I hope the busybody doesn't take much lon*

I stopped writing.

There were footsteps behind me.

I flipped the front page of the notebook back down — no use exposing "scribble scribble scribble" to the world — and turned.

A thirtyish, bushy-bearded, bespectacled man was coming across the street toward me. He was wearing black jeans and red Chuck Taylors and a bright green cardigan over a plaid shirt. He looked like every hipster tech nerd in every cell phone commercial of the last five years.

"Hi," he said.

"Hello."

"I couldn't help noticing you out here."

I said nothing to that. I just looked at the man expectantly, not friendly but not unfriendly either. All business.

"Uhhh . . . are you with the police?" the

man said.

"No," I told him.

I could let my shoes say I was a cop, but I wasn't about to. Because shoes don't get charged with impersonating an officer.

The man wilted. "Oh."

"I'm an insurance investigator," I said. Because there's no law against impersonating an insurance investigator, for people or shoes.

The man perked up.

For his purpose — gossip — an insurance investigator would be almost as good as a cop. It's practically a private eye!

"I'm Paul. I live right over there." The man jerked a thumb at a cute little ranch house across the street. "I didn't see anything, but I'd be happy to help. What happened to Bill, anyway? I heard he'd been in jail for a while. Does it have something to do with that or does it look more like a random crime? A home invasion? We're not really used to that kind of thing around here. It's usually pretty quiet."

I can tell, I almost said.

The guy was so desperate for excitement I was surprised he hadn't brought a bowl of popcorn and a lawn chair with him.

"The police haven't come to any conclusions yet," I said. "What time did they show up this morning?"

"A little after four. I heard a car pull up in a big hurry, so I got out of bed and looked out the window."

Paul glanced down at my notebook, looking disappointed.

I lifted it up and started writing on it.

"A little after four," I said as I wrote.

"Yeah. Exactly. There was a big, bald lumberjack-looking guy on the Riggs's front porch. Even from across the street I could tell he was freaked out. He said something, pointed to the front door, then kind of stumbled off into the driveway while one of the cops went inside. The guy obviously didn't want to see what was in there again."

"Why do you say he looked like a lumberjack?"

"He was in a flannel shirt and jeans and big work boots — you know the look. He wasn't really a lumberjack, though."

"Oh?" I said, as if this was quite the revelation.

Berdache is in the middle of a desert. There aren't many lumberjacks around.

Paul nodded, looking pleased with himself.

"There was a big work truck in the driveway. A pickup with two-by-fours and stuff in the back. When I went out to talk to some of my neighbors — people started kind of milling around when more cop cars showed up — I noticed writing on the side: 'Huggins Construction.' "

That *was* a revelation.

Riggs sold timeshares for a golf resort outside Sedona. The management company had one of those generic bullshit names — Excelsior Enterprises Inc. or Superlative Hospitality Industries or something like that. I couldn't remember what the name was, but I did know what it wasn't: Huggins Construction.

"The Former Co-Worker" didn't seem to work for the same company Riggs had. What kind of co-worker is that?

I wrote down "??Huggins Construction??" while Paul went on describing the comings and goings at the Riggs's house.

Cops came. Then more cops came. Then "some CSI-looking guys" came. Then "a coroner-looking lady" came.

Then Bill Riggs left. In a body bag.

Before the cops left, too, they'd spread out to the surrounding houses to ask if anyone had seen or heard anything suspicious the past few days. The neighborhood consensus, according to Paul: nope.

"Had you ever seen the Huggins Construction truck there before?" I asked.

"No."

"How about a highway patrol cruiser? Have you noticed one on the block lately?"

"Come to think of it, yeah, I have. Two or three times this week."

"Did the police ask about it?"

"No. It didn't come up."

"Do you happen to remember the name of the officer who interviewed you?"

"Sure. Bublé. Or maybe it was Beiber. Something like that, anyway. He looked like he belonged on the cover of *Tiger Beat.*"

"Detective Burby."

"Yeah, that's it," Paul said. "So was the highway patrol staking the Riggs place out? Do they even do that kind of thing?"

"I'm afraid I can't discuss it," I said.

Because I didn't know. But I meant to find out soon.

"What else did Burby ask about?" I said.

"Whether I'd seen Riggs's wife around, whether I'd seen her and Riggs fighting, whether there'd been any trouble with the neighbors — that kind of thing."

"And you said . . . ?"

"No, I haven't seen Marsha in weeks, and no, I never saw them fighting, though they never looked happy when I saw them, that's for sure. And yes, there'd been trouble with the neighbors — or one neighbor, anyway.

It probably would've been more if Riggs wasn't so standoffish. I lived across the street from him for two years and I don't think he said more than five words to me the whole time. He was the kind of guy you wave to who doesn't wave back."

"So who was the trouble with?"

Paul pointed at another ranch house across the street — a drab gray one with a bed of rocks for a lawn.

"Tom Nord," Paul said. "He used to let his cat wander around the neighborhood. Riggs would get pissed because it crapped in his yard sometimes. Of course, it crapped in everybody's yard, but Riggs was the only one to get bent out of shape about it. I guess it was an excuse to stomp over and yell at somebody, so he took it. And Tom yelled right back. And the fourth or fifth time Riggs brought over a bunch of the cat's turds — he'd scoop these, like, football-size dookies into a plastic bag and try to hand it to Tom — he said if he ever caught that cat, he was going to break its neck."

Paul paused for dramatic effect.

"Then, on Friday, Son of Kong vanished," he said.

It didn't have quite the effect Paul intended.

"Uhhh . . . Son of Kong?" I said.

"The cat."

"Oh."

"He was big."

"Oh."

"That's why he used to leave such big . . . well, anyway. He disappeared. And Tom was sure Riggs was behind it. Called the cops on him and everything, but nothing came of that. So Tom started talking about taking matters into his own hands."

"And you told all this to Detective Burby?"

Paul nodded.

"He didn't seem to take it very seriously, though. Whenever I started talking about Tom, he'd give me a 'yeah, yeah, whatever' vibe, you know?"

I knew. Because Burby's mind was already made up.

"Thank you, Paul. You've been very helpful."

"My pleasure," he said. And his smile told me that wasn't just an expression.

Of course, neighborhood gossip is a two-way street. We'd gone my way. Now I was supposed to go his.

Meaning: it was time for me to dish.

"So how was Riggs killed, anyway?" Paul said. "Do the cops think it was just one person or more than that? Could it have been a gang thing? Do you think we should we set up a neighborhood watch?"

I opened my mouth to say the modern equivalent of "I think I hear my mother calling me": "Excuse me — I just got a message."

And then a miracle happened.

I got a message.

"Excuse me — I just got a message," I said.

I turned away and pulled my cell phone from my shoulder bag.

The message was from Victor.

HEY ALANIS JUST WANTED TO THANK YOU FOR LAST NIGHT. MOM HAD A LOVELY TIME — AND SO DID I. TALK SOON. V.

Well, how about that? A follow-up from Victor Castellanos. And now, apparently, we weren't just on a first-name basis. We were on a first-letter-of-first-name basis.

Coming from Victor, that was like a dozen roses.

I typed a response.

I HAD A LOVELY TIME TOO. LET'S DO IT AGAIN SOMETIME. A.

Short and sweet — but not too sweet. That

might send Victor running for the hills again. And who feels up for "sweet" when they're at a crime scene?

I hit send, then started to put my phone away.

"So how often do you see this kind of thing, anyway?" Paul said. "I mean, is this normal for an insurance investigator? I didn't think you guys handled murders."

"We don't. I'm just here to make sure the car's all right," I said. "Excuse me again. I'm vibrating."

"You're what?"

I waggled my phone.

"Gotta take this. Sorry."

I turned, speed-dialed Eugene Wheeler, put the phone to my ear, and went striding off toward Tom Nord's house.

"Dana Tanna here," I said. "Don't worry — the Camaro's fine. Tell the boss we just saved Geico $500."

Eugene picked up four rings later. By then Paul was a good forty feet behind me, so I didn't have to keep up any act.

"Alanis," Eugene said.

"Eugene," I said. "What are you doing?"

"Working. What are you doing?"

"Getting out of an awkward conversation."

I peeked over my shoulder at Paul.

He was standing in the Riggs's driveway looking like a dog watching someone walk off with his favorite bone.

"Well, I'm glad I could be of service," Eugene said. "I'll send you a bill."

"There's more. Bill Riggs was murdered two nights ago. They just found his body this morning."

"*Jesus.* Is Marsha all right?"

"I hope so. I still don't know where she is."

"*Jesus!* Are the cops sure Riggs was murdered? He didn't kill himself?"

I knew what Eugene was thinking. The old, old story.

Wife leaves psycho husband. Psycho husband kills wife. Psycho husband kills self. The end.

I told Eugene the good news: Riggs was beaten to death.

"Thank god for small favors," he said. "That'll make it harder for the police to pin it on Marsha, too. He was the one with the army training. She doesn't look like she could beat a gerbil to death."

"Anyone can get lucky with a baseball bat."

"Is that what he was killed with?"

"That or something like it."

"*Jesus!*"

"I think Jesus is out of town right now," I said. "You're stuck with me. Look — I need you to do me a couple favors."

"Favors?"

Eugene said the word as if he'd never heard it before.

"Billable favors," I told him. "I need to know the name of the state trooper Bill Riggs tangled with when he was arrested. And it looks like Riggs got into some kind of fight when he was in jail, too. Left him with a shiner. I want to know who popped him."

"Anything else?" Eugene asked sarcastically.

"Yeah. You can look up Huggins Construction for me, too. Find out how it was connected to Riggs."

That's what you get for being sarcastic with *me.*

Eugene sighed. "You know, Alanis, I usually do wills, estates, trusts — nice, quiet, boring stuff."

"Then you should be grateful I'm bringing you something interesting."

Eugene sighed again. "You'll hear from me soon," he grumbled.

He hung up, which was perfect timing. I'd reached the front door of Tom Nord.

My first suspect.

BASTONI
BATONS

7

WANDS
BASTOS

STÄBE

STAVEN

So you're cornered and you're outnumbered and your enemies have breadsticks just as long and crusty as yours. There's going to be a fight, and the odds aren't in your favor. But don't throw down your baked goods and start begging for mercy yet. You've got the high ground and can see the bad guys coming. That means you've got a chance . . . well, so long as there aren't more bad guys sneaking up the other side of that hill.

Miss Chance, *Infinite Roads to Knowing*

I walked up to the small, drab home of Tom Nord and, once upon a time, Son of Kong. Before I knocked on the door, I did what Biddle told me you should always do when you might be facing a killer.

I smiled.

No one answered, so after a minute I knocked again. And kept smiling.

I heard a gruff, muffled voice from somewhere inside, the words indistinct but the meaning unmistakable.

I'm coming, but I'm not happy about it.

I brought up my notebook, readied my pen, and took a deep breath.

The door opened, revealing a tall, broad hulk of a man. If the cat was Son of Kong, this must be Kong.

The guy could've snapped Bill Riggs in half — forty years ago. Now he looked like He-Man after two decades of retirement and two thousand visits to the Golden Corral's all-you-can-eat buffet.

If he'd killed Riggs, he hadn't done it with a baseball bat. He'd done it with a walker.

I stifled a sigh behind my smile.

"Tom Nord?" I said.

"Yes," he said suspiciously.

"Human companion of . . ." I glanced down at my notepad. "Son of Kong?"

Nord's craggy, saggy face sagged even more. "What's this about?"

"Today is Son of Kong's lucky day," I said. "You've won a free three-week supply of Puss'n'Boots Gourmet Supreme Canned Cat Feasts. All you have to do is agree to keep an easy-to-use customer satisfaction log tracking Son of Kong's reaction to the new Puss'n'Boots flavors he'll be —"

Nord held up a hand and shook his head. "You're wasting your time."

"You won't be saying that when Son of Kong gets his first taste of Puss'n'Boots Surf'n'Turf Medley. Hearty chunks of genuine imitation crab, lobster, and Chilean sea bass with succulent soy steak in a creamy —"

"Son of Kong is gone," Nord said. The last word came out quivering.

"Gone?" I said. "As in . . . passed on?"

"As in killed," Nord said, his voice hardening.

"Oh, no. I'm so sorry. What happened?"

"You wouldn't believe me if I told you."

"Try me."

"He was killed by devil worshippers."

Well, whadaya know? I thought. *The guy was right.*

I didn't believe him.

"Devil worshippers?" I said. Not in a challenging way, though — a tell-me-more way. Which worked.

Nord pointed at the Riggs's home across the street.

"The guy who lived there. Bill Riggs. He was a Satanist. I think he snatched Son of Kong for one of his black masses. Son of Kong had his revenge, though. The sick son of a gun got himself killed."

"By Son of Kong?"

Nord looked at me like *I* was the crazy one.

"No. By other Satanists, I assume, which would be just what he deserved."

"And how is it you know Riggs was a Satanist?"

"Well, here's the thing. He started coming over here raving about Son of Kong, waving around big baggies full of cat doo, making threats. Then Son of Kong disappeared. The cops wouldn't do anything about it, so I decided to investigate myself. Went over to

140

Riggs's place at night with a shovel. Looking for —"

Nord paused for a long, ragged breath. He was winded just *talking about* going to the Riggs's place. There was no way he could have gathered enough breath to kill somebody there.

"— looking for fresh holes," he went on. "I didn't find anything, but before I left I took a look inside the house. Just, you know . . . in case Riggs was keeping Son of Kong prisoner or something."

I nodded as if that made sense.

Guy gets mad about giant cat turds in his yard, so he takes the cat hostage *in his house.* Sure, why not?

"And do you know what I saw Riggs doing?" Nord asked.

My nod turned into a shake of the head.

"The guy was sitting there at his kitchen table" — Nord leaned forward, looming melodramatically, which was a little scary, actually, since it was pretty easy to imagine him losing his balance and falling on me — "painting a human skull."

"Oh," I said. As bombshells go, this one seemed like a pretty big dud.

"And you think Riggs was going to use his painting in some kind of satanic ritual?" I asked.

" 'His painting'?" Nord said, looking confused.

"The painting of a skull."

"No no no. I don't mean he was painting a skull. I mean he was painting a *skull.*" Nord opened his eyes wide and waited for the bombshell to go off.

Boom.

It finally did.

"You're saying Riggs had an actual human skull?" I said.

Nord nodded.

"And he was painting it?"

Nord nodded again. "With Son of Kong's blood," he said.

"Blood" came out Vincent Price–style: *buh-luuuuud.* All Nord needed was a flashlight to hold under his chin, and the moment would've been perfect.

"How horrible," I said. "So you saw Son of Kong's body?"

Nord blinked at me and straightened up, the campfire ghost-story spell suddenly broken.

"What? Oh. No. I didn't see Son of Kong."

"So how do you know Riggs was painting the skull with Son of Kong's blood?"

Nord shrugged. "Well, it just stands to reason. The guy's painting a skull with some kind of sticky-looking red stuff, Son of

Kong had just gone missing — it's the only logical explanation. I mean, this town's lousy with devil worshippers. Right downtown we've got three or four stores for 'em. House of Whatever and that other place and . . . what's it called? The White Magic Something Something Something?"

"Something like that," I said.

A sign began flashing in my mind like the *Eat. At. Joe's.* you used to see in old cartoons.

Wasting.
Your.
Time.

I needed to wrap this up and move on to leads with more potential and less cray cray.

"So you went home and called the police but they didn't believe you and now you figure Riggs's coven turned on him and maybe even killed him as a sacrifice to their dark lord Lucifer, prince of darkness and father of lies."

Nord blinked at me. "Yes. Exactly. How did you know?"

I shrugged. "It just stands to reason."

I thanked Nord for his time, told him how sorry I was about Son of Kong, and turned to go.

"Mew," someone said behind me.

It didn't sound like Nord.

I looked back and saw Nord leaning down laboriously — he had to brace himself in the doorway — and scooping up what looked like a grapefruit-sized cotton ball trying to slip past his feet.

"Mew," the cotton ball said.

"Son of Son of Kong?" I asked, nodding at the kitten Nord was cradling.

"Her name's Mothra," Nord corrected me. "Hey — could we sign *her* up for the free food deal?"

"Sorry. She'd need Puss'n'Boots Junior. It's a whole different division. Have a good one, Mr. Nord!"

"You, too."

I hurried off before Nord could think of the question he *really* should have been asking.

How did the people at Puss'n'Boots know he had a cat named Son of Kong?

"Mew," Mothra said one more time, and I heard the door close behind me.

Back in the Caddy, I tried not to think about Martha sporting an orange jumpsuit. Sweet, mousy Martha in prison. She wouldn't last past breakfast.

It was too bad Nord hadn't panned out, but there'd be plenty of other would-be murderers for a guy like Bill Riggs. The challenge would be finding the right one before Martha was modeling the new black.

I couldn't push the image of Martha behind bars out of my head. Then something pushed it out for me.

A Berdache police cruiser was parked in front of the Riggs's house — a cruiser that hadn't been there ten minutes before. Amazing what can happen behind your back when you're busy flogging Puss'n'Boots Gourmet Supreme Canned Cat Feasts.

The cops had already searched and sealed the house. Why were they back?

Before I could take a guess, the front door of the house swung open and a cop came striding out. I slid down behind the wheel but kept an eye on him. No one I recognized — tall, a little paunchy, with sandy hair and a long nose. He was headed to his cruiser with a laptop tucked under his arm.

Question answered: he'd come for the laptop, probably after he — or, more likely, Detective Burby — got a warrant to seize it.

Either the net was being thrown wider in the search for Bill's enemies or Doogie Howser, Homicide Detective, was trying to draw the net tighter around Marsha.

As the cruiser cruised off, my cell phone started playing the song "The Jean Genie." Eugene was calling.

"That was fast," I said. "You must not have heard me say this was billable."

"I could pretend to work on it some more and call you back in an hour if you want."

"No, that's all right. You can tell me now."

"You have something to write with?"

I picked up my pen and notebook again. "Hit me."

"All right. The state trooper who got into it with Riggs is one Michael LoTempio." Eugene spelled it out. "I've got the name of the guy Riggs fought with in jail, too. Get a load of this: George Washington Fletcher. And Huggins Construction is . . . well, a construction company. Owned by a guy named Huggins."

"There's a twist. Back to that Fletcher guy. Can you find out if he was still — ?"

"Locked up at the time of the murder?" Eugene cut in. "Sorry. Yes, he was."

"Damn."

I'd just lost a potential suspect.

"What was he in for, anyway?" I said.

"You're not gonna believe this."

"Yeah?"

"Yeah. *Loitering.*"

"Ahhh," I said.

" 'Ahhh'? What does 'ahhh' mean?"

"It means I *do* believe it when you say he was locked up for loitering."

"Who gets arrested for loitering?"

"Well, not you, Eugene. And not me — anymore. I think. But once upon a time . . ."

"Tick tick tick, Alanis. I am still on the clock. If you're trying to say something, just say it."

"The cops know him. And they don't like him."

"Ahhh," Eugene said.

"How'd you get those names, anyway?"

"I'm Berdache's most successful attorney-at-law, Alanis. You don't think I have friends at the courthouse?"

"Of course. Tell you what — why don't you call back your buddies over there and see if you can get me more than a name for Fletcher."

"What is it you want? His social security number?"

"That'd help. But I'll settle for an address."

"I think that's doable. But, Alanis . . . what are you going to do with all this information, anyway? I know it looks like Martha's in trouble, but you need to leave all that to the professionals."

"Eugene?"

"Yes, Alanis?"

"When it comes to trouble, I *am* a professional."

I knew a good exit line when I heard one. I hung up.

Ten minutes later, Eugene called back with an address for the prisoner Riggs had fought with.

Fletcher's last known abode was the Rest E-Z Motel.

He wasn't there, of course. Like he was going to give the cops that address on his arrest report, then actually stay there.

According to the middle-aged Indian woman who ran the place, he hadn't been there in weeks. From the scowl on her face, I could tell he'd left something for her to remember him by, though: an unpaid bill.

I was quickly getting a feel for Mr. George Washington Fletcher.

I started making a tour of the skankiest motels in town.

The tart Moor Log was number three on the list. I assume it was actually the Stardust Motor Lodge, but the busted-up sign out front read "-tar—t Mo-or Lo-g-." According to the sign, there was air-conditioning and a color TV in every room. Swanky!

Someone really should have fixed that. Someone really should have fixed a lot of things — the cracks in the walls, the potholes in the parking lot, the dingy half-filled swimming pool. But no one had or ever would. A few cars were scattered throughout the lot, parked in front of rooms with scuffed doors and windows with tattered, sun-bleached curtains.

Barbra and Biddle and I had stayed in a hundred such dumps over the years. Home sweet home.

I suppressed the urge to barf as I walked to the front desk.

A tattooed twentysomething in a faded Eminem T-shirt sat crouched behind the desk. He was jabbing at his cell phone while muttering things like "now" and "that's it" and simply "ha!"

I stood there a moment, unnoticed. Then I cleared my throat.

"Yeah, okay, hold on," he said without looking up. "I've just got to get past this . . . no! *Noooooooooooooo!*"

He collapsed forward onto the desk.

"Are you all right?" I asked.

"One more row," he whimpered. "One more row, and I would've gotten past level 40. Can you believe that? Level. 40. No one gets past level 40 without paying for it. And I blew it in the last row."

"I'm deeply sorry for your loss."

The motel clerk raised his head and squinted at me.

"You don't play Mint Squasher, do you?" he said.

"No."

"Well, if you did, you'd understand."

He looked me up and down.

"He's not here, by the way," he said.

"Who's not here?"

"Whoever you're looking for."

"How do you know I'm not here to rent a room?"

The clerk chuckled. "Good one," he said, then went back to his game.

That's what I got for showing up still dressed like an upstanding citizen.

"So . . . this level 40," I said. "How much does it cost to buy your way through it?"

"I think I could do it with a Sugar Boss powerup and a Place-Saver add-on for insurance. It'd be, like, four b—"

He caught himself just in time. Before he got the "-ucks" out, he realized he was being offered a bribe.

"Forty bucks," he said.

I took out two twenties and put them on the counter. I kept my hand on them, though.

"George Fletcher," I said.

The clerk paused his game and looked up again.

"You know what? I was wrong," he said.

"He *is* here."

He reached out for the bills.

I kept my hand on them.

"He's got a delivery. An envelope sent to this address from the city prosecutor's office," I said. "You should tell him to come get it."

The clerk sighed, picked up the motel's phone, and punched in some numbers.

"Fletcher? Got something for you. Letter from the city prosecutor. How should I know how they found you? A snitch? Me? Gee, thanks, Fletcher. And I thought we were friends."

The clerk hung up, then reached for the money again.

"One more thing," I said, still not moving my hand. "Describe him."

The clerk shrugged.

"He's a guy. Pretty regular. Maybe a bit better than regular."

I could tell that was the best I was going to get out of him, and I didn't have much time.

I lifted my hand.

"Give my regards to level 41," I said.

The money disappeared.

Before I could walk away, the clerk was already muttering to himself again.

"That's it. Over there. Almost got it. Ha!"

■ ■ ■ ■

Outside, twenty numbered doors faced the parking lot. I walked to the nearest car and pretended to fumble with the nonexistent keys to someone else's ancient Buick.

Behind me, a door opened and closed. Then I heard quick footsteps headed in my direction. When they were just a few feet away, I turned and stepped in front of the wiry, dark-haired man who was hurrying toward the office.

I couldn't see his face. He was glancing back over his shoulder, more worried about someone he didn't see than the nicely dressed, harmless-looking woman he could.

His mistake.

"George Washington Fletcher?"

My mistake. Specifically, saying it when I was within arm's reach.

In one smooth movement, the man grabbed me by the shoulders, pushed me to the side, tripped me over an outstretched ankle, and spun around to run in the opposite direction.

It was a thing of beauty. The guy was the Michael Jackson of assault and battery.

And I was about to hit the pavement. Hard.

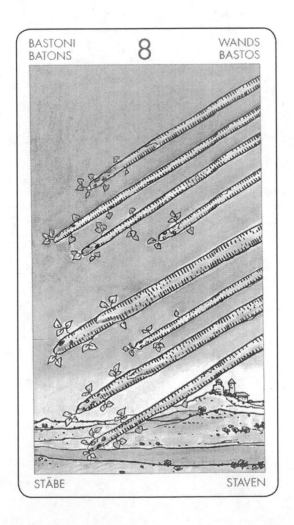

Look out below! Here comes a barrage of baguette bombs! They may bring a message, a warning, or simply imminent impalement. So you might as well get your butter and your bread knife ready because whatever's coming down, it's coming down on *you.*

Miss Chance, *Infinite Roads to Knowing*

I managed to stop my fall with my hands, not my face. For which my face was grateful.

My hands — not so much.

Or my knee.

Or my pride.

"Shit! That hurt!" I wanted to howl. But there wasn't time for stating the obvious.

I could hear Fletcher's pounding footfalls as he did a hundred-yard dash out of the parking lot.

"I'm not a cop!" I yelled.

The footfalls slowed.

"Not a bail bondsman! Not an insurance investigator! Not a process server!"

The footfalls stopped.

I sat up and looked myself over. There was a nice new tear over the left knee of my gray slacks, and the skin underneath was scraped raw.

A skinned knee. I hadn't had a wound like

that since my youthful nights scaling fences for Barbra and Biddle. Otherwise, I was just a little bruised and a lot chagrined.

George Washington Fletcher stepped around the Buick next to me and looked me up and down.

"You know what?" he said. "I believe you."

Because, presumably, a cop, bail bondsman, insurance investigator, or process server wouldn't be so easy to lay out on the pavement.

It wasn't a compliment. But it wasn't meant as an insult, either.

Fletcher smiled and offered me his hand. "Sorry about the shove. Usually when I sweep a lady off her feet, it's not so literal."

I let him help me up.

"Thanks," I said, dusting off my clothes and stealing a better look at him. He wore a faded flannel shirt and tattered jeans. His hair was dark and tousled.

And he was better than "regular." Way better, in fact. If this guy was your average jailbird, I'd been hanging out at the wrong jails. He had a handsome face, a strong jaw, and hazel eyes that sparkled with good humor — and shrewdness.

"So . . . I know what you *aren't,*" he said. "That still leaves me wondering what you are."

157

"I'm Alanis McLachlan. Private citizen."

"And what do Alanis McLachlans, private citizens, do?"

"At the moment, they ask questions about Bill Riggs."

Fletcher gave me a blank stare. It was pretty convincing — though I got the feeling the guy could be a fine actor when he needed to be.

"Never heard of him," he said.

"You should have. Apparently you beat him up in jail."

He frowned.

Then recognition dawned.

"Right. Riggs." The frown turned into a smirk. "Total asshole."

"I completely agree. But his wife is a friend of mine."

Fletcher's smirk grew even smirkier.

"So you're here to beat *me* up?"

Fletcher found the thought so amusing he laughed, the cocky SOB.

Time for a little sobriety.

"Riggs is dead," I said. "Murdered. Two nights ago."

Fletcher tensed, his smile fading as he went back two nights in his mind. When he realized he had the best alibi anyone could ask for, he relaxed again — but not entirely.

"I was in jail two nights ago," he said.

"You're following the wrong lead, Nancy Drew."

"I'll be the judge of that, *Sherlock*," I said. "And I know you didn't kill Riggs. I was just hoping you could tell me if there was anyone else who might have wanted to — someone else Riggs rubbed the wrong way in jail, maybe."

Fletcher shrugged. "He rubbed everybody the wrong way. He was sandpaper, that guy. But I don't know of anyone who'd want to murder him over it."

"So he wasn't worth killing, just punching?"

"That sums it up pretty well."

I gave Fletcher a skeptical look.

He squinted back at me, obviously wondering whether this was a conversation worth continuing.

He smiled ever so slightly.

For some reason, he'd decided yes.

"Look," he said, "Riggs was a pain. Kept whining that he'd been framed, someone had it in for him, it was a conspiracy. The usual. I didn't believe him, and I said so — but not to be a dick and not even to him. He got all up in my grill about it, though. It was pretty obvious he wanted to fight with someone. He didn't seem like a very Zen person, you know what I mean? He was

159

pissed, and he needed a whipping boy. So he picked me."

Fletcher's smile widened.

Bad call, it said.

"Did anyone else get into it with him?" I asked.

Fletcher shook his head.

"He didn't have so much fight in him after he and I were done. After that, he mostly kept to himself. He was only in another day or so anyway. Then he finally managed to scrape together bail, and he was out."

"If Riggs could barely make bail, how is it he could afford such a hotshot lawyer?"

Fletcher's brows drew together. "What hotshot lawyer?"

"Charles Dischler. I'm told he's a big deal around here — and that he doesn't come cheap."

"True and true. I had no idea he was Riggs's lawyer." Fletcher rubbed his chin. "Which is weird. It seems like the kind of thing that big-mouth bastard would've bragged about. You know — 'Whoever did this to me is gonna pay. Charles Dischler's gonna see to that.' Or 'Touch me again, Fletcher, and my boy Charles Dischler will sue you for every cent you'll ever have.' But he never mentioned it."

"You're right. That does sound like the

kind of crap Riggs would say. But if he didn't hire Dischler till after he put up bail, where'd the money come from so fast? He should've been broke."

"Are you asking me or just thinking out loud?" Fletcher said.

"The latter."

"Good. Because if it was the former, you'd be SOL. I've told you everything I know."

I looked into Fletcher's eyes. For a down-and-out jailbird troublemaker, he seemed pretty sincere.

"All right, then," I said. "I've taken up enough of your time. Thanks."

I turned to go — and instantly found Fletcher blocking me.

"Hold on there," he said. "I didn't have a chance to ask any questions."

"Who says you get to?"

"Common decency and fair play."

"Never heard of 'em."

Fletcher's smile returned even wider than before, and his eyes gleamed. It almost looked like his first question was going to be "Will you marry me?" and the second, "How soon?"

"Please," he said. "I just have two questions. That's a lot less than you asked me. And you tricked me into coming out here right in the middle of the best *Judge Judy*

I've seen in weeks. I might *never* find out who's going to pay for all those dead gold-fish."

I sighed, though it was a bit of a put-on. I actually liked his big smile and the gleam in his eye.

"Fine. Two questions."

"Good. Question one: Why are you stick-ing your nose into this Riggs business? That's what cops are for, and it sounds like you know the guy was a tool anyway."

"I told you. His wife is a friend."

Fletcher shook his head and spun his hands slowly in the air.

Not good enough. Give me more, he was saying silently — maybe so he wouldn't have to use up his second question.

"Riggs *was* a tool," I went on. "The kind who knocks his wife around, and that's got the cops following the path of least resis-tance. Enough?"

Fletcher nodded slowly, his expression so-bering.

"I get the picture. Okay. Question two."

Fletcher's smile returned. I got the feeling it was never gone for long.

"Who are you, Alanis McLachlan?"

"I'm me," I said. "Well . . . most of the time."

Fletcher shook his head and spun his

hands again. *More.*

"Okay," I sighed. "I own one of the fortunetelling places in town. The White Magic Five and Dime. I just inherited it from my mother. Marsha — that's Riggs's wife — was one of my mother's customers. Now she's my friend, so I'm trying to help her. That's who I am. Good enough?"

As I spoke, Fletcher's smile faded and his expression sobered. When I was through, he surprised me by reaching out and gently taking my hands in his.

"I am so sorry for your loss," he said. "What happened to Athena was such a shock."

Shit, I thought. *It figures.*

Athena Passalis was also known as Barbra Harper. Who was also known as Mom.

He'd known my mother.

Slowly but firmly I pulled my hands from his.

"It wasn't a shock to everyone," I said. "Thanks again for your time, Fletcher. I've really gotta go now."

"Please — call me GW," Fletcher said softly, his eyes filled with pity. "All my friends do."

"Yeah, well . . . bye."

I turned and started to walk away. After a few steps, I glanced back.

Fletcher was still watching me solemnly.

"Goodbye, Alanis," he said.

I kept walking. After a few more steps, I turned to look back again.

Fletcher hadn't moved. He still stood there by the old Buick, staring after me with big sad puppy eyes.

"Good luck," he said.

On I walked. As I was about to head around the corner of the tart Moor Log, putting the parking lot out of sight behind me, I glanced back one last time.

And there it was. His irrepressible, perhaps irresistible, smile. It was small, but it was back.

"I hope I'll see you again sometime," Fletcher said.

The smile seemed to add that it was more than a hope.

GW Fletcher was going to see that it happened.

BASTONI · BATONS · 9 · WANDS · BASTOS · STÄBE · STAVEN

That's quite an impressive collection of giant pretzel sticks you've pulled together, isn't it? But you didn't get it without paying a price. You're a little bruised, a little battered, and someone stole your pants. So now you're paranoid. Where are your enemies going to come from next time? From your left, you're thinking . . . or maybe your right. Well, don't think those pretzels are going to protect you. The most devastating attack usually comes from behind.

Miss Chance, *Infinite Roads to Knowing*

I drove back to home base. My HQ. My Batcave. The White Magic Five and Dime.

I'd had dozens of home bases over the years, but they were really just oversized closets. Rooms where I could dump my stuff. And me.

I still wasn't sure if the five and dime was going to feel different — if it could put the *home* in home base. But I was willing to give it a chance.

I went to the front window and reached for the neon *open* sign. Before turning it on, I took a moment to stare out at the street. There wasn't much to see.

A few tourists strolled up and down the main drag, Furnier Avenue, while others cruised through in dust-covered cars on their way to someplace more interesting. Beyond the buildings, tall rocky mountains glowed a burnt red as the late afternoon sun sank in the sky.

I was looking at a scorched, bone-dry desert podunk.

Why did I want to stay again?

"Well, are you going to open the place or not?" someone said behind me.

I turned to find a dark, tall, gawky figure moving up the hall from the back of the house.

Clarice.

I turned on the sign.

"Good," Clarice said. "We can't live on the money Athena left us forever."

"You're right. Good thing we've got so many customers banging down the door."

If you listened very, very carefully, you might have heard the sound of a tumbleweed rolling past outside.

"So what happened to you?" Clarice asked.

"What makes you think something happened?"

Clarice nodded at my scuffed knee. "Did you fall off your bike?"

"Oh. That. Yes, actually. I wiped out trying to pop a wheelie."

"Fine," Clarice said with a shrug. "Don't tell me."

"That's the plan."

"Why? Because you're trying to be a responsible big sister and keep me out of trouble?"

"Bingo again."

Clarice had reached the end of the hall now. She leaned against the wall, cocked her head to one side, and gave me her best *you are sooooooo lame* teenage eye roll.

Her best was quite good, too. It made me feel like I'd just told her to turn off that rock-and-roll racket and come watch Lawrence Welk with the rest of the family.

"It's not like you have to worry about being a bad influence," she said. "I grew up with Athena for a mom. I've been around bad influences my entire life, and I haven't killed anybody yet."

I walked past her to the store's display counter and opened the laptop we kept there for Web surfing and solitaire when business was slow.

It got a lot of use, that laptop.

I opened a browser, went to Google, and typed in MICHAEL LOTEMPIO ARIZONA HIGHWAY PATROL.

Riggs's neighbors had been a dead end. GW Fletcher had been a dead end. Now it was time to see if the cop Riggs had tangled with was yet another road to nowhere.

"So," I said, "how was school today?"

Clarice went up on her tiptoes to peer over me at the computer screen.

"Great," she said. "I learned how to use the Internet to find important stuff that can help get friends out of trouble. Got an A+ on it and everything. Want me to show you?"

I turned the laptop so she couldn't see the screen. It was full of search results — a directory page for the Arizona Department of Public Safety, a newspaper article about Traffic Safety Day at a local preschool, etc., all of them mentioning Officer Michael LoTempio.

So step one was a complete success: I had confirmed the man's existence.

Step two — figuring out if that mattered in the slightest — wasn't going to be so easy.

"Some other time, maybe," I told Clarice as I scrolled down the page. "I need to catch up on Facebook. I haven't posted anything in, like, hours. No one even knows what I had for lunch."

"And it looks like they might have to wait a little longer to find out."

I glanced over at Clarice and found her nodding at the front door. Through the glass I saw a fiftyish woman in a baggy coral pantsuit reaching out for the door handle. She had iron-gray hair cut in an angled bob and yellow-framed glasses so large and round I could picture Elton John wearing them circa 1979. One hand was clutching a cherry-red handbag.

She opened the door and smiled broadly when she noticed us watching her.

"Oh! I'm so glad you're open!" she said as she walked inside. She pointed toward the front window. "I'm a returning customer, like it says on the sign."

I nodded in an encouraging but neutral sort of way. "You don't say."

She nodded back. "Yes! The last time I was in was maybe . . . oh, two months ago." She leaned to one side to look down the hallway behind Clarice. "Is Athena in today?"

Awk-warrrrrd, as I believe they used to say on Facebook. But at least it settled my question about her. She wasn't another cheapskate trying to scam her way to a bargain.

"I'm afraid Athena is no longer with us," I said. "But I'd be happy to do your free reading if you're interested."

Usually all it takes is the word *free* to seal the deal. Not this time, though.

The woman shook her head, her smile turning tentative.

"That's not actually what I came for. I need . . . well . . . to consult, I guess. To start off, anyway. But I'm not sure if you can do what Athena did. And it's" — her voice dropped to a whisper, and her gaze

172

flicked from me to Clarice and back again
— "a little sensitive."

Message received.

I stepped to the hallway that led to the
back of the building and stretched out an
arm.

"I understand," I said. "Step into my parlor."

"Thank you," the woman said, looking
relieved.

She walked past me and Clarice, heading
for the small reading room halfway up the
hall.

"The store's all yours," I told Clarice.

"Can I have that in writing?"

"I mean you're in charge," I said, adding
"smart-ass" in a whisper.

I followed the woman into the reading
room, where there was a table and some
chairs and a waist-high bookcase loaded
with faux-mystical bric-a-brac — an oversized crystal ball, a bag of rune stones, a
box of Kleenex (which wasn't faux-mystical
but did sometimes come in handy).

There were tarot cards, too, of course. My
favorite deck: the Universal Tarot. I like the
illustrations' clean lines and modern style.

Some tarot decks seem like they're trying
to give you the vibe of stained glass or
medieval parchment. The Universal Tarot

feels more like a Marvel comic book.

Not that it mattered just then. The deck wasn't even going to get a shuffle.

"So," the woman said once we'd sat down and introduced ourselves with an awkward handshake, "how are you with curses?"

"Applying or removing?" I said without a blink. Biddle would have been proud.

"Removing."

"Oh, that I can do. Is that something you and Athena discussed?"

The woman — who'd introduced herself as Liz White — nodded.

"We did more than discuss it. Athena lifted a curse for me."

"Just out of professional curiosity," I said, "what was the curse and how did Athena lift it?"

I knew what Liz was going to say before she said it.

An inheritance. Cursed money and/or valuables. Solution: give some or all of it to the medium . . . who would (supposedly) return some or all (ha!) when the curse had lost its power.

It was an old, old story. Liz told me her version. It involved a dead uncle and $10,000 in a will and a sudden run of bad luck.

Athena had taken care of the problem by

holding the $10,000 and working to "dissipate the evil in it" over the course of a month. When half the cash was "clear," Athena gave it back to Liz.

"And now you're hoping the other half is ready," I said.

Liz shook her head. "Oh, no no no! I'm worried that the curse wasn't lifted after all. I thought maybe I should bring back the $5,000 Athena gave me."

This time I blinked.

"The past two weeks have just been horrible," Liz went on. "First Paul finds out he has type 2 diabetes, then somebody keys my Impala at Albertsons, then I get not one but two ingrown toenails, and then this morning Mr. Feathers just fell off his perch dead as a doorknob."

I had no idea who Paul and Mr. Feathers were. I could only assume that they were, respectively, Liz's husband and Liz's pet bird, and not vice versa.

"If that's not being cursed, what is it?" Liz asked.

Life, I wanted to say. But this had to be handled delicately.

"Here's what I'm thinking, Liz," I began.

As I spoke, Liz opened her handbag, pulled out a wad of bills big enough to choke a grizzly, and plopped it on the table.

I guess delicate wasn't really her thing after all.

"Here's the money," she said. "See if you can feel anything."

"All right."

Liz watched me intently as I held a hand out over the money. She seemed to be expecting something — glowing eyes or speaking in tongues or a puff of sulfurous smoke — so I began to silently recite my favorite anti-curse incantation: "Hungry Like the Wolf" by Duran Duran.

"No," I said when I got to the "Do-do do-do do-do do-do do-do do-do-do-*DO-DO*" part the second time. "I don't feel any negative energy coming off this at all."

Liz didn't look relieved. "But there has to be *some.* Why else would our luck be so bad?" Her eyes narrowed. "Maybe you're just not sensing it. Maybe you're not as good at removing curses as you think you are."

She started to reach for the stack of bills.

I had a vision of the future without the help of my tarot cards or crystal ball.

Liz takes the money. She bounces around to other occult shops looking for someone who'll "lift the curse." Some fake mystic scumbag — maybe even one of the Grandis — eventually says yes. Liz never sees her money again.

I slapped my hand over the cash.

"Tell you what," I said. "Why don't you give me a little more time? Let me try a few more spells, consult my curse books, see what the spirits say."

Liz's face brightened. "Oh, would you? That would be wonderful! I confess, when I saw that sign in the window — 'under new management' — I thought I was a goner! So how long do you think this will take?"

"Come back this time tomorrow. I should have an answer for you by then."

Liz beamed at me. "Oh, thank you! You don't know how much this means to me! You're a lifesaver!"

"Hey . . . that's what I'm here for."

I walked Liz to the door, suffered through a bear hug, and said goodbye. When the woman was gone, I turned to find Clarice smiling at me smugly from behind the counter — and the laptop.

"Google was only going to get you so far on Officer LoTempio," she said. "Fortunately, when it came to researching marks, Mom left most of the computery stuff to me."

She spun the laptop around so I could see the screen. Two files were open on it. I stepped closer and started to read them.

One was a credit report — complete with current address.

The other was a complaint filed with the Yavapai County Superior Court six months before. Someone had tried suing the Arizona Department of Public Safety and one of its employees — Officer Michael LoTempio — for $100,000.

Clarice thumbnailed the suit so I wouldn't have to wade through all the legalese.

"Looks like Mike's got a temper," she said. "Riggs wasn't the first citizen to get into it with him during a traffic stop."

"Which helps explain how Riggs was able to land that big shot Dischler as an attorney. A prior complaint is blood in the water. That'll draw the sharks. He'd still need money for a retainer, though. Guys like Dischler don't work for high hopes and promises . . ."

My words trailed off as I tried to think it through. The money was still a mystery, but at least we'd made progress on LoTempio. The kind of progress that gave us a strong new suspect.

Hey, I thought, catching myself. *What's with this "we" and "us" stuff?*

Clarice cleared her throat and gave me a significant look.

"Thank you, Clarice. Nice work," I said.

"And no — I still don't want you helping me."

She pouted and gave me an "awww."

"This isn't a game, Clarice. It's —"

The phone rang. The caller ID said UN-AVAILABLE.

Usually I'd assume it was a scammer. But pay phones often don't have IDs either.

I picked up the phone and said simply, "Yes?"

"Alanis! Thank god you're there!"

It was Marsha.

I didn't let myself feel relieved — not until I knew more.

"Are you all right, Marsha? I've been try-ing to reach you."

"No, I'm not all right, Alanis. How could I be after what's happened? Bill's dead!"

"I know."

"He wasn't the best husband, I know. But . . . I loved him. And now he's gone. I can't believe it!"

"Just take a deep breath and try to calm down, Marsha. We need to talk things through. The police are looking for you."

"I know. I've been talking to a detective — Burby. He's asked so many questions, I can't think straight anymore. I just picture Bill. Dead. Murdered!"

She started to cry.

"Where are you?"

The crying grew more intense, almost hysterical.

"Where are you, Marsha?"

Her response came out between strangled sobs.

"I'm . . . at the . . . police station."

I went very still, and my next words were very quiet.

"Don't say another word, Marsha. I'm going to find Eugene, and we'll be right there to get you."

"Don't say another word? But —"

"Don't. Say. Another. Word."

Marsha finally stopped crying.

She didn't stop panicking.

"Why would you say that? Do you think that . . . that the police . . . think that *I* . . . ? But that's crazy!"

"I know it is. So you have nothing to worry about. Just sit tight and stay quiet. I'll see you soon."

I started to hang up.

Before I could disconnect, I heard Marsha.

"But I didn't do anything," she said.

I hung up and dialed Eugene, Marsha's words still ringing in my ears.

But I didn't do anything.

Poor Marsha.

She had no idea that made no difference at all.

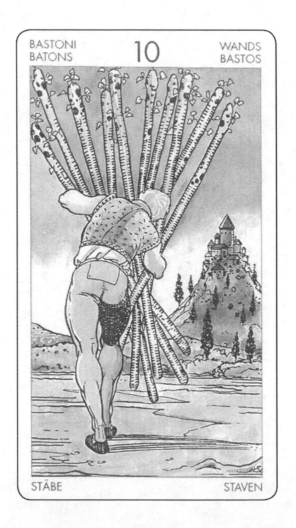

Now you've done it. Those giant Twizzlers looked pretty tempting, so you picked up a few — then a few more. Then you offered to carry one for Aunt Gladys and for Uncle Joe and your neighbor Ann. Before you knew it, you were loaded with a whole heap of heavy. And once you've picked all that up, it's not easy finding someone willing to share the load. So you'd better rent a U-Haul . . . or steel yourself for a long, exhausting road ahead.

Miss Chance, *Infinite Roads to Knowing*

The Berdache Police Department is headquartered in a two-story building that was probably pretty spiffy around the time I was conceived. Now it just looks like a big beige sun-baked box. Parked out front were three cruisers and one me.

"I'll wait here," I told Eugene as I plopped down on a bench near the sidewalk. "I think I'll do more harm than good if I go in."

Eugene shot me a puzzled look. He still didn't know the whole truth about my mother, how I'd been raised, and my less-than-cordial relationship with law enforcement. But he was too preoccupied to ask any questions.

I was picking up the tab for him to be there, but I wasn't his client. *She* was inside with the police, who might or might not decide to let her leave with him.

"Suit yourself," he said. "But you might end up waiting a long time."

"I won't mind. I can entertain myself." I looked up at the clouds drifting by overhead. I pointed at one. "Hey — that one looks like a bunny," I said. "See?"

Eugene just grunted, spun on his heel, and headed inside.

After ten minutes, I started pacing. After another ten minutes, I started jonesing for a cigarette. Not that I smoke. It just seemed apropos for pacing in front of a police station.

After another ten minutes, the building's front door opened.

I turned toward it with a smile on my face.

I got a sneer in return.

It wasn't Eugene and Marsha stepping outside. It was a crooked bail bondsman named Anthony Grandi.

I knew he was crooked from stories I'd heard from Eugene. Oh, and the fact that Grandi and his sister had almost killed me once. That's enough for "crooked" in my book.

The Grandi family had been my mother's biggest competitors for local suckers, and they didn't like me showing up just when she was finally out of their way. There was a truce between us — or at least no Grandis had tried to kill me lately — but I didn't expect that to last forever.

Anthony Grandi was a burly, bald-headed man who favored black T-shirts and leather jackets and scowls, one of which he kept pointing my way.

I met his gaze and kept on smiling.

As Grandi stalked past me, he growled out an insult under his breath.

"Sorry — you'll have to speak up," I said. "Did you say 'glow truck yourself'?"

Grandi didn't look back.

"Well, anyway . . . have a good one, Mr. Luthor!" I called after him.

It was a bad day. I had to take my pleasure where I could.

There was more waiting. More pacing. More longing for a pack of Kools. Then —

"Alanis!"

I turned, and there she was.

Marsha. Finally.

She was coming out of the police station with Eugene. *On* Eugene, really. She was leaning into his doughy body at a 70-degree angle.

The woman was a mess. Puffy eyes, frizzy hair, wrinkled clothes.

I hurried to her side.

"It's all right now, Marsha," I said to her. "Everything's going to be okay."

There were sharp footsteps on the sidewalk behind me and Marsha stiffened, her eyes wide.

I glanced back.

A Berdache cop was walking our way. He gave us a not particularly curious look, then passed us and went inside.

Marsha whimpered and slumped even more against Eugene.

"Why don't we go to my office?" Eugene said. "It's nice and quiet there."

He threw me a look that added *and private.*

Eugene's office is indeed quiet and private. Whether it was nice would depend on your definition. If you find dark faux-wood paneling and plastic ferns and small, stuffy rooms with all the zest and color of a funeral home nice, then sure. It was very nice. Otherwise . . .

"Just when I was finally going to leave Bill . . . maybe . . . someone killed him. And the police act like it was *me,*" Marsha moaned, wiping tears from her cheeks. She swiveled in her chair to face me. "Could this be a punishment? For making the wrong decision?"

"No," I said firmly.

The tears kept coming.

Eugene leaned across his desk to offer

Marsha a white handkerchief he'd drawn from his pocket, which says a lot about the kind of guy Eugene is. He carries hankies and wears short-sleeved white work shirts and probably relaxes after a hard day's work by firing up the turntable and listening to Pat Boone 45s.

Marsha took his handkerchief and buried her face in it. I waited till her sniffles stopped to speak again.

"Where did you go after you left the White Magic Five and Dime yesterday?"

Marsha lifted her head and peeped over at me warily. "Promise you won't laugh?"

"Why would I laugh?"

"Because you're not the person I thought you were. You must think I'm so *dumb.*"

I reached out and put a hand over hers. "I don't think that, Marsha. I swear I don't."

Her expression didn't change. She still looked timid — scared — of *me.* Because I'd hurt her.

I gave her what I hoped was a reassuring smile.

"I *am* the person you think I am, Marsha," I said. "There's just more to that person than you know. You'll know it all eventually. That's a promise. For now, though, the important thing is I'm here to help. And I can't help if I don't know everything. So, please . . . tell me where you went."

Marsha looked down at the floor and bit her lower lip. Then she looked up into my eyes again.

"I went walkabout," she said.

It took all my self-control to stifle a *huh*?

"I see," I lied instead.

I looked at Eugene. He was staring back at me with a cold intensity I'd never seen in him before.

And then the word — *walkabout* — came back to me from the distant past.

All those afternoons I'd been left to entertain myself in malls and motel rooms as a kid. All those hours I'd filled with fake friends and fake family from TV shows and movies while my only real family and my only real friend — Mom and Biddle — were off somewhere doing grown-up things like lying and cheating and stealing.

That's how I knew what walkabout was. From one of those fake friends who'd once made my life bearable.

"You went into the desert," I said to Marsha. "You wandered in search of yourself."

Marsha's eyes went wide, and then she smiled. Just a little bit. I'd gotten it right and at just the right moment to win her back.

189

Thank you, Crocodile Dundee.

"Athena told me once that if a truly sensitive person went walkabout in the desert here, like the Aborigines do in the outback, the vortexes would reveal themselves," Marsha said. "They would share their energy. Share their wisdom."

Her tentative smile faded.

"But they didn't, of course. I was so confused and frightened . . . and I found nothing out there. Nothing," she said. "Because Athena was a fraud, wasn't she?"

I sighed. And I nodded.

"So you drove out into the desert on walkabout," I said. "And you were out there for . . . ?"

Marsha squinted, obviously doing the math.

Eugene had already done it. And he didn't look happy with the answer.

"About thirty hours," he said.

"Did anyone see you?" I asked Marsha.

I already knew pretty much what she'd say. It's why Eugene was so unhappy.

"A few tourists," Marsha said with a shrug. "Nobody I knew or could ever find again. I was mostly walking around Juniper Mesa, which isn't very popular, I guess. When I wasn't down by the parking lot, I didn't see anybody at all."

So as her husband's bloodied body lay spread out in her house, Marsha was supposedly on a spiritual journey in the desert with no one but coyotes and vortexes and untraceable just-passing-through visitors around to notice.

Detective Burby must have *loved* that.

Speaking of which . . .

"How did Burby find you?" I asked.

"I'm not sure. I assume he had someone watching the motel. I'd only been back about twenty minutes when he showed up. I knew it wasn't good news as soon as I realized what he was. I assumed Bill had been arrested again or something. But then he told me that Bill had been . . . had been . . ."

Marsha swallowed hard, fighting back more tears.

"*. . . murdered,*" she said firmly, as if accepting the truth of it for the first time.

"And then he suggested that you come in with him," I said. "Just to clear up some questions."

Marsha nodded. "When we got to the police station, he started asking if we'd been fighting. So of course I said that we had. A lot . . . though our fights were never really fights. They were Bill yelling and me waiting for it to be over. Because of Bill's temper, you know? And Detective Burby

191

seemed to find that real interesting. He asked me what I thought about the arrest and the drugs and gun in Bill's car. Did I think he could have been set up, like he kept saying?"

"And what did you say to that?" I asked, keeping my expression blank, my body still, my tone calm. I was working so hard to seem placid, I could have qualified to be a yogi.

"Well, I told him it was possible. Bill wasn't exactly popular," Marsha said. "He didn't get along with some of our neighbors. Or *anyone* at Oak Creek."

My wall of calm cracked a bit — not because of nerves. Because of excitement.

I smelled a new lead. "Oak Creek's where Bill sold timeshares, right?"

"Yeah. Oak Creek Golf Resort. It wasn't an easy place to work. There was always so much pressure to bring in new buyers and close deals. I'm surprised Bill lasted as long there as he did, actually. He *hated* Harry Kyle, his boss. And Harry knew it." The corners of Marsha's mouth twitched. "Bill wasn't very good at hiding his feelings."

"How did Burby react when you talked about Oak Creek? Did he seem interested?"

Marsha shrugged listlessly. Suddenly she looked very, very tired.

"Not particularly. He went back to asking me what Bill and I had been fighting about, why I was leaving him, whether I" — Marsha's eyes began to glisten — "loved him . . ."

The tears returned.

I patted Marsha's bony shoulder and looked at Eugene.

I didn't expect a happy wink and a thumbs up, but I didn't expect what I was getting either. Eugene was giving me a steady, stony stare. A glare, almost.

He knew. About my mother, about me. It must have come up when he was in the police station with Marsha and Burby.

Great. Mr. Straight-Laced knew I was Ms. Crooked. Just what I needed right then.

I didn't know what to say. So it was almost a relief that I didn't get a chance to say anything.

"It's time I spoke with Marsha privately, Alanis. Attorney to client," Eugene said. "After that, I think, Marsha should get some rest."

"Of course. Good idea. Do you want me to wait outside until — ?"

"You've done enough waiting today. I can drive Marsha back to her motel when we're through here."

"Oh. All right."

I'd been about to suggest that Marsha stay at the White Magic Five and Dime. I looked over at her to see if she'd bring it up herself.

She didn't. She just wiped at her eyes and sniffled and gave me another tentative, tremulous smile.

"I'll call you later," she said. "I . . . have some questions for you."

Eugene kept glowering at me in a way that said *yeah, me too.*

I gave Marsha's shoulder a squeeze, then left.

Back at the five and dime, the OPEN sign was still glowing in the window, and Clarice was behind the counter where I'd left her hours before.

"How's Marsha? Are the cops holding her? Has she been charged? What does Eugene think?" she asked quietly as I stepped inside.

"Marsha's fine and free. No charge for now. As for what Eugene thinks, I don't know . . . except that I'm some kind of scumbag."

Clarice looked confused for about three-quarters of a second.

I'd told her about the conversation Marsha had overheard a couple days before, and the kid was quick with two plus two.

"He was gonna find out the truth about us sooner or later," she said, voice still strangely low.

"Yeah, and *later* would've been my choice," I said, matching her hushed tone. "By the way — why are we whispering?"

Clarice jerked her head toward the back of the store. "Your five o'clock is here. He's waiting in the reading room."

It felt like I'd swallowed a bowling ball pulled out of a freezer.

I didn't have a "five o'clock."

"Oh, right. Almost forgot," I said, perfectly calm. On the outside, anyway.

No reason to spook Clarice. Yet.

I sorted through possibilities as I headed for the reading room.

A Grandi showing up to turn that OPEN sign off forever?

Bill Riggs's killer making a preemptive strike on the meddler out hunting for him?

Or maybe it was —

Yes. It was.

Bachelor number three.

"What are you doing here?" I said when I saw him.

George Washington Fletcher looked up at me from the reading table. My tarot deck was spread out in front of him.

He'd been trying to play solitaire with it.

"What does it look like?" Fletcher said with a grin. "I'm here to see my future."

FANTE DI BASTONI   KNAVE OF WANDS
VALET DE BATONS   SOTA DE BASTOS

BUBE DER STÄBE   STAVEN SCHILDKNAAP

The last few cards have been pretty rough, so congratulations are in order. You've made it to the Knave (sometimes known as the Page). You can take a breather, strike a heroic pose, and contemplate different paths and fresh adventures. Who knows? You're sure to attract admiring attention thanks to that bitchin' skirt and those shapely gams. But don't get cocky, dude. You're standing by a cliff. You might want to glance back over that manly shoulder and take stock of what's behind you.

Miss Chance, *Infinite Roads to Knowing*

"I'm sorry, but now isn't the best time," I told Fletcher.

"I understand," he said.

He didn't get up, though. Instead, he scooped up the cards in one smooth motion, shuffled them three different ways — weaving, overhand, and the riffle — then left them in a neat stack in the center of the table.

It looked like he'd been a dealer once upon a time.

I could guess why he wasn't a dealer anymore.

"I see how busy you are," he said, nodding languidly at the empty shop down the hall and the also-empty sofa and chairs where no customers waited for readings. "So as much as I might like to while away the time reminiscing about Athena, we can just get right to the reading."

He patted the cards and smiled.

I sat down across from him, the smooth son of a bitch. The chance to learn more about my mother was the bait — and I was biting.

I picked up the cards and shuffled them again. I did the weave, the overhand, and the riffle, then threw in a pile shuffle, a Hindu shuffle, and a scramble, just because I could.

Fletcher whistled appreciatively.

Then I remembered that the client is supposed to shuffle before a reading. I'd been so intent on one-upping Fletcher — or maybe impressing him — that I'd smeared my karma all over the cards for no reason.

I put the deck down in front of him. "Do you have a particular question you want to ask?"

"I do," Fletcher said.

After that I got silence. And a smirk.

"And . . . ?" I said.

"Oh, I'd rather keep that to myself."

"Suit yourself. Shuffle the cards again, but this time be thinking about your question while you do it. Then cut the deck into three piles." I paused. "With your left hand."

He picked up the deck and started to shuffle. He started off simple, almost clumsy this time — like a seven-year-old with an Uno deck — as if he didn't want to try to compete after what he'd seen me do.

Then he launched into the Mexican spiral mixed with the Mongean shuffle topped off with the Zarrow before cutting the deck into three perfectly even piles.

"Why the left hand?" he said casually.

"The energy's better out of the left," I said.

Really, I had no idea. I just remembered hearing that somewhere — probably from Josette.

Fletcher nodded as if it made sense, then just looked at me expectantly.

"Now pick one of the piles," I told him.

He pointed at the middle one, and I picked it up with my right hand while sweeping the rest of the cards off to the side with my left. Then I began laying out five cards in a cross shape. When the cross was done, I placed a sixth card sideways over the middle card.

"Okay, then. Here we go."

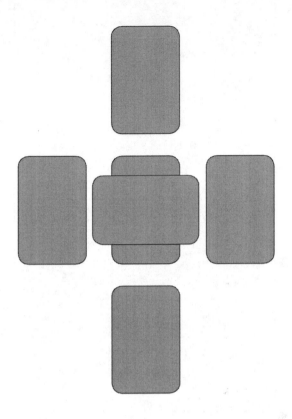

I reached toward the sideways card at the center of the cross, slipped out the card beneath it, and turned it over.

"This card represents you: the Two of Wands. Looks like you've had some success lately — trips to the clink notwithstanding. See this guy holding a globe? He's got the world in his hands."

Fletcher nodded and grunted in a neutral, unreadable way.

I flipped the sideways card next.

IL CARRO / LE CHAR — VII — THE CHARIOT / EL CARRO

DER WAGEN — DE ZEGEWAGEN

"This card represents the issue at hand — the crux of the matter: the Chariot. Whatever success you've had, you've achieved it through sheer force of will. See how the black-and-white sphinxes are angled in different directions? They don't work well together. You've controlled them through the strength of your mind or the force of your personality, but you have to watch out.

All that control can make you overly rigid."

This time Fletcher scoffed. "I am the least rigid person you're ever gonna meet. I'm like a Slinky or something, I'm so flexible."

"That might be what you tell yourself," I said cryptically, "but the cards are saying something else."

Fletcher gave me a deadpan look that seemed to say *I'll bet you say that to all the suckers.*

And the look wasn't all that wrong. I had used the line whenever a client said something like "that's not me at all!"

"Moving along," I said.

I turned over the card beneath the crossed cards at the center.

"Wands again — the three this time, in the near future position. Wands is the suit of action. So what we've got here is someone who wants to *do* something — specifically, set off in a new direction — but he's blocked. Before he can do that, he has to get beyond that wall in front of him — a wall he put there himself for his own protection. He has to step out of his comfort zone, in other words. Are you thinking about some big new project, Fletcher?"

It was Fletcher's turn to be cryptic. "Always," he said, and left it at that.

I flipped over the card to the left.

"The Four of Pentacles. This position shows what's holding you back, and it's fear again. Look at that guy. He's scared. That pentacle over his head tells us what he wants: money. But he's so worried someone's going to take away what he's got that he hoards it, cuts himself off, leaves himself alone. Sound familiar?"

I looked across the table at Fletcher, expecting another scoff. He didn't give me one, but he looked tempted.

"Are you telling me I'm afraid of commitment?" he said. From the look on his face, it was obvious this wasn't the first time a woman had said such a thing to him.

"I call 'em like I see 'em," I said.

I turned over the next card — the one above the crossed cards in the center of the spread.

"The card in this position shows us how you can overcome the things that are blocking you. You've got the Seven of Pentacles, which I'd usually tie to job satisfaction or a sense of fulfillment and accomplishment, but it's reversed here. So you're getting the job done, but you're *not* satisfied. I think you need to ask yourself why."

"Wow," Fletcher said. "I think I'm gonna

get my fortune told, and I end up getting analyzed by Dr. Phil. I can't wait to hear how my troubled relationship with my mother diminished my ability to love."

"You want your fortune told? Fine. Let's look at your future."

I flipped the final card.

"I'm going to hell?" Fletcher said. "I've heard that one before, too."

"This isn't you going to hell — not literally, anyway. It's you giving in to something — an obsession or a destructive worldview. That's the path you're on if you don't change your ways. This isn't you being chained by the devil; it's you chaining yourself."

My words seemed to hit close to home. Fletcher's expression shifted and sobered, and he nodded thoughtfully for a moment.

"Hmm. Chained by the Dark Side you are not," he said. "Chained by yourself you are."

He was doing a perfect Yoda imitation.

I wasn't annoyed. I wasn't amused. I wasn't going to give him the satisfaction either way.

I just said, "Yeah. Something like that," then changed the subject. "How did you know my mother?"

Fletcher opened his mouth to answer, and I got the distinct impression he was about to croak out something like "worked with her often I did, young Jedi." Wisely, he changed his mind and replied in his normal voice.

"She was a colleague, I guess you could say. Never an actual partner, though. Things never got that far. But we kicked around

212

the idea of a collaboration once or twice."

"How did you meet?"

"Oh, you know. Word gets around about this and that. She sounded like a real interesting lady, so I made sure we got acquainted. It wasn't hard to arrange."

Fletcher grinned at me.

"You came in for a reading," I said.

The grin grew larger.

"When you say word got around," I said, "do you mean you know who some of my mother's clients were?"

I cocked my eyebrow just enough when I said *clients* to make it clear what I meant.

Marks.

"I hate to tell you this, Alanis," Fletcher said, "but you're being awfully presumptuous."

"I am?"

"Yes. You are. You're acting like my reading's over, but you never answered the question I was asking the cards."

"The question you wouldn't tell me."

Fletcher nodded. "That's the one."

"The cards are what they are, Fletcher. You don't get to choose your answer."

"But I don't feel like I got an answer at all. Your mother, she gave good fortune — *you're going to come into money, beware of a red-headed man with a limp* — juicy stuff.

213

You sound like a self-help book. It's almost like . . . well . . ."

His words trailed off, but I knew where they led. *Almost like you actually believe what you're saying.*

That was a conversation I didn't want to have with Mr. GW Fletcher.

"Don't want an unsatisfied customer," I said.

I picked up the cards again and gave them a quick shuffle. Then I spread them out in an arc on the table.

"Think of the question and pick a clarifying card. That'll be your final answer."

It was a move I'd read about in *Infinite Roads to Knowing* but hadn't tried yet — because I hadn't needed to.

Fletcher pulled one card from the middle of the deck. He examined it for a moment, then placed it on the table between us.

"Looks like I've got a new woman in my life," Fletcher said with a smirk.

"Not necessarily," I said, deadpan. "The High Priestess card doesn't represent a specific person. It relates to intuition and magic and mystery and secret truths buried deep in the subconscious."

Fletcher added a cocked eyebrow to his smirk.

"Okay, screw it — I don't know what it means," I said. "I can never figure out that goddamn card. You may as well have drawn from a Pokémon deck."

Fletcher ran a finger lightly over the card, almost caressing it. "Well, I'll just stick with my interpretation, then. After all, I did meet a magical, mysterious woman today. And I can't believe she didn't come into my life for a reason. What do I owe you?"

"Didn't you see the sign? Returning customers get a reading free. I'm sorry yours wasn't as . . . *definitive* as you wanted."

Fletcher shrugged dismissively. "Who needs definitive? I'm Mr. Flexibility, remember?"

He reached into his shirt pocket, pulled out a folded piece of paper, and put it on top of the High Priestess card.

"In lieu of payment," he said.

I made no move to pick up the paper.

"Thanks for the freebie, Alanis . . . and good luck keeping that friend of yours out of jail."

Fletcher stood up and started to go, then paused and flashed me another of his thousand-megawatt smiles.

"I'll be seein' ya."

He left the reading room.

I heard him say goodbye to Clarice, then open the front door of the five and dime.

Only after I'd heard the door close did I pick up the slip of paper he'd left on the table.

Written on it were ten numbers. Nothing else.

The cocky bastard had left me his phone number.

I started to crumple the paper in my fist. I stopped.

Good luck keeping that friend of yours out of jail.

Yeah, I was going to need some luck. And some help.

I refolded the paper and stuffed it into my pocket.

Cocky.

Bastard.

I stepped out to the front of the store to find Clarice watching Fletcher walk down the sidewalk.

"Better looking than most of our customers," she said.

"I didn't think he was your type."

"He's not. But that doesn't mean I don't know hot when I see it."

Clarice waggled her eyebrows suggestively.

I ignored it.

"Ever seen him before?" I asked.

"Yeah, I've noticed him around town. He's pretty noticeable."

Clarice gave me another eyebrow waggle. When I didn't react, she threw in a wolf whistle. I think she was trying to see if she could embarrass me.

She should've known better. People born and raised to lie, cheat, and steal don't embarrass easy.

"Who is he?" Clarice asked me.

"No one," I said — though what I wanted to say was *trouble*.

The man was shady. Shifty. Slippery.

Perfect for what I'd decided to do next to help Marsha. Unfortunately, I couldn't trust GW Fletcher to be untrustworthy in just the way I needed.

Clarice stepped up and waved a hand in front of my face.

"Hey — you still there?"

I blinked and shook my head.

"Sorry — I was just thinking about an errand I have to run tomorrow."

"Oh?" Clarice said, cocking her head and folding her arms across her chest. "Can I help?"

She couldn't know what the "errand" was specifically, but she'd obviously guessed that it had something to do with Marsha.

"Yes. You can help," I said.

I walked to the register, opened it, and took out a twenty-dollar bill.

"You can run down to El Zorro Azul and get us some dinner. I'm starving."

Clarice looked annoyed, but of course that didn't stop her from taking the money.

"Can I invite Ceecee over to eat with us?"

I opened the register and pulled out a ten.

"Thanks!" Clarice said, snatching the money from me and hurrying toward the door.

When she was gone, I picked up the phone we keep near the counter.

I needed a partner for what I was planning. A grown male one.

GW Fletcher? Too sketchy.

Eugene? Too square.

Victor Castellanos? Too square, too — but maybe I could do something about that.

I dialed.

"Hey, Victor. It's Alanis," I said. "What are you doing after school tomorrow?"

CAVALLO DI BASTONI   KNIGHT OF WANDS
CHEVALIER DE BATONS   CABALLO DE BASTOS

RITTER DER STÄBE   STAVEN RIDDER

It's time to hit the road, and your horse is raring to go. You've got your armor and your battle club, and you're ready for a ruckus — even though you don't know who you're fighting or why. In fact, you don't have a clue where you're going, either. So you might want to hold your horse and check your GPS before you set out. It's way too easy to get lost in the desert, and all the bravery and determination in the world won't keep you from cooking in that suit of armor.

Miss Chance, *Infinite Roads to Knowing*

"I'm not sure this is a good idea."

We were in the black Caddy heading down Route 89A toward Sedona. Victor Castellanos was slumped beside me in the front seat looking like I was taking him in for a root canal.

"You didn't have to say yes, you know," I told him. "You could have told me you'd be washing your hair tonight."

"That would have been lying," he sighed. "And for some reason I find it hard to lie to you."

"Why — you're afraid I'll call your mom?"

Lucia Castellanos had been one of my mother's most loyal customers, which was how my mother had ended up with so much of her jewelry. I'd returned it all, yet Victor still didn't trust me.

Lucia, on the other hand, didn't just trust me. She seemed to think I was her handsome fortysomething son's last, best shot at wedded bliss.

Victor slumped in his seat even more. Any lower and he'd be a puddle on the floorboards.

"My mother has nothing to do with it," he said. "I'm happy to be your go-to guy for . . . whatever this is."

He turned his head to look out at the brush-pocked desert and jutting buttes we were passing.

"And what *are* we doing, anyway?" he said. "Why make it a big secret?"

"Okay, you're right. Cards-on-the-table time." I saw the turnoff I'd been looking for and put on my signal. "What's your preference? Gas station or 7-Eleven?"

"For what?"

"To rob, of course. You're going to be the getaway driver."

Victor's eyes went wide.

"I'm kidding, silly," I said. "You don't stick up one of those places in broad daylight. We're hitting a bank!"

Victor finally got it. He shook his head and let out a growly sigh.

"Funny. So where are we really going?"

"We're going to look at houses in Sedona."

"Look at houses?"

Victor looked even more alarmed than he had a few seconds before. I could see the

223

terrifying question burning in his eyes.

Did Mom put her up to this?

"There's a housing development I want to check out, that's all," I said. "You're my beard."

"Your beard?" Victor squeaked. "Why do you need a beard?"

"The usual reason. The house is in a Christian gated community, and I bat for the other team."

Victor squinted at me, then shook his head again.

"No, you're not," he said. "Not the way you kiss."

"Oh, yeah? How many lesbians have you kissed?"

"None," he said. "And that includes you."

"Don't get out much, do you?"

Victor finally smiled. A little.

"See? This is fun, right?" I said. "It's called joking. You should do it more often."

"Are you telling me to lighten up?"

"Let me guess — you've heard that before."

Victor folded his muscular arms across his broad, manly chest and pouted like a five-year-old.

"I can be light," he said. "I'm light all the time. I — hey!"

He'd noticed the sign pointing toward

Sedona. I was turning us in the opposite direction.

"You said the development was in Sedona."

"It is."

He jerked his thumb at the sign behind us. "Sedona's thataway."

"I know. But Cottonwood's thisaway."

"What's in Cottonwood?"

"Don't worry. This is just a little detour. Why don't you show me how light you can be?"

Victor went back to pouting instead.

I parked the Caddy on the corner of a quiet street lined with squat one-story ranch houses and even squatter scrubby trees.

"Well, that's a relief," Victor said.

"Yeah?"

He pointed out the window.

"No 7-Elevens or gas stations," he said.

I reached out and pinched his cheek old-school grandma–style.

"Thatta boy! There's that fabled Castellanos lightness! Keep working on it till I get back."

I picked up the notebook and pen I'd brought along and got out of the car.

"How long are you going to be gone?" Victor asked before I could close the door.

"Anywhere from ten seconds to forever, depending on how this goes. I'm guessing it'll be somewhere in between."

I started to close the door, then stopped myself.

"By the way, I left the key in the ignition. Just in case."

"Just in case *what*?"

"Oh, you'll know."

I closed the door before he could ask how.

It didn't need saying.

Gun shots. Screams. Sirens.

Even Victor Castellanos would know he was really my getaway driver.

I walked a winding half-block to 3801 Pioneer Drive — home of Michael LoTempio, Arizona State Trooper.

The house was cute. A little candy-pink bungalow with a yard of white stones. A mesquite tree filled with twittering birds stood to the right of the walkway.

More importantly, there was only one car in the driveway. A Subaru Forester.

A wife car. A mom car. A not–Michael LoTempio's car.

Or so I hoped.

If it were Michael LoTempio in the highway patrol car that had been lingering around the Riggs's house . . . and *if* LoTempio saw me when I'd spotted the car a few days before . . . and *if* LoTempio had bashed Riggs's not-exactly-ample brains out for getting him in trouble with that bust gone wrong . . . and *if* LoTempio were home now . . . and *if* he recognized me . . .

If all that? I was about to be in a hell of a lot of trouble.

I comforted myself by counting all those ifs as I walked up to the house. How unlucky would I have to be for this to go suddenly, disastrously, murderously wrong? Pretty damned.

But I couldn't help remembering something Biddle said, too: *luck is a sucker's game.*

Never count on being lucky . . . or not being lucky. Sure bets or nothing, that was the way to play.

This was not a sure bet.

I rang the doorbell anyway.

The classic two-note chime — *DING dooooonnnng* — echoed through the house. A moment later, the door opened and I found myself facing what I could only assume was Mrs. Michael LoTempio. If it were Mr. LoTempio, it was pretty amazing how much he looked like a slightly pudgy, long-haired Ellen DeGeneres.

"Can I help you?" Mrs. or Mr. LoTempio said.

"That's what I'm hoping." I smiled and stretched out a hand. "Gladys Kravitz. I'm new to the neighborhood."

"Nice to meet you, Gladys. I'm Marion LoTempio."

The woman returned the smile and gave my hand a dainty, ladylike shake.

"Did you move into the Rogers's place?" she said. "I saw the moving van there a couple weeks ago."

My smile widened. It looked like relying on luck hadn't been such a bad bet after all.

"That was us!" I said. "Pioneer Drive's newest pioneers!"

"Well, welcome. I'm sorry I haven't popped by to say hello. Things have been" — Marion's gaze slipped away to the side, her eyes going glassy; then she blinked and looked me in the eye again — "you know," she said. "So how's the neighborhood suit you so far?"

"That's just what I'm here to talk to you about, actually. We've loved it here. Really, truly loved it. It's been so beautiful. So *quiet*. Except for Sunday night."

I let that hang there as if Marion should know what I was talking about.

"Sunday night?" she said, blinking at me

in bafflement.

I nodded. "The night of the party."

"Party?"

There was more blinking.

"Yes," I said. "Those neighbors of ours — what a blowout they had! The talking, the laughing, the fireworks — I don't think it stopped until dawn."

"Are we talking about the McNallys or Joyce and Herman?"

Something about the names "Joyce and Herman" made me think they weren't party animals.

"The McNallys," I said. "Abner and I didn't get a wink of sleep because of them. That's why I'm going around today." I waggled my notebook. "I wanted to see who might sign a petition calling for a block curfew."

Marion eyed the notebook warily.

"I'm really sorry you had that experience," she said. "But we've never had any problem like that ourselves."

"So you didn't notice anything strange Sunday night."

"No."

"Not even the mariachi band?"

"Mariachi band?" Marion blinked again, then narrowed her eyes. "I'm surprised my husband didn't notice anything. He was working a late shift Sunday — got home sometime in the middle of the night — and he didn't say anything about fireworks."

"Well, those sort of came and went. So what kind of work does your husband do?"

"He's an Arizona State Trooper."

"You don't say! And he always has to be on patrol in the middle of the night?"

"No, not usually. There was some kind of last-minute scheduling mixup and he ended up covering for a friend. If you want, you can talk to him about that night yourself."

"He's . . . here?"

I tensed.

Marion shook her head.

I relaxed.

"No," Marion said. "But his shift was over forty minutes ago. He'll be home any second."

I tensed again and did something about it.

"Hey, that's perfect!" I said, starting to back away from the door. "I'll pop back and talk to him once I've spoken to some of the other neighbors. Thanks for your time. It was lovely meeting you!"

I gave Marion a little wave, then turned and hurried off up the street.

After maybe half a dozen steps, I heard the LoTempio's door close behind me.

That didn't stop my hurrying, though. Because any moment Michael LoTempio was going to come cruising up the street — and I knew now that he didn't have an alibi for the night Bill Riggs had died.

Now here's a woman who knows what she wants and how to get it. We can only assume that one of the things she wanted was a skirt so poofy you could park a golf cart under it. What's she got down there? She's not telling. What she's *not* hiding is her familiar: the black cat at her feet. This queen doesn't make things happen with a royal decree. She's got some black magic mojo, and she's not afraid to use it.

Miss Chance, *Infinite Roads to Knowing*

I made it back to the Caddy without being spotted, recognized, and run over by Michael LoTempio.

"Something wrong?" Victor said as I swung down into the driver's seat, started the engine, and drove off almost — but not quite — quickly enough to do a *Dukes of Hazzard*–style peel out.

"Everything's ducky," I said. And I almost told him why.

We had a strong suspect lined up, and hopefully we were on our way to line up more. Slowly but surely we were getting Marsha Riggs off the hook.

Then I looked over and saw the way Victor had his big hands braced against the dashboard, long legs stiff and straight to push him back into his seat, teeth gritted, one eye closed. All because I was suddenly going 35 in a 25 zone.

I could just imagine his reaction when I

told him we were poking our noses into a *murder*. So I didn't tell him.

"Ready to look at some real estate?" I said.

"Sure," he grunted, still bracing for an imminent crash. "But I'm not in any *hurry*."

I got the message and eased off the gas.

For the moment.

The signs started ten miles outside Sedona.

A handsome, grinning gray-haired man clenching a fist and raising a club in victory as a golf ball rolls toward a hole.

OAK CREEK GOLF RESORT
AND ESTATES
THE PERFECT PLACE TO
PUTTER AROUND!
A EUREKA RESORTS
INTERNATIONAL DESTINATION

Then: a regal gray-haired woman dressed in immaculate white laughing with three other Stepford Wives as a waiter brings them fruity drinks by a pool.

HEAVEN HAS A NEW NAME
. . . AND DAIQUIRIS
OAK CREEK GOLF RESORT
AND ESTATES

Etc.

"Is that where we're headed?" Victor asked after the fifth sign.

"That's right."

"I'm not sure I'm going to fit in."

Victor's skin isn't all that dark, but he was Darth Vader compared to the Casper the WASPy Ghosts on the billboards. The only brown-skinned person in any of the ads had been the guy bringing the daiquiris.

"Just try to think like a Republican, and you'll be fine," I said.

"I *am* a Republican."

I glanced over to see if Victor was joking. He wasn't.

"Well, then this'll be easy," I said.

I hoped I was right.

There was a gate with a guard, but all I had to say was "we're here for a presentation" and we were waved through.

Despite the sign, Oak Creek Golf Resort and Estates didn't seem like heaven to me. It looked like your typical housing development/timeshare getaway targeting upper–middle class families and retirees from back East. I knew such places well, though I'd never actually been to one. For years I'd peddled timeshare units like these over the phone. In a way, it was nice to see that they actually existed. Sometimes it had felt like I was selling rainbows and unicorns.

We drove past rows and rows of tidy two-story townhomes and villas with the occasional tennis court, swimming pool, or fountain to break up the monotony. Some of the houses were half done and there were stretches of empty street where construction had yet to begin, but it was clear what was coming: more of the same.

Then I noticed who was building it. A sign in front of one of the nearly finished houses told me.

ANOTHER QUALITY HOME BROUGHT
TO YOU BY
HUGGINS CONSTRUCTION

The "former co-worker" who'd found Bill Riggs's body had driven to his house in a Huggins Construction truck. So now I knew the connection . . . sort of.

It seemed a bit unlikely that a front-office guy like Riggs would pal around with someone from the construction crew. And even if he did, why was his buddy dropping by his house early on a Tuesday morning?

Curiouser and curiouser.

And then even curiouser still.

As we cruised past, I noticed two work-men — Huggins Construction employees, presumably — scrubbing graffiti off the side of the unfinished house. The red paint was faded now, but you could still read the message.

INDIAN LAND FOR INDIANS!
INDIAN LIBERATION FRONT

"Is this really Indian land?" I asked Victor. He shook his head.

"Couldn't be. They would never have got-ten permission to build here if it was."

I nodded as if that were true.

There's no such thing as never, Biddle used to say. *Just a higher price.*

But tribal politics wasn't my concern just then.

We'd passed Oak Creek's sales office on the way in. I turned around, headed back to the small lot in front of the building, and parked the car.

"Before we go in, there's something I need to give you," I said.

I dug into my purse and pulled out two plain gold bands. One I slipped onto my ring finger. The other I gave to Victor.

He looked at it as if I'd just dropped a scorpion onto his palm.

"Oh, come on," I said, rolling my eyes. "We're supposed to married, remember?"

Victor pinched his ring in his fingers and held it up to give it a better look.

"Where'd you get these?"

"Don't worry," I said. "They're not hot."

Not anymore, anyway. I'd taken the rings from my mother's stash of jewelry in the White Magic Five and Dime, so their previous owners — whoever they were — hadn't had them for a while. That made them lukewarm at best.

"Just put yours on and try not to act like it's giving you cooties," I said. "And let me do all the talking. You're the strong but silent type, okay?"

"I'll do my best. But I wouldn't say acting is my best skill."

Victor slipped on the ring and tried to smile.

He was right. He was a terrible actor. But it was too late to change partners now.

I got out of the car and headed for the sales office.

Show time.

A pretty young blond at a reception desk greeted us when we walked in. Behind her was a wide room filled with low-partitioned work cubicles. In each one a salesperson sat huddled with a couple, talking intensely.

A presentation had just wrapped up — probably a video playing to an audience lured out to Oak Creek by the promise of gift cards or free meals. Now, if they wanted to collect their freebies, they had to hear the rest of the pitch face to face — and resist the hard sell.

"I'm so sorry. You just missed the presentation," the blond said with a smile. "The next one's not till five."

"Oh, we've already been through all that," I said. "We came back to see the salesman we talked to last time." I went up on my tiptoes to scan the room. "I hope he's here today. Bill Riggs?"

The blond's smile stiffened.

"I'm afraid he's no longer with us," she said.

"Oh, no! We'd already worked out most of the details with him."

I turned to share a look of disappointment with Victor.

"Uhh . . . bummer," he said.

I reached out and took his hands in mine and squeezed them. Hard. *Really* hard.

Victor got the message. He pinched his lips together tight.

"You can talk to another sales representative as soon one's available," the blond told us.

"No," I said. "We want to talk to Bill."

The blond's smile was so stiff by now it looked like rigor mortis had set in.

"That's not possible," she said.

"Anything's possible . . . especially if you want to close a deal," I said. "We'll be waiting right over there."

I put a smug look on my face, as if I were pleased with myself for pulling off a negotiating trick I'd just read about in an Internet article called "10 Ways to Knock 10 Percent Off Your Down Payment."

"Come along, Jonathan," I said, tugging Victor with me as I walked away.

"Jonathan?" he whispered once we were settled on a pleather couch near the sales office's front door.

"You're not happy with your alias?"

"Why do I even need an alias? Why did you just lie to that woman? What's going on?"

"Shhh. Watch."

I nodded at the work cubicles.

One of the couples was getting double-teamed. An older man — fiftyish but looking fit in a sleek, well-tailored suit — had joined the salesdrone for the full-court press. I could see he'd resorted to an old salesman's trick: writing a bunch of jargon down on a notepad and forcefully underlining and drawing arrows toward the selling points. The end result:

Commit now

Read the fine print later

Asking questions is for losers

Payment is non-refundable

100% your money → → → US = YOU HAPPY!!!

And it worked. The couple looked at each other with wide, cowed eyes, exchanged a few words, then nodded.

The older man grinned and turned to the blond receptionist.

"Sophia," he said.

She hopped up and hurried off around a

corner. When she returned a few seconds later, she was carrying a silver tray with glasses and a bottle of champagne balanced on it. She delivered it to the work cube where the couple was now signing form after form after form.

"Congratulations, Paul and Shari Rodes!" the man boomed. "And welcome to Oak Creek Golf Resorts and Estates!"

He popped open the champagne, and the other salespeople applauded.

As the man poured glasses of bubbly for a beaming Paul and Shari, a different couple — this one looking confused and embarrassed — was quickly hustled toward a back door by a stone-faced salesman. No one else would look at them. The salesman didn't give them a kick in the pants as he practically shoved them out the door, but that was only because they weren't worth the trouble.

They were nobodies. Losers.

Because they were smart. They'd said no, so they had to go.

It takes a special kind of person to thrive in a business like this — coddling and manipulating the gullible while coldly discarding the uncooperative and unprofitable. "Assholes," I think they're called. Or "sociopaths," if you want to be more scientific about it.

In my case, "Mom" also fit the bill.

The older man moved on to another cube. He leaned in over the couple there and put his hand on the husband's back in a way that was supposed to seem friendly but was really assertive and domineering. Everything was a power play with this guy. A battle for dominance he had to win.

I didn't have to wonder how someone like Bill Riggs would get along with him. I knew.

"Alanis — you need to tell me. *Now,*" Victor said. "Why are we really here?"

"To see him."

I nodded at the man. I knew another name for him.

Harry Kyle. Bill's boss.

And perhaps suspect #2.

RE DI BASTONI · KING OF WANDS
ROI DE BATONS · REY DE BASTOS

KÖNIG DER STÄBE · STAVEN KONING

Presented for your consideration: a king upon his throne. Why does he keep it outside, where every passing lizard will feel free to crawl around on it? So that he can measure everything in his kingdom against his royal rod. (And if that sounds Freudian . . . well, it is.) His authority isn't just a tool for maintaining order. It's a license to judge. He likes his lands and subjects just so, this king, and anything that doesn't measure up is going to bring down his wrath.

Miss Chance, *Infinite Roads to Knowing*

It took the Oak Creek sales force thirty minutes to clear the room. In the end, it was fifty-fifty — six couples got the bum's rush out the back, six got champagne — which is an amazing sell-through percentage. These guys were good.

Harry Kyle was on hand for every score, always managing to materialize just before a couple broke down and said yes, always the one to turn and signal for the Korbel. Did that make him a control freak who didn't trust his team to do its job or a glory hog who had to muscle his way into every success?

My verdict after watching the man work: both.

Sophia, the young receptionist, seemed to know better than to get in his way while there was blood in the water. But once the prospects had all been properly sorted — profitable over here, unprofitable out the door — she sidled up to his side and spoke to him softly.

His gaze darted our way. When he saw me watching him, he smiled.

I smiled back.

This was going to be interesting.

"I'm so pleased you decided to come back," Kyle said as he ushered Jonathan and Jennifer Hart — Victor and me — into his office. "Can I get you anything? Water? Coffee?"

"I'm fine," I said.

Victor wasn't taking any chances. He just grunted and shook his head.

I did a quick scan of the room and didn't see anything I didn't expect.

Mahogany desk — check.

Plush office chair big enough for Captain Kirk on the bridge of the Enterprise — check.

Shelves lined with large leather-bound books that looked impressively official (and had no doubt never been opened) — check.

Framed inspirational poster featuring a soaring eagle and a drippy sentiment ("*DARING:* You'll never know how high you can fly until you spread your wings") — check.

Kyle seating himself and gesturing for us to sit in the chairs on the other side of his desk — check.

"It must have been a while since you were in for a presentation," he said as we sat.

"I think it was two or three months back," I said. "Right, dear?"

Victor looked surprised to be addressed.

He grunted and nodded.

"Well, that explains it," Kyle said. "Otherwise, I'm sure I'd remember you. And Bill left us weeks ago."

"Where'd he go?" I asked.

Kyle shrugged and gave me a non-answer answer: "Oh, it was just one of those things."

"One of what things?"

"It didn't work out for Bill here."

"Why not?"

"I probably shouldn't talk about it, Jennifer. Now this deal you and Bill were discussing —"

"Why shouldn't you talk about it?"

Kyle really was smooth. He only clenched his jaw and gritted his teeth for half a second.

"There are legal implications," he said blandly.

"Oh. I get it," I said. "You're afraid he'll sue you."

"No. I'm not afraid Bill will sue me," Kyle said. And the little smirk he allowed himself told me something extremely important.

He knew Bill Riggs was dead.

"Look," he said, "wouldn't you rather talk about Oak Creek? You must be excited about coming here. Who wouldn't be, right? Five pools, four restaurants, thirty-six holes of USGA-rated golf, a four-star day spa just steps away from —"

"Yeah, yeah — we know all that," I cut in. "That's why we're here. But you have to understand: we had something special with Bill. A real bond. We trusted him, you know?" I turned to Jonathan/Victor. "I don't know about you, dear, but I'm a little nervous about doing this without him."

My "husband" took a chance and spoke.

"Umm . . . me . . . too?" he said.

I'd been right to tell him not to talk. A natural actor he was not. Compared to him, Keanu Reeves was Sir Laurence Olivier.

I turned toward Kyle again.

"Bill being gone so suddenly . . . I think it just makes us wonder what's going on out here."

Kyle's chair let out a little squeak as he leaned forward and hit us with his best super-sincere "let me level with you folks" look.

"I understand. And let me assure you: Bill's departure had nothing to do with the quality of the Oak Creek lifestyle or the value of an Oak Creek home. It was simply a case of a square peg in a round hole."

I cocked my head and gave Kyle a look of squinty-eyed puzzlement. Out of the corner of my eye, I could see Victor trying to copy it. It looked like someone had squirted lemon juice in his face.

"Bill wasn't what you'd call a team player," Kyle said. "There were . . . disagreements. With me, with the other sales associates. Sometimes even with prospective vacation club members or buyers like yourselves."

I turned the dial on my puzzled look up to eleven: complete and utter bewilderment. I didn't dare peek over at Victor, but I could only assume he was still trying to look stupefied, too.

Kyle's expression didn't change, but his face was starting to flush just the teeniest bit pink.

We were getting to the guy.

"Bill had a hard time keeping interactions professional," he said. "Eventually there were legal repercussions, and we had to let him go."

"Oh!" I said, sitting up straight in my chair. "He got in fights."

The pink on Kyle's cheeks deepened to red.

"Not fights. Disagreements."

"About what?"

The red deepened to purple.

"About everything," Kyle grated out. "Bill Riggs was an . . ."

He stopped himself just in time.

Mustn't speak ill of the dead. Or call the dead an asshole.

". . . an extremely opinionated man," Kyle said.

"That's so hard to believe. He was always sweet as pie to us," I said. "And I know we weren't the only ones who got along with him. He was tight with one of the guys on the construction crew, am I right?"

The purple vanished, with no red or pink in between. Kyle's face just went straight to bleached-sheet white.

"What do you mean?" he said.

"It's just something Bill mentioned when he was telling us how well the houses here are built. The construction company only uses the best this and the strongest that and the most dependable other thing, and he knew because he was buddies with . . . oh, what was his friend's name again, dear?"

"Uhhh," Victor said.

I circled my hands in the air as if the name was right on the tip of my tongue. "You know. The guy from Higgins or Huggins or Muggins Construction?"

Victor gave me another "uhhh."

"Jack Schramm?" Kyle suggested, his voice quiet and quavery.

I snapped my fingers and grinned.

"Jack Schramm! That's the name I was hunting for!"

"Oh, yes," Victor said woodenly. "That was it."

Kyle was more than wooden. He suddenly looked petrified.

"I'm sorry," he said. "You'll have to excuse me for a moment."

And he stood stiffly and lurched swiftly out of the room.

"Where do you think he's going?" Victor said.

"If the movies have taught me anything, that is a man who's about to splash his face with water from a bathroom sink, then give himself a long, hard look in the mirror."

"But why? What are you up to here, Alanis?"

"Please. Don't break character. It's Jennifer."

I hopped out of my chair and leaned over Kyle's desk. Apparently, Kyle was a traditionalist: he still used a real paper appointment book. It was sitting beside his phone, spread out to show the week's schedule.

I scanned it for highlights or lowlights or

anything interesting, but the only standout was STAFF/MEMBER MIXER PICNIC!!! blocking out a three-hour chunk of the next day. I reached out and flipped back a page to see the previous week's appointments.

"He's going to be back any second, *Jennifer,*" Victor growled.

"Much better, *Jonathan,*" I said.

Harry Kyle was a busy man. His days were packed with meetings, presentations, and conference calls. But only one, I noticed, took place after six o'clock.

It wasn't clear what it was or where it was, but I had a hunch who it was with.

It was scrawled on the line for 9 PM Friday night.

J.S. — #235

"Are you all right, Harry?" I heard a woman say. "You look —"

"I'm fine," Harry Kyle snapped.

When he walked into his office two seconds later, I was in my seat, legs crossed.

"God, could you stop going on about that, Jonathan?" I was saying. "I swear, all you ever do is gab, gab, gab."

Victor just gaped at me.

"Sorry about that," Kyle said as he walked around his desk and sat down again. "I just remembered something I had to take care of."

His face looked moist.

"So," he said, rubbing his hands together with unconvincing enthusiasm, "shall we get down to business?"

My phone started playing "The Jean Genie."

Good timing. My business in Kyle's office was done, and now I could give myself an excuse to leave before I had to start faking my way through a bogus real-estate deal.

I dug out my phone.

"It's from Sabrina," I said to Victor.

"Oh. Okay," he said blankly.

"The babysitter," I explained to Kyle.

I put the phone to my ear.

"What's going on, sweetie? I hope Reggie didn't get into the liquor cabinet again."

"Alanis?" Eugene said.

"He did *what*?" I said, bulging my eyes wide.

"Alanis, is that you?"

"Is it still on fire?" I said.

"Is this some kind of joke?"

I hopped out of my chair.

"Well, *how did he get a lawn mower into the house in the first place?*" I cried in horror.

"Stop playing games, Alanis," Eugene growled. "I've got something important to tell you."

"Just hang on! We'll be right there!" I lowered the phone and faced Kyle, who was staring at me with a dazed look on his face. "I'm sorry, Mr. Kyle, but Jonathan and I need to leave immediately. Thank you for your time. You'll be hearing from us again soon."

Victor followed as I scurried out the door, the phone pressed to my ear again.

"For god's sake, don't touch it if it's still running, Sabrina!" I barked. "The firemen can figure out how to get it out of the bathtub!"

"I'm just going to sit here quietly until you can knock off the nonsense," Eugene said.

A few seconds later, Victor and I were out in the parking lot, headed for the black Caddy.

"All right. Nonsense knocked off," I said. "What's going on, Eugene?"

"Marsha's being charged with the murder of William Riggs."

I came to such a sudden stop that Victor actually bumped into my back.

"What?" I said.

"She's already in jail," Eugene told me. "Burby took her in about half an hour ago."

"That smug, overeager rookie dipshit."

"Maybe not."

"What do you mean, 'maybe not'?"

"He had his ducks in a row. More than enough probable cause for an arrest warrant."

It was a warm, dry Arizona evening . . . and suddenly I felt very, very cold.

"What could Burby possibly have on Marsha?" I asked.

"Well, he claims he has proof she hired a hit man to kill her husband," Eugene said. "And the thing is, Alanis — she's not denying it."

■ ■ ■ ■

PART 2
REVERSALS

■ ■ ■ ■

Suddenly everything's been turned on its head — including you! It's a wonder your crown hasn't fallen off. At least you've got your rod to cling to; instead of being a symbol of mastery, now it's a lifeline. Keep holding onto it — and the skills and confidence that got you that crown in the first place — and maybe, just maybe, you won't drop head-first into oblivion.

Miss Chance, *Infinite Roads to Knowing*

Eugene filled me in as I stood there in the parking lot.

Burby had found incriminating Internet searches on Marsha's laptop. She'd used keywords like "hit man" and "assassin" and "kill for money Arizona," and then she'd done more than Google killers: she'd hired one.

When Burby asked her if she'd been in contact with a hit man, she didn't say no. She said, "Yes, but I hadn't actually —"

That was as far as Eugene got. In the distance I heard a muffled voice barking out unintelligible words.

"Here we go again," Eugene groaned. "That was my bathroom break, Alanis. Burby wants me back in the interview room for round two with Marsha."

"Thanks for being there for her, Eugene."

"Don't thank me yet. My specialty is estate planning. If you wanted Matlock, you've come to the wrong guy."

"I'm sure you're doing great."

"Well, Burby seems to hate me, so I must be doing something right."

"Tell him I'm coming to see him."

"He's already counting on it."

"And tell Marsha everything's going to be okay."

There was a pause. Then a sigh.

"I'm not sure how you do business, Alanis," Eugene said, "but I *never* lie to my clients."

And he hung up.

I had Victor drive us back to Berdache. I wanted my hands free to wring and my mind free to brood.

"Is this when you finally tell me what the hell this is all about?" Victor said as we pulled out onto the highway.

"This is when I was going to, yes."

Victor glanced over at me expectantly.

We went by a billboard letting us know that we'd just passed paradise: Oak Creek Golf Resort and Estates was one exit behind us.

A minute later, we passed the sign letting us know it was two exits behind us.

Victor was still waiting for an explanation. "Alanis . . . ?" he prompted.

"How about if I said it's complicated and you should just trust me?"

"I'd say, 'What kind of fool do you take me for?' "

"And I'd say, 'A really nice one whose help I deeply appreciate.' "

"And I'd say, 'Stop trying to butter me up and just tell me the truth.' "

"And I'd say —"

"Good god, Alanis!" Victor roared. "Do you really think this is an acceptable way to behave? Is this *normal* to you?"

I thought it over. "Now that you mention it, I never saw the Bradys do it."

"I'm not joking!"

"Neither am I. My mother was a sociopathic con woman, Victor. Watching *The Brady Bunch* alone in a hotel room was as close to normal as I got growing up."

"Well, I hate to point out the obvious, Alanis, but you're all grown up now and your mother isn't here."

I'd been slumped in the passenger seat, but now I suddenly sat up straight. It felt like someone had just attached electrodes to my toes and given me a jump start.

"What is that supposed to mean?" I asked Victor. But part of me knew already.

"It means if you expect me to keep dancing around for your amusement like some mindless puppet, doing whatever you want without any thoughts or questions or feelings of my own, that's not on your mother. That's on you."

Victor's words gave me another jump start. If I sat up any straighter, my head would pop through the roof.

Goddamn that goody-two-shoes tightass. How dare he judge me. And how dare he be right.

"I'm sorry, Victor," I said. "I haven't been very . . . respectful, have I? I guess I was afraid if I told you everything up front, you wouldn't help me."

Victor gave me a surprisingly warm, gracious smile. Just like that, all was forgiven.

"It's all right, Alanis. Just tell me what the trouble is."

So I took a deep breath and told him. Not quite everything — there was no reason for him to know how I'd set Bill Riggs up to get arrested — but it was enough.

"Meth?" he said when I told him what the cops had found in Riggs's car.

"Murdered!" he said when I told him what had happened to Riggs.

"Hit man!" he said when I told him what Eugene had just told me.

His smile disappeared fast, and I could tell from the way he clenched his jaw and gripped the wheel and stared straight ahead at the ribbon of blacktop winding through the desert that I'd been right about him in the first place.

He wasn't going to help me.

The rest of the ride back to town was very, very quiet.

Victor dropped me off at the police department and told me he'd leave my car at the White Magic Five and Dime. There was no talk of him coming inside with me.

I knew I could trust him to leave the Cadillac at my place. I'd probably find it washed and vacuumed.

Victor was a good man. A nice man. A law-abiding man.

Which was why we had no future.

Burby didn't keep me waiting long when I told the cop behind the glass at the reception counter that I was there to see him. I'd barely settled myself in one of the waiting-area chairs when the door by counter opened and Burby waved me through it.

"In my office," he said.

I followed him through narrow halls underlit by fluorescent lights, checking every door to see if it was the one Marsha might be behind. We didn't pass an interview room or holding cell, though.

We did pass several uniformed officers. Their stares ranged from merely hostile to downright murderous.

My reputation doth precede me.

Finally Burby led me into a small room and closed the door behind us. The walls were bare, the floor clean, the desk free of clutter. It was obvious the office hadn't been Burby's for long.

He walked around the desk and plopped into the seat there. He didn't invite me to sit, but I took the chair across from him anyway.

"The Fixer," Burby said.

"The Fixer?" I said.

Burby nodded. "The Fixer."

I narrowed my eyes. "The *Fixer*?"

Burby narrowed *his* eyes. "The. Fixer."

"Are you saying I'm the Fixer?"

"*Are* you the Fixer?"

"I don't know. What the hell is 'the Fixer'?"

"So you're saying you're *not* the Fixer."

I repeated myself. "What the hell is 'the Fixer'?"

Burby leaned back in his chair and steepled his fingers and regarded me coolly. He was trying to appear wily and enigmatic, I think, but his bland baby face ruined the effect. It looked more like he was about to launch into a Dr. Evil imitation.

"You know what?" he said. "I believe you."

"I haven't told you anything."

"It's the way you haven't told me anything that I believe."

I managed not to roll my eyes.

"Look," I began.

"You're about to tell me that I'm making a terrible mistake, am I right?" Burby cut in.

"About that, yes. You are making a terrible mistake. I mean — you arrested an abused woman for murder because she googled 'hit man'? The DA's gonna have you busted down to crossing guard."

Burby smiled faintly.

"We've got more than Google searches. We've got emails, too," he said. "Your friend Marsha paid someone to murder her husband."

"That's bullshit. Marsha Riggs wouldn't ask someone to swat a fly for her, let alone kill Bill."

"Well, I guess that settles it then. If an upstanding citizen like you is willing to vouch for her character, I suppose we should just release her right now."

"You know she's flat broke, right? How do you think she was going to pay this supposed hit man?"

Burby's smile turned into a smirk. "I think maybe a friend was going to give her the money."

He practically waggled his eyebrows at me.

The little shit was determined to make me an accessory one way or another.

"Michael LoTempio," I said.

"Michael LoTempio?" I expected Burby to say.

"What about him?" he said instead.

Suddenly the bombshell I'd wanted to drop was looking more like a firecracker. But I had to try dropping it anyway.

"He's the state trooper Riggs had a fight with," I said.

"Yeah, yeah — I know," Burby said impatiently.

"Some of the neighbors saw a state patrol cruiser hanging around the Riggs's house last week. And LoTempio doesn't have an alibi for the night of the murder."

The bit about the alibi was a stretch. Easy enough for the guy to lie to his wife about working late. Happens all the time.

Only this time, it hadn't.

"LoTempio not only has an alibi, it's the best one anybody in the world could possibly ask for," Burby said. "At the time William Riggs was murdered, Officer LoTempio was answering highway patrol calls twenty miles away."

"But all he'd need is half an hour to drive to Berdache and —"

"Haven't you ever heard of a dash cam, McLachlan?" said Burby with the sneering self-assurance of someone who'd personally checked LoTempio's dash cam video. "I might look young," he said, "but that doesn't mean I don't know what I'm doing."

"All right, then. What about Harry Kyle?"

"Harry Kyle?"

"Bill Riggs's boss. They didn't get along, and —"

"You're clutching at straws, McLachlan."

"Kyle —"

"I don't want to hear it."

"If —"

"We're through here."

"Please —"

"You're free to go."

"Burby —"

"Go."

"But —"

Burby pushed his chair back and stood. He looked ready to step around his desk and take me by the arm and drag me down the hall. To the door, maybe, or to a cell.

"Go."

I went.

■ ■ ■ ■

Burby hadn't wanted to talk to me, hadn't wanted to listen to me. He'd just wanted an answer to one question. And when he thought he had it, he'd thrown me out.

It was a pisser but not a total waste of time.

Now I knew the next question *I* needed to be asking.

The Caddy was parked behind the White Magic Five and Dime, as promised. The keys were inside the store. Clarice jingled them at me when I walked in. Ceecee was with her behind the counter.

"What did you do to Mr. Castellanos?" Ceecee asked as I took the keys. She'd redone her hair since the last time I'd seen her. It was even more blue than usual.

"I told him the truth."

Clarice winced. "The whole truth and nothing but the truth?"

"No. But enough."

Clarice and Ceecee looked at each other.

"No wonder he seemed so pissed," Ceecee said.

"What were you and him doing this afternoon, anyway?" Clarice asked me.

"Trying to help Marsha."

"It didn't look like he'd be helping you much anymore," Ceecee said.

"He won't be. I don't think Victor has the biggest comfort zone, and being around me took him *way* out of it."

"Awww. Too bad," Ceecee groaned.

"You are such a shipper," Clarice said to her under her breath.

"It's all right," I said. "Fortunately, I've got other people I can turn to for help."

"You do?" said Clarice.

I gave her and Ceecee a long look.

"Oh! Us!" she said. "It's about time! What do you want?"

"I need you to use those Internet skills of yours to find somebody."

"Cool," said Ceecee. "Who?"

My answer had their eyes popping wide.

"An assassin," I said, "called the Fixer."

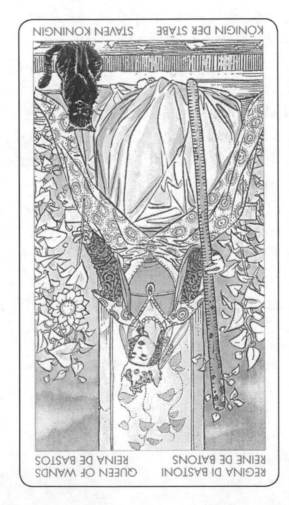

KÖNIGIN DER STÄBE　　STÄVEN KONINGIN

REGINA DI BASTONI　　REINE DE BATONS
QUEEN OF WANDS　　REINA DE BASTOS

Hanging around upside down is for the bats, though your cat has taken to it pretty well. You, solid fire queen, can handle it — or at least you think you can. You've been the first to rush in and help in a crisis, the first to offer guidance . . . and also the first to become bitter and cynical when everything goes topsy turvy. You'll probably also be first to get a massive migraine from the blood rushing to your head. Maybe you should just hang out a while in that comfortable (though upside-down) garden of yours. But then again, that's probably a wasted suggestion, since you're much better at giving advice than receiving it.

Miss Chance, *Infinite Roads to Knowing*

I explained the situation to the girls — Burby's accusations about a hit man and Marsha's supposed confession — and they had the same initial reaction as me.

No way.

"Then we've got to find this Fixer guy so he can tell Burby that Marsha didn't hire him," I said. "Assuming he even exists."

"The Fixer," Ceecee mused. "Sounds like a Batman villain."

"If he's real, we'll find him," said Clarice.

She swiped the laptop off the counter, and she and Ceecee raced off up the hall toward the stairs to the second floor. They were obviously excited by the weirdness and intrigue. It would have been cute if Marsha's life weren't on the line.

Oh, didn't I mention?

Arizona has the death penalty.

I went to the window to turn off the *OPEN*

sign and wondered if I should ever turn it on again. I'd been so sure I could take over the White Magic Five and Dime and just flip its karma like a pancake: turn wrongs into rights, help instead of hurt, make amends for all my mother's crimes. And the result: Bill Riggs in a morgue and Marsha Riggs in a jail.

Maybe I'd been fooling myself. About Marsha. About everything.

I wasn't even totally sure Marsha was innocent anymore. I used to think I was the perfect judge of character because I'd been well trained by someone who had none. But what if Burby was right? What if Marsha's helpless innocence was all just an act — one I'd been all too eager to believe because it had made me feel like some kind of hero?

It might depend on who this Fixer was. Burby hadn't come right out and said the Fixer was the hit man, but it was obvious he'd been testing me when we first started talking. He wanted to see if the name meant anything to me.

It didn't, but I was still a stranger here. If I were a local with friends in low places — like the Grandis, say — I might know all about the Fixer. It even occurred to me that it might *be* a Grandi. I had a good candidate in mind, too, given the nickname. But I wasn't about to stroll down to Anthony Grandi's bail bonds office and ask where he'd been the evening of October 3.

Then I remembered that I did have a friend in low places — or an acquaintance anyway.

I went to the small office at the back of the building and opened a drawer in the desk there. Sitting on top of a box of paper clips was a folded piece of paper I'd put there the day before.

I took it out, unfolded it, and picked up the phone.

Nrrrrrr. Nrrrrr. Nrrrrr.

Click.

"Hey there! You have reached the voice mailbox of GW Fletcher. If you've got something nice to say, wait for the tone. If you don't, do us both a favor and hang up now, asshole. Ha! Just kidding, Mom! You can go ahead and leave a message, too."

Beeeeeeeep.

"It's Alanis McLachlan, Fletcher. I need to know if you've ever heard of someone who calls himself the Fixer. He might be some kind of hit man, he might be a plumber — I don't know. Either way, I need to find out everything I can about him. Sorry if that doesn't qualify as 'something

278

nice.' How about . . . you don't seem to smell bad? Hope that's nice enough for you."

Cli-beep.

"You don't seem to smell bad"?

It occurred to me that my flirting skills were more than a little rusty.

Then it occurred to me that I shouldn't be flirting with a guy like GW Fletcher at all.

And then it occurred to me that if Marsha *had* paid the Fixer to murder Bill, I might be digging up the very proof that would get her the death sentence.

I couldn't stand by and do nothing, though. I had to keep my faith in my friend's essential goodness and hope for the best.

Somewhere deep inside me, my mother heard that and laughed.

I went upstairs to check on Clarice and Ceecee's progress. They'd made more than I was expecting.

A *lot* more.

"We found him!" Ceecee reported cheerfully.

"Already? That was fast."

"He made it easy," Clarice said. "He's got

an ad on Greylist."

"It's like Craigslist but skeevier," Ceecee explained.

I chuckled as I walked up to look at the laptop, which was on the kitchen table in front of the girls.

They were looking at a Greylist page. A blue headline ran across the top.

PRIVATE CONTRACTOR WILL FIX YOUR PROBLEMS — PERMANENTLY (AZ)

I stopped chuckling.

"Wait . . . you weren't joking about the ad?"

"Huh? Joking? No," Ceecee said.

"It's totally real," said Clarice. "The Fixer advertises in the same place as, like, hookers and guys looking to get together in rest area men's rooms."

I leaned in closer to read the ad.

If you're having trouble with someone, I am the solution. I provide killer service. It'll be a hit, man. Assassing the results afterward, you will be very pleased. Discretion guaranteed. Reasonable rates. Discounts for seniors. Reply to TheFixer@greylist-responses.com.

Clarice pointed at the screen. " 'Killer,' 'hit man,' 'assassin.' They're all in there. So if you do a search on any of those, you'll find this ad."

"It's pretty smart," Ceecee said. "If he'd put 'Want someone killed? I'll do it for money!' even Greylist would take the ad down. But this way, no one notices unless it's exactly what they're looking for."

I read through the ad a second and then a third time.

" 'Discount for seniors'?" I said dubiously.

Clarice shrugged. "Hit men can't have a sense of humor?"

"The ones I've known didn't," I almost said.

It wasn't a memory I wanted to dwell on, let alone joke about.

"Well, I guess the next step is to send the guy a message and see what happens," I said. "Let me sit down."

Clarice and Ceecee looked at each other. Neither made a move to get out of my way.

"What?" I said.

"We already sent a message," Ceecee said.

"What?"

"Don't freak out," Clarice told me. "We used a fake gmail account. There's no way it can be traced back to us."

"Well, what did you say?"

281

"Not much," Clarice said. " 'I've got a problem that needs fixing — a people problem. Willing to pay to make it go away for good. Write back for details.' Something like that. Vague . . . but clear enough."

"Oh god," I groaned. "I've known you less than a month, and already you might have a hit man for a pen pal thanks to me."

Ceecee and Clarice grinned.

"Yeah," Ceecee said. "Isn't it great?"

"Look," I said. "No more tonight, okay? And next time you'll ask before you do anything beyond googling, right?"

Clarice and Ceecee nodded.

"Okay," said Ceecee.

"Next time we'll ask," said Clarice.

I didn't believe them for a second.

I pulled out a twenty-dollar bill and tossed it onto the table. "Go get something to eat. You've earned it."

They both reached for it. Clarice was a little faster.

"Don't you want to come with us?" she asked me.

"I'd love to, but I have things to do."

Clarice started to open her mouth.

"Ask what and I'll take that twenty back," I said. I reached out for the bill.

Clarice was faster than me, too. She shoved the money into her jeans and bolted for the stairs.

"Come on! Let's go to El Zorro Azul!"

"Again?" Ceecee said as she got up to follow. "I'm getting kinda sick of that place . . ."

Once I heard the back door open and slam shut downstairs, I unplugged the laptop and hid it in the one place I knew Clarice would never look: the dishwasher. She seemed to think that if you left all your dirty dishes in the sink, the washing elves would come take care of them in the middle of the night.

Then I headed down the stairs and out to the black Caddy. I had some backtracking to do, and I didn't want the girls zooming ahead while I did it.

I drove through the darkening desert to the little town called Cottonwood and 3801 Pioneer Drive.

There were two cars in the driveway now. The Subaru Forester I'd seen there earlier and a decidedly more masculine Dodge Charger.

State Trooper Michael LoTempio was home.

I walked up to the house and rang the doorbell. I heard voices inside, then footsteps. The porch light came on.

The door opened.

I found myself facing a fortyish man with the burly build of a linebacker and the down-to-the-bone buzz cut of a marine. He was wearing a loose-fitting hockey jersey and cargo pants, but it was obvious he'd been in uniform not long before that.

The expression on his face was pleasant, solicitous.

Then suddenly it wasn't.

He had sharp eyes. We'd been half a block apart when I'd spotted his cruiser outside the Riggs's house, but he recognized me.

"Yes?" he said gruffly.

"I need you to come outside and talk to me."

"About what?"

"You know. You've seen me before. And I've seen you."

LoTempio put a hand on the door and took a step back. He was about to close the door.

"You'd better leave. Now."

"You were stalking Bill Riggs," I said quickly but quietly. "That's enough to cost you your job. I don't want to make a stink about it, but I can."

The door stayed open.

There were footsteps behind LoTempio.

"I'm Gladys Kravitz," I whispered. "I'm back to talk about the party at the Mc-

Nallys' Sunday night."

"Who is it, Mike?" a woman said.

"It's Gladys Kravitz," said LoTempio. "She's back to talk about the party at the McNallys' Sunday night."

I peered around LoTempio and saw his wife watching us from the hallway.

"Hi, Marion! Can I borrow your husband for a minute? He just offered to talk to the McNallys with me and clear all this party business up once and for all."

Marion smiled and fluttered a hand at LoTempio's broad back.

"Keep him for as long as you like. He already washed the dishes, so I'm through with him for the day."

"Thanks, Marion! Come on — let's go, Mike."

I turned and walked away. When I looked back, LoTempio was following me and scowling.

"I don't like being threatened," he growled once the house was far enough behind us.

"And I don't like threatening people. So we both have good reason to get this over with quick. Why were you hanging around Bill Riggs's house?"

"Riggs claimed the meth I found in his car was planted there. I wanted to find proof that he really was using or dealing."

"So you investigate by hanging out on his block in a state patrol cruiser?"

"I was trying to identify his associates."

"No. You were trying to intimidate Riggs. You knew Charles Dischler was his attorney and there was a good chance he was about to sue the state over the way you roughed him up. Your job was on the line, and you were trying to send Riggs a message."

We'd followed the road as it curved and climbed until we were out of sight of LoTempio's home. There were other houses lining the road, but they were silent and still aside from the gray flicker of a television here or there.

No one was around, it was dark, and I'd just called a large, hotheaded man a liar.

I've never taken an IQ test, but there are times I wonder how I'd do.

"That's not it," LoTempio said. "I mean . . . not entirely. I wasn't really thinking it through. I just wanted Riggs to know I was out there. I wanted him looking over his shoulder, wondering where I was. I wanted him to sweat. But that's all it was. Just an 'eff you' to a guy who deserved it."

I stopped walking. My Cadillac was just a dozen yards beyond us now — within quick sprinting distance, if it came to that.

"Now *that* story I believe," I told LoTempio. "So here's what I really want to ask you. You spent the last week or so basically staking out Riggs's house. Did you see anything?"

"What's it to you? Who are you, anyway?"

"A friend of Bill Riggs's wife. I don't particularly care that Bill is dead. But I do care that she's being charged with murder."

LoTempio took a moment to process that. It was too dark to clearly see the expression on his face, but it looked like the processing took a lot of effort.

"Okay," he finally said. "I may as well tell you 'cuz I can't tell anyone else. I did see something. A delivery."

"A delivery? Like Fed-Ex?"

"Like *drugs*. A guy goes up to the house with a backpack, talks to Riggs, goes inside, then comes out a minute later without the backpack."

"When was this?"

"Sunday."

"Sunday?"

LoTempio nodded.

Bill Riggs had been murdered Sunday night.

"What did this guy look like?" I asked.

"Big. Bald. Muscles. Flannel."

"And driving a pickup with Huggins

Construction printed on the side, am I right?"

"Yeah, that is right. You know who he is?"

"Not yet. But I know that he and Riggs used to work for the same people."

LoTempio's eyebrows shot up. "Meth dealers?"

I shook my head. "Real-estate developers."

LoTempio frowned as if that was just as bad.

"Did you see anything else important?" I asked him.

"No. I was only there three or four times, and I never stuck around long."

"Okay. Thanks. You won't see me again."

I turned and started toward my car.

I didn't get far.

LoTempio reached out, grabbed me by the wrist, and jerked me back.

"Thanks?" he snarled. "You come to my house, speak to my wife, blackmail me into answering your questions, and then you say *thanks*?"

His grip felt hard as steel. Maybe a knee to the groin or slap to the ear would get him to loosen up enough for me to break away and run. But then again, maybe it wouldn't. And if it didn't work, there'd be a steep price to pay.

I decided not to resist him. Yet.

He pulled me so close we were practically rubbing noses, and when he spoke again I caught the sour smell of Budweiser on his breath.

"Yeah, lady, I'd *better* not ever see you again. Because if I do, you're going to end up looking worse than Riggs."

He shoved me away and let me go, and I stumbled and tripped and almost fell. When I had my feet firmly under me again, I simply turned and moved quickly — not *quite* running — to the Caddy.

It was not the time for a snappy comeback. I had what I'd come for, as well as all of my teeth. That was a win.

If you're always trying to get the last word, Biddle used to tell me, *one day they'll be your final words.*

The point: sometimes you just shut up and go.

Which is exactly what I did.

I was jittery and jangled as I drove away. Confronting LoTempio alone had been dumb. Who knows? If he'd downed one more Bud before I showed up, maybe making a threat wouldn't have been enough for him.

I needed backup. But where was I supposed to get it?

My phone started playing "Desperado" — a song I'd picked out for a certain phone number just an hour before.

I took the call.

"Thanks for calling me back, Fletcher."

"Please. It's GW to my friends, remember? And of course I was going to call you back. I'm not about to let you mess with the Fixer on your own."

"So you've actually heard of the guy?"

"Heard of him? He's a legend — the bad kind. Like Dracula or the Wolfman."

"So he's not a plumber."

"I don't know. He might be in his spare time, when he's not killing people."

"Shit. I was hoping he was . . . hell, I don't know what I was hoping. But not this."

"How are you mixed up with him?"

"I'm not. Yet."

"Well, what can I do to help?"

I drove in silence for a moment.

I needed someone to watch my back.

I needed a wingman who was unburdened with scruples or respect for the law.

Damn it. It looked like I needed GW Fletcher.

"Alanis? You still there?"

"I'm still here. As for how you can help . . ."

I went silent again.

Was I going to say it?

Yes, I was going to say it.

"GW, how would you feel about a little breaking and entering tonight?"

RITTER DER STÄBE   STAVEN RIDDER

CAVALLO DI BASTONI   CHEVALIER DE BATONS
KNIGHT OF WANDS   CABALLO DE BASTOS

Whoa — a knight thrown from his horse. Pretty humiliating. There'll be a lot of pointing and laughing the next time you're in Camelot. Don't worry, though; you can still continue your quest. You just have to get back in the saddle, but be more careful this time. That trusty steed you're riding doesn't seem to be so trusty after all — and the next time you end up under its hooves, even your armor might not protect you.

Miss Chance, *Infinite Roads to Knowing*

Fletcher met me at 1703 O'Hara Drive —
until recently, the home of William Riggs.

"That's a good look for you," I said as he
slipped into the Cadillac.

"That's a good look for *you*," he replied.

We were dressed almost identically in dark
sweatpants and hoodies and running shoes
for either pretending to be late-night jog-
gers or, if need be, *running.*

"So . . . you want to tell me again why
I'm about to commit criminal trespassing?"
Fletcher said.

I ran through the story one more time, as
I had on the phone an hour before. A friend
was in trouble. Her husband murdered. The
killer had been looking for something. I had
reason to believe it might be a backpack —
and I had no idea what was in it.

"And that's really it?" Fletcher said.
"We're just doing a good deed for a friend
in need?"

"You sound skeptical."

"Well, burglary usually isn't quite so altruistic."

"This time it is."

Fletcher nodded. "That's good enough for me." He pointed at the Riggs's house. "That's the place?"

There was still police tape across the front door. Not that it mattered to us. We didn't plan on going in that way.

"That's the place," I said.

Fletcher leaned forward to gaze up at the sky.

"Crescent moon," he said. "Perfect for a B&E . . . not that I've ever B&E-ed before."

"Of course not. You've just read about it in books."

Fletcher smiled. "I'm very well-read."

Fletcher reached into his hoodie and pulled out two pairs of blue rubber gloves. One he handed to me.

"Playtex gloves? For a burglary?" I said.

Fletcher tugged his on, then rubbed the fingers together. "Better grip than cloth. And thinner, too."

"Or so you've read."

"Exactly." Fletcher nodded at the house. "We'll try the back door first. Always better to walk in than climb, if you can. Shall we?"

"Not quite yet. Before we do this, I want

to hear more about the Fixer."

"He's bad news. I'm not sure what else to tell you."

"Well, how about his name, where he lives, who he usually works for?"

"You want his social security number while I'm at it? Because I don't know that either, Alanis. He's a freelancer with a good reputation for being bad; that's all I know. Now we really ought to get moving. Every second we sit here gives someone another chance to notice us. The books are very clear about that."

"All right, fine. Let's go."

We got out of the car and walked casually toward the house — just two upstanding citizens out for a midnight stroll dressed as ninja dishwashers.

When we reached the back door, Fletcher knelt down by the knob and pulled what looked like a small black loaf of bread from under his hoodie. He rolled it out to reveal pouches filled with screwdrivers and pliers and miniature flashlights and metal tools I didn't recognize. He chose one — an L-shaped something-or-other — and grinned when he noticed me cocking an eyebrow at it.

"Tension wrench," he whispered. "You put it into the lower part of the keyhole, like so, then apply some light pressure. That tells you which way the key turns to open the door." He extracted a thin pick from his case and stuck it into the upper part of the keyhole. "This helps you feel the pins in the lock."

"Or so the books say."

"They're very detailed books."

While Fletcher fiddled with the door knob, I took a quick look around us. Nothing moved, and all I could hear was the occasional car driving by in the distance. Of course, that didn't mean someone wasn't watching us from their darkened home, maybe saying something like "Quick, Phoebe — call the police! A couple blue-handed people are breaking into the old Riggs place!"

"Interesting," Fletcher said.

"What?"

Fletcher slid his tools back into the case, then put his hand on the door knob and gave it a twist. The door swung open.

"Looks like I read all those books for nothing," Fletcher said.

"The door wasn't locked?"

"It couldn't be. Lock's busted."

"*Very* interesting," I said.

We were going in the same way the killer had.

Fletcher handed me a flashlight, took one out for himself, then rolled his tools up and stuffed them back under his hoodie.

We went inside. Once the door was closed behind us, we turned on the flashlights, making sure the beams were aimed low.

We were in the kitchen. Every cabinet door was open, and boxes of cereal and macaroni and cake mix had been swept off the shelves and onto the floor.

We found the same kind of mess in the dining room. Papers littered the floor and the well-worn maple table, and all the drawers of a matching hutch had been pulled out and upended. In the living room, the furniture had been pulled away from the walls, and the back of the couch had been slashed open to reveal the crisscrossing wood and springs inside it. A roll-top desk had been tipped over and its back panels smashed.

And that wasn't all that had been smashed there. Dark red splatters stained the carpet and walls.

"How'd the guy die?" Fletcher asked.

"Baseball bat," I said.

Fletcher winced. "Ouch."

"That's a bit of an understatement."

"May we — ?"

Fletcher gestured toward a hallway to our left.

"Good idea," I said.

We continued our search elsewhere, finding the same destructive mess in the bathrooms and bedroom and closets.

"The cops said the place had been ransacked, but this is more like demolished," I said.

"Yeah. Someone put a lot of energy into it. Not a lot of smarts, though."

"What do you mean?"

"Well, the books offer plenty of tips for where to look when you're doing this kind of thing, and I saw three perfect hiding places that haven't been checked yet."

"Oh?"

I gave Fletcher a look that said *impress me.* He turned and waved for me to follow him.

"Check out this closet in the hall, for starters. The killer pulled everything out but left the carpeting in place."

"So?"

Fletcher knelt by the closet. He reached down and picked at a corner of the carpeting, then lifted it up to reveal a square in the floorboards beneath.

A trapdoor.

"Crawl space?" I said.

"Either that or we're in a horror movie and it's the doorway to hell."

"My money's on crawl space."

There was a bolt locking the trapdoor, and Fletcher slid it open. Then he found a small metal latch, grabbed it, and pulled up. The trapdoor opened.

I stepped forward to shine my flashlight through the hole in the floor.

It was a crawl space, all right. I saw reddish-brown clay and shards of broken brick and the tip of something dark blue off to one side.

"Geronimo," I said.

I stepped forward and dropped to the dusty floor below. It was only about a four-foot fall. When I crouched down and moved my flashlight around, I saw what I'd been looking for.

A blue backpack.

I picked it up — then let out a gasp and fell backwards onto my ass.

"What is it?" Fletcher said. "Spiders? Snakes?"

"No, but thanks for the inspiration," I said, suddenly very aware of how completely creepy it is to be in the crawl space under a house.

Not that I needed any further inspiration.

A grinning human skull lay before me on

the floor. It was surrounded by what appeared to be shards of broken terra-cotta pottery. The skull and the pottery were nearly the same color — a dull, mottled copper.

"Oh my god," I blurted out. "So he wasn't crazy after all."

"Who wasn't crazy?"

"One of the neighbors. He told me he peeked in the window one night and saw Riggs painting a skull for a satanic ritual."

"What?"

Fletcher's head and arm popped down through the hole in the floor. He searched with his flashlight till he spotted the skull.

"Jesus! That is freaky!"

Then he noticed the backpack.

"Given what Riggs kept in his basement," he said, "I'm not a hundred percent sure I want to see what's in that."

"I know what you mean. But if it's going to help get Marsha out of jail . . ." I stood up, cradling the backpack in my arms. "On the count of three?"

Fletcher nodded.

"One . . . two . . . three."

I took hold of the backpack's zipper and pulled. It opened easily.

"Well, would you look at that?" Fletcher said.

He was a lot more articulate than me. All I could manage was "whoa."

We were looking at money. Lots and lots of money. All of it neat and tidy in $10,000 bundles.

"So . . . you're just helping out a friend, huh?" Fletcher said, a strained, hostile tone to his voice.

I started to look up at him.

"Yoink," he said.

With his right hand, he grabbed the backpack and tore it away from me.

With his left hand, he shoved me back down onto my butt in the dust.

"Wait, GW! Don't!" I cried.

But it was too late. He was already slamming the trapdoor shut above me.

A second later, I heard him lock me in.

BUBE DER STÄBE   STAVEN SCHILDKNAP

FANTE DI BASTONI   VALET DE BATONS
KNAVE OF WANDS   SOTA DE BASTOS

So here you are: an upside-down knave. A flip isn't quite as bad for you as it was for the king and the queen and the knight. You don't have a crown to lose or a mighty stallion to smash you flat, and apparently you don't even have to worry about your skirt flopping down. (How much starch do you put in that thing?) You're a simpler guy with simpler problems and a simpler approach to solving them, but don't be simple-minded about it. You got thrown for a loop because you didn't think things through in the first place. If you don't want to go head over heels again, *slow down.*

Miss Chance, *Infinite Roads to Knowing*

"Let me out of here!"

"Shhh. You'll wake the neighbors," I heard Fletcher say.

The floorboards above me groaned. Fletcher was standing up.

"Stop," I said. "You can't leave me down here."

"Oh, don't worry. You'll find a way out. Sooner or later."

"You son of a bitch —"

"You shouldn't have lied to me, Alanis."

"What are you talking about? I've never lied about anything."

I heard Fletcher scoff.

"I meant to you, Fletcher. I've never lied to *you.*"

"My friends call me GW," said Fletcher.

And he walked off. I could hear his footfalls fading as he went back up the hall and through the living room, the dining room, the kitchen.

Then there was silence. Complete and utter.

He was gone. I was alone — except for a human skull and whatever spiders and snakes happened to be down there with me.

I tried pushing up against the trapdoor, but the bolt held firm. I was stuck.

"Shit," I said.

Then I said a few more things, most of them unflattering descriptions of GW Fletcher — his provenance, his hygiene, and his sexual habits.

When I finally ran out of vulgarities (it took a minute or two), I started exploring the crawl space, moving the flashlight methodically over the dirt floor and cement walls.

"You'll find a way out," I said, imitating Fletcher's smug, lightly accented drawl. "Bastard."

And then I saw it: a way out.

Maybe. If I were a really strong opossum.

About thirty feet from me was a squat rectangle of metal mesh: ventilation for the crawl space. I hoped it wasn't as small as it looked. Slowly, walking doubled over like the Hunchback of Notre Dame, I made my way to it.

It wasn't as small as it had looked. It was even smaller. About fourteen inches high and twenty across.

I sat down in the sod, planted my feet against the ventilation screen, and pushed. And pushed. And pushed.

And kicked. And kicked. And kicked.

And cursed.

And kicked again.

The screen popped out and flew off into the darkness.

I crawled to the opening it left behind and tried to figure out how a grown woman was going to get through it. Maybe if I had some full-body Spanx and a bucket of Vaseline . . .

But I didn't. So I started doing it the hard way. And hard it was.

I tilted my head sideways and got it through, then managed to follow it with most of my shoulders. Since leaving the rest of my shoulders behind wasn't an option, I had to squirm and thrust and writhe until they were fully through. Then it was a matter of wriggling and contorting and not minding the scraping and abrasions as I slowly, slowly, slowly pushed my arms and chest outside. (For not the first time in my life, I was grateful to be a B cup and not a D.) Then, after I'd given myself a minute to catch my breath, I had to get my hips through. I knew what fate awaited me if I failed: I'd show up in one of those "dumb criminals" stories people love so much.

SHE BROKE INTO A HOUSE — BUT SHE COULDN'T BREAK OUT AGAIN!

Or

BUBBLE-BUTT BANDIT GETS CAUGHT IN THE (REAR) END

A fate worse than death. The sheer horror of it gave me the motivation I needed to worm my way out.

Once I was free, I took another moment to rest before getting up off the ground and heading around the house to the street. I felt like I'd just been squeezed out of a toothpaste tube, but that didn't slow me down once I was moving. I was already envisioning how things were going to go once I was behind the wheel of my Cadillac.

I saw myself cruising the streets of Berdache.

I saw myself spotting Fletcher walking along the road.

I saw myself veering from my lane just long enough to squash Fletcher flat.

I saw myself smiling.

It was a fun fantasy, anyway, and fantasy was all it would be.

The Caddy was gone.

I recycled some vulgarities, but it really shouldn't have come as a surprise. Fletcher had the tools of his trade with him. If he could open the back door of a house with them, why couldn't he hot-wire a car?

I suddenly felt very, very tired — too tired to face the four-mile walk home. But who could I call to come get me? Clarice and Ceecee didn't have a car — and they might try to steal one if they thought it would help. Marsha was obviously a no go. And I didn't feel like explaining to Eugene what I was doing outside the Riggs's house dressed like I was. I may as well have had a black eye mask on and a big bag over my back with SWAG written on it.

That was about it for friends and family.

Except . . . there was a neighbor I could try. She'd probably come get me — if she owned a car. For all I knew, she went everywhere via unicorn or astral projection.

I pulled out my phone (my sweatpants had pockets or I would have been *really* screwed) and looked up the home number of Josette Berg, owner of the House of Arcana, the occult shop across the street from the five and dime.

It was after midnight, but she answered after the second ring.

"Hello, Josette? It's Alanis. You're not busy at the moment, are you?"

I asked Josette to pick me up at a corner six blocks away. As I headed toward it, I stripped off my Playtex gloves and dumped them and my flashlight in the first trash can I saw. Then I started jogging. Isn't that what people in sweatpants and hoodies and running shoes are supposed to do late at night?

Five minutes later, I was at the corner, only panting slightly, when a Cadillac pulled up beside me.

A *white* Cadillac.

The window on the passenger side rolled down, and Josette poked her head out.

"Hop in!" she said.

I climbed into the back.

A tubby, gray-haired man with a walrus mustache was in the driver's seat. He looked a bit like Wilfred Brimley's not-quite-as-suave younger brother.

He was wearing striped pajamas, and Josette was in a fluffy white bathrobe.

"Alanis, this is my husband, Les," Josette said. "Les, this is Alanis."

"Nice to meet you, Les," I said. "I really appreciate you coming out to get me so late."

"Alanis?" Les grumbled. "You Athena

311

Passalis's kid?"

"That's right."

Les snorted. "If I'd known we were giving the competition a ride, I'd have stayed in bed."

Josette gave him a playful swat. "Oh, you grumpy old bear."

Les growled.

"So . . ." Josette turned to pin me with her gaze. "How'd you get stranded out here?"

"I'm too embarrassed to say."

"Oh, come on — you're among friends."

"Speak for yourself," Les muttered.

Josette ignored him. "There's no reason to be embarrassed."

"Okay. Well. To be completely honest with you . . . I went for a run and got lost."

Les burst into gruff guffaws.

"In Berdache? Lost?" he crowed. "That's like getting lost in a cardboard box."

"Oh, stop it, you," Josette told him with another little swat. I got the feeling she hit him like that about a thousand times a day.

"I told you it was embarrassing. I'm just grateful someone could come get me."

"It's our pleasure," Josette said. "We were just lying there reading anyway."

"I was sound asleep," said Les.

"You know, it's funny — I was actually

thinking about you, Alanis," Josette went on.

"Now I'll be up all night," Les said.

Josette shushed him, then continued again.

"I keep going over that reading I did for you the other day. You remember all the reversals? The Ace of Cups reversed, the Fool reversed, the Magician reversed. Reversals can be so complicated. There are so many different ways to interpret them. Some people try to make it easy by just going with the exact opposite of the upright card, but that's not always right. A reversal can also mean the energy of the card is increased or decreased depending on what the rest of the cards in the reading say."

Les started snoring loudly. Fortunately, he wasn't asleep at the wheel; he was just showing what he thought of all this shop talk. Josette didn't even bother hitting him this time.

"Well," she said to me, "I think I missed something. I think there's a connection between those three cards you had reversed, Alanis. Like maybe someone's trying to charm you *and* use his powers to deceive you. And please don't take this the wrong way — I know you're a very worldly woman — but I'm afraid there's a chance he might actually fool you."

I sighed. "Thanks for the warning, Josette."

"Not a problem. I probably should have called you right when I thought of it, but things got hectic. A tour bus stopped by, and I had a *ton* of customers — more than I could handle. I tried to send some your way, but the five and dime was closed."

"Always helping the competition," Les grumbled. "It's a wonder we're not broke."

Most of the homes and businesses we were cruising past were dark, but the lights were still on in one office.

"Looks like Anthony Grandi's working late tonight," Josette said sourly as we went by Star Bail Bonds. The Grandis are the only thing I've ever seen put a damper on Josette's good vibes.

"Now that's a dependable business," Les said. "All you have to do is sit back and wait for schmucks to get in trouble. I wonder who it is tonight."

I did, too. One thing I knew: It wasn't Marsha keeping Grandi at work. Eugene would make sure she took her bail bond business elsewhere — if she got lucky enough to get out on bail at all. Allegedly hiring a hit man would get you a charge of first-degree murder with aggravating circumstances; bail wouldn't be a given.

We turned onto Furnier Avenue, and half a minute later Les was slowing to a stop in front of the White Magic Five and Dime. He ended up parked behind a black Cadillac.

My black Cadillac.

Was that SOB searching the store, looking for more money now that I was (supposedly) out of the way?

I looked up at the second floor. The lights were on.

Clarice.

"Thanksgoodnight," I said quickly as I jumped out of the car and rushed to the front door.

"Such gratitude," I heard Les say. "What manners."

I guess I hadn't made a good impression. I didn't care.

The front door was locked, but that didn't mean anything. Fletcher would have gone in the back way whether the door was locked or not.

I unlocked the door, ran through the store, and tore up the stairs.

"Whoa," Clarice said when she saw me. "What's the hurry?"

She was sitting at the kitchen table with the laptop and a bowl of Froot Loops in front of her.

"You're all right?" I said.

Clarice put a spoonful of cereal in her mouth.

"Do I not look all right?" she said as she chewed.

"You haven't noticed anything weird?"

Clarice swallowed, then nodded.

"I have, actually," she said. "You busting in after midnight wearing sweatpants and a hoodie. Since when do you dress like Eminem?"

I let out a sigh of relief.

Obviously Fletcher hadn't broken in. He'd simply dropped off the car where he knew I'd eventually find it.

So the man wasn't a complete tool. Just 99.9 percent.

"Anyway," I said, "it's a school night. What are you doing up?"

"Waiting for you, of course. I had to show you this."

She jabbed her spoon at the laptop. On the screen was what looked like an email message. When I moved closer, I could see who it was from.

The address was TheFixer@greylist-responses.com.

When will you learn? Your whole world's been turned upside down, and *you're still holding on to those damned Twizzlers*! The burdens you've taken upon yourself are just as heavy as ever, but now you can't even count on gravity to keep the earth under your feet. You ought to think about throwing away the whole kit and caboodle now. Because if your world can do a loop-de-loop once, it could do it again any second.

Miss Chance, *Infinite Roads to Knowing*

The price is $2,000 per fix, the message read. *Half in advance, in cash, in person. Details are only discussed face to face. If you agree, I'll let you know the time and place for the meet.* DO NOT PROCEED IF YOU ARE NOT SERIOUS.

"So," Clarice said. "What next?"

"That's obvious," I told her. "You're going to bed."

Clarice dropped her spoon into her Froot Loops. "What? Come on! That's not fair!"

"It's not fair that I'm making you go to bed at 12:37 on a school night and not letting you stay up all night writing emails to assassins?"

"Yes!"

"You have a warped sense of fair, kid."

I closed the laptop, unplugged it, and put it under my arm.

"Well, good luck finding a better hiding place this time," Clarice said. "The dishwasher was the first place I looked."

She got up and marched off to the bathroom, leaving her bowl and spoon for the washing elves.

I took the laptop to my bedroom, closed the door, and got to work.

I am DEADLY *serious,* I typed. *Just tell me where and when, and I'll be there with the money.*

The next morning, Clarice was even louder than usual as she got ready for school. I heard stomping feet, clattering dishes, music, an electric toothbrush that sounded like it was being used vigorously right outside my room, and finally a slamming door.

It was my sister's revenge for being cut out of the action the night before.

Fair enough. It beat a flaming bag of dog crap and a knock on the door. And I needed to get up anyway.

First order of business: checking for another reply from the Fixer.

There wasn't one.

Second order of business: making myself look and feel like a human being.

That took a little time — and I didn't quite get to finish. Just a few seconds into my own tooth brushing I heard a faint, distant *rap-rap-rap.*

I stopped brushing and listened, and there it was again.

Someone was knocking on a door downstairs.

I spat out my toothpaste, rinsed out my mouth, and headed down to the first floor.

The rapping was coming from the front door — the entrance to the store. As I walked up the hall toward it, I could see someone peering in through the glass. When she noticed me approaching, she smiled and waved.

It was Liz, the woman who'd left $5,000 in "cursed" cash with me a few days before.

I opened the door and let her in.

"Sorry to come before you're open," she said, "but I was so excited to find out if you've lifted the curse. I just found out my cousin won one hundred dollars on a lottery scratcher card, and I thought, 'I bet that's a sign! I bet Alanis did it!' "

"Yup," I said. "It's a sign, all right. I did a few more spells and couldn't find any curse at all."

Liz blinked at me in astonishment from behind the large round lenses of her glasses.

"No curse at all?"

"Nope."

I walked over to the cash register, turned

it on, and opened it. Inside was the stack of bills Liz had given me.

I took the money out and offered to her.

"Spend it in good health," I said. "You have nothing to worry about."

Liz was still blinking. She made no move to take the money.

"But your mother . . . she was so sure . . ."

I shrugged. "Misdiagnosis. It happens." I gave the money a little waggle. "Please. Take it."

"I don't know. I'd hate to even touch it if the curse isn't lifted."

"But it is, Liz," I said through gritted teeth.

"Maybe you didn't have enough money to detect the curse. I could bring in more."

Now *I* was the one blinking at *her.*

Some people just won't be satisfied until you have all their money, Biddle used to say.

And I knew he was right. Some marks practically throw their life savings at you. But there was something else Biddle used to say.

We'd be out of business in a heartbeat if people just remembered one thing: if it sounds too good to be true, it's too goddamn good to be true.

"Tell you what," I said. "How about I show you proof the money's been cleansed?"

"You can do that?"

"Absolutely. Follow me."

I led Liz down the hall to the reading room and motioned for her to take a seat. I put the money on the table as I sat across from her, and then I picked up the deck of tarot cards that I keep there.

"We'll let the tarot tell us," I said. "Three cards should do the trick."

Liz hesitated, then nodded. "Okay."

I shuffled the cards, then held them out to her. "Cut them with your left hand and make three piles."

She did as I said.

I turned over the top card on the first pile.

"Ahh, the Moon reversed. Usually this card tells us things aren't what they seem. In the half-light of the moon, it can be difficult to see what's true; there are too many shadows. Reversed, this energy can be increased."

I said a silent thank you to Josette for her mini seminar on reversals the night before.

"So what does that tell us?" Liz said.

"A lot — if you believe in the tarot. But we'll know more when we see what's next."

I turned over the top card on the middle pile.

"Interesting. See how this card shows a guy sneaking off with a bundle of swords? Look at his expression. Confident, smug. He thinks he's getting away with something, but he's not as smart as he thinks: he's left two swords behind. He's careless. His plan was impulsive. He didn't think everything through. His theft is going to be discovered — and so is he."

"So that's you, maybe?" Liz said. "You made a mistake when you said the money wasn't cursed?"

"No. I don't think so."

"Well, what does it mean then?"

"Let's see the final verdict."

I turned over the top card on the last pile.

"The King of Cups — and look at that: it's reversed. You know something weird? I've had a lot of reversals pop up in my readings lately. What do you think that might mean?"

Liz shrugged. "You're the tarot expert."

I didn't tell her how wrong she was. The tarot was still very, very new to me. I was just beginning to understand how useful it could be — and how revealing.

"Well," I said, "upright, the King of Cups is a creative person. But reversed, he's someone who uses his talent to deceive and cheat. He's not always what he appears to be."

I looked into Liz's eyes.

"Like you," I said.

She didn't flinch. And I knew then that I — and the cards — were right about her.

Too goddamn good to be true.

"You didn't come here to get a curse taken off that money," I said. "You came to give me the chance to steal it."

Soft, hapless, harmless Liz vanished, replaced in an instant by a woman with cold, hard eyes and a sneering smirk.

"Told ya it wouldn't work," she said. "The bitch ain't stupid."

It took me a moment to realize she wasn't speaking to me.

"Of course. You're wearing a wire. Trying to entrap me," I said. "Who sent you? Burby?"

The woman just got up and walked out of the room. The trap had failed, and now she wasn't even going to bother talking to me.

I followed her as she headed for the door, showing her contempt for me by strolling slowly, utterly without fear. When she was out on the sidewalk in front of the store, I darted around to cut her off.

"Just let me say one thing," I said.

She cocked her head and gave me a scornful, heavy-lidded look that seemed to say, "Do your worst, biatch. I don't care."

I leaned in so close to her my face was less than an inch from her breasts — where I figured the mic was stashed.

"DUUUUUUUUUUUUUUCK YOOOOOOOO OOUUUU!" I shouted at the top of my lungs. Only I didn't really mention any birds.

A plain white work van was parked just a few feet away. I heard my own voice coming from it, as well as feedback and a yelped "ow!"

The woman shoved me back and told me to go duck myself. (Again without the bird reference.) Then she walked around to the back of the van, opened the doors, and climbed in. She slammed the doors shut before I could see who was back there with her, but a moment later a scowling middle-aged man with dark hair and a thick black mustache slipped into the driver's seat, started the engine, gave me the finger, then peeled out.

As they drove away, I noticed Josette watching from across the street. All the yelling about ducks (or things that rhyme with them) had drawn her out of her shop.

"What was all that about?" she asked as she crossed the street to join me.

"That woman was trying to catch me running a scam, but I wouldn't play along."

Josette scowled in a way that she usually reserved for one subject, which she promptly brought up. "Trying to catch *you* running a scam? That's ironic."

"What do you mean?"

Josette pointed at the van as it zoomed away up Furnier Avenue.

"That was Madame Jezebel. She has a phony fortunetelling parlor on the other side of town," she said. "She's one of the Grandis."

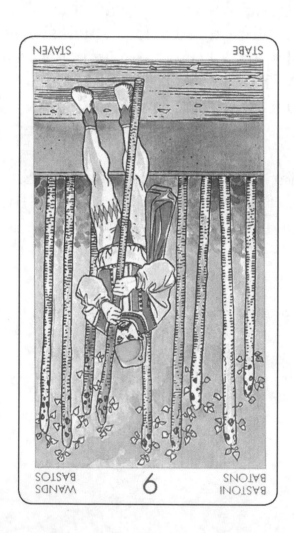

Your first line of defense — the breadstick stockade — has been upended. All the effort you put into erecting it was for nothing. It failed. *You* failed. You couldn't keep the danger at bay. That means it's time to take off your fez and put on a thinking cap, pal. You need a new game plan.

Miss Chance, *Infinite Roads to Knowing*

I didn't know what the Grandis planned to do with whatever they got on me. Take it to the police or the DA or a TV station, maybe. Maybe try to blackmail me into leaving town.

Whatever their scheme, it hadn't worked. But I didn't fool myself thinking I'd foiled the Grandi family for good. They'd be back again. And again. And again. As long as it took to get rid of me.

I couldn't worry about that just then, though. I had other nooses to stick my head in.

I thanked Josette for the ID and the ride the night before, then went back upstairs to check for new email messages on the laptop. There were three.

One was an offer to increase the size, strength, and "stanima" (I assume they meant stamina) of my nonexistent penis. Another was an urgent message from a

Nigerian bank manager who needed help with a million-dollar wire transfer. (How do those people find new email addresses so quickly? It was something even I had never figured out.)

The third message was from TheFixer@greylist-responses.com.

Noon today. Red Rock Factory Outlets. The fountain. Bring the down payment in a Mc-Donald's bag. COME ALONE.

I turned on the White Magic Five and Dime's OPEN sign and tried to pretend I cared whether anyone saw it or not. I couldn't stop thinking about Marsha. While I'd had a pretty crappy night — getting locked in a crawl space, losing a backpack full of cash (and evidence) — it was probably nothing compared with hers.

Her first night behind bars. I could only hope it was her last, too. My plan to make sure it was:

1. Get the Fixer to admit Marsha hadn't hired him (assuming she hadn't).
2. Learn why one of Riggs's co-workers was making house calls with bundles of money.

    2A. Get said bundle of money
       back.
    2B. Kick GW Fletcher's ass.
3. Find out why Riggs had taken up
   skull painting in his spare time.
4. Pray Marsha made bail.
5. Stop trusting assholes.
6. Start having much, much better
   luck.

Foolproof it was not. But it was all I had.

I was thinking I might start with 2A and 2B — since that was going to be one of the more satisfying parts of the plan — when my cell phone began playing "The Jean Genie."

I answered, not bothering with hello or good morning but going straight to "How is she?"

"As good as can be expected," Eugene said.

I winced.

I expected something pretty bad.

"Has her first appearance been scheduled?" I asked.

"That's what I'm calling about. It's set for 10 o'clock."

"Do we know the judge?"

"It's Crowell."

I winced again. I hadn't been in Berdache

long, but I already knew about Judge Crowell. He had a harder ass than the Venus de Milo.

"Maybe he'll take pity on her," I said.

"Maybe. After all, he is human . . . supposedly."

"I'll be there."

"Can you come a little early? There's something I'd like to discuss with you — in person."

"This is a hell of a time to propose, Eugene."

Silence.

"I'll be there," I said.

Eugene hung up.

I was four or five years old. We were in another nameless (to me) Midwestern city. The older buildings were brick; the newer, more "now" ones were groovy black glass and chrome.

And then we drove past a building that towered over the rest. It was made of imposing gray granite, with a golden dome that thrust high into the sky like it was trying to compete with the sun.

"What's that, Mommy?" I asked, pointing.

My mother glanced at it and sneered.

"That's where the stupid people go," she said.

"Not necessarily stupid," said Biddle. "Just sloppy."

So of course I thought it was where all the hippies lived.

Like I said: I was four or five.

A couple years later, we passed an identical building in an identical nameless city, and this time I saw the brass sign bolted to the cornerstone.

It was a county courthouse.

I went where the stupid, sloppy people go. It didn't look like the ones I'd seen when I was a kid, though. No imposing gray granite for Berdache, Arizona.

It was groovy black glass and chrome.

Eugene was waiting on a wooden bench outside one of the courtrooms. He didn't get up when he saw me. He just sat there forlornly, waiting for me to come to him like a graying, 250-pound bump on a log.

I walked over and sat next to him.

"You're quitting," I said.

"Not necessarily."

"Is it because of me or because you're in over your head?"

"I'm willing to stay in over my head until it starts harming Marsha."

"So it's me."

"It's you. The money you're paying me with — where did it come from?"

"You know that. My mother."

Eugene gave me a long, silent look.

"And yes," I said. "What you've heard from Marsha and, I assume, Burby is true. My mom was a con woman. *I* was a con woman — or a con girl, I guess. That's why I eventually ran away from her. It's why I was so surprised when she left me the five and dime."

"So why did you keep the store open? Why take over your mother's business?"

"Just look who I've met because I stayed — who I've been spending that money on. I'm atoning for my mother's sins. That's why I asked you all those questions about the cop who arrested Riggs and the guy he fought with in jail and Huggins Construction, too. That wasn't idle curiosity. I'm trying to help."

"I'd like to believe you, but I'm not sure I should," Eugene said. "My trust is nothing to trifle with, Alanis. I give it once. Once it's gone, it's gone for good."

"Are you saying you can never trust me again?"

"No . . . because I never entirely trusted you in the first place. But I can't keep going with this — taking money from you and feeding you information — if I can't believe in you."

"What do you want me to say, Eugene? 'I am not a crook'?"

Eugene mulled that over — then nodded. "Yes. That. Exactly."

I put up my right hand with the three middle fingers pointing straight up, scout's-honor style.

"I am not a crook." I brought down my hand and made an X across my chest. "Cross my heart and hope to die."

"All right, then. That's good enough for me," Eugene said. "You'll be getting my first bill for Marsha tomorrow."

He gave me a small, sly, sad smile.

I was trusted by Eugene Wheeler. And I was grateful.

"So what are you going to be saying in there?" I asked.

"That Marsha admits she exchanged emails with an anonymous individual who claimed to be an assassin, but that she never asked him to do anything, never paid him anything, and in fact broke off contact with him when he pressed her to make a commitment. She was a scared woman having an idle conversation that didn't lead to any harm to anyone. That's all. So if the Google

340

searches and emails are the only proof the DA's office has, they may as well drop the charges now so we can skip the whole conversation about bail."

"Sounds good," I said with an approving nod. "You'd think you actually know something about criminal law."

Eugene mock-grimaced. "Thanks."

"So how's our girl holding up?"

Eugene sighed, and the grimace turned real.

A court clerk came out to let Eugene know that Marsha's case was next. We stood and walked into the courtroom together. Eugene sat at the defendant's table. I sat right behind him.

I looked over at the prosecutor's table and found the bony, ponytailed, fiftyish woman sitting there staring right back at me.

"Howdy," I said.

The woman held my gaze another moment, then started sorting the papers spread out on the table before her.

A minute later, a dead-faced female marshal came in with a handcuffed Marsha.

Marsha looked like she'd aged ten years in a single night. Her face was ashen, her eyes puffy and pink, her shoulders stooped, her gait a stumbling shuffle.

When she saw me, a little life came back to her eyes.

"Oh, Alanis," she said. "You —"

The marshal stepped in front of her to remove the handcuffs, then pointed to the chair beside Eugene.

"Sit there," she said tonelessly.

Marsha sat.

I leaned forward and stretched out a hand, wanting to pat her on the back, but the marshal gave me a pretty good stink-eye for someone who seemed to be a zombie. So I sat back and just said "Hang in there" instead.

A moment later, the bailiff stood and called out, "All rise. Yavapai County Circuit Court. The Honorable Judge Crowell presiding."

The Honorable (I'd heard various other adjectives) Judge Crowell swept into the courtroom from his chambers. With his long strides and swirling black robes, he looked like he should be escorted by a squad of Imperial Stormtroopers. He was a pale Darth Vader with a bad comb-over and pair of glasses perched on the end of his nose.

He took his seat on the bench, lifted his gavel, and brought it down hard. Most of us flinched.

I got the feeling Crowell liked that.

"State of Arizona versus Marsha Riggs," he said. "The accused is charged with murder in the first degree. How does your client plead, Mr. Wheeler?"

Eugene rose. "My client pleads not guilty, Your Honor."

Crowell looked at the paper in front of him. "You are asking that the defendant be released on her own recognizance."

"That is correct, Your Honor."

Crowell kept his head tilted down but lifted his eyes to meet Eugene's. Then he shifted his gaze to Marsha.

I looked hard into the man's dark eyes, hoping there was a soul in there somewhere.

Crowell turned to the DA's table.

"Does the prosecution have anything to say about this?" he asked dryly.

"We do, Your Honor," the skinny woman said. "We believe that Mrs. Riggs engaged in a conspiracy to plan and execute the murder of her husband. That — combined with the fact that the defendant is known to associate with criminal elements in Berdache — makes her a flight risk. We request that the defense's motion be denied."

" 'Criminal elements'?" Marsha said to Eugene. "What is she talking about?"

"Later," Eugene whispered to her, throwing a worried look at Judge Crowell.

The guy was already reaching for his gavel, but he sat back and relaxed when he saw that Marsha had stopped talking.

"Go on," he said to the prosecutor.

And she did. At length.

She talked about the brutality of the crime and the cold calculation that preceded it and the need for Marsha Riggs to answer for what she'd done. And as she spoke, Marsha sank lower and lower and lower in her chair until I worried she was going to slip under the table and form a puddle on the floor.

Then Eugene got his chance. He rose and talked about the fact that Marsha had no prior record and, despite the prosecutor's reckless and defamatory comments, no association with criminals of any kind. Given the weakness of the state's case and the emotional trauma his client had just gone through, it would be unconscionable not to release her immediately.

It wasn't exactly Perry Mason, but it sounded good to me.

When Eugene finished, the judge leaned back in his chair for a moment and squinted at Marsha over his glasses. Then he sat up and wrapped his hand lovingly around his gavel.

"Given the gravity and circumstances of

these charges, the defense's motion is denied, and bail is denied. Trial date is set for one week from Monday. Next case."

And he banged the gavel quickly, sharply, like he was squashing a bug that had dared crawl across his bench.

"So I have to go back?" Marsha said, her voice wobbly. "I have to go back?"

Eugene leaned close and put his hands over hers and whispered something in her ear.

She nodded, obviously trying to look brave — then began weeping anyway as the marshal told her to stand, put the cuffs back on her, and led her away. It all happened so quickly that all I could do was call out "We're gonna get you out, Marsha! I promise!" before she and the marshal disappeared through the side door they'd come in through twenty minutes before.

I felt a hand on my back.

It was Eugene.

"I can go talk to Marsha privately now," he said. "Is there anything else you want me to tell her?"

"I have some things I need you to *ask* her. I was hoping we'd all talk it over at the five and dime after the hearing, but . . . well . . . obviously . . ."

I had to stop and suck in a deep, trembling

345

breath. I knew bail had been a long shot, yet I still felt like Crowell had just punched me in the gut. I was going to have to figure out what kind of car the guy drove.

One of these days, the old bastard was going to get a banana up the tail pipe.

"I need you to ask Marsha why Jack Schramm from Huggins Construction would have been bringing cash to the house for Bill," I said. "Lots of it."

Eugene's eyebrows shot up.

"And why mentioning Jack Schramm and Bill in the same breath would give Bill's boss, Harry Kyle, the vapors."

Eugene's eyebrows went even higher.

"And why Bill was keeping old pottery in the crawl space under the house."

Eugene's eyebrows went so high they almost left his forehead.

"And why Bill would paint a human skull red."

Eugene's eyebrows crashed back down hard and fast to form a glower.

I put my right hand up with the three middle fingers pointing at the ceiling.

"Scout's honor again. I wouldn't joke about this," I said. "You need to ask Marsha about it."

The glower lifted. Slightly.

"Like you were ever a scout," Eugene

muttered. "All right — I'll ask. You'll hear from me soon."

"Thanks, Eugene. For everything."

He nodded curtly, then walked up the center aisle toward the courtroom doors. I paused for another deep breath, then turned to follow him. I was halfway up the aisle when the ambush began.

One of the men came at me from the seats on the left; the other, from the seats on the right.

"Alanis, I want to say I'm sorry," said the first.

"Alanis, I came to apologize," said the second.

They stopped and stared at each other.

"Who are you?" said Victor Castellanos.

"Who are *you*?" said George Washington Fletcher.

"You've got to be ducking kidding," said I.

Without the bird.

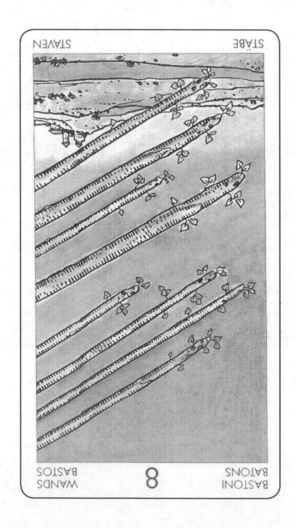

STABE STAVEN

BATONI WANDS
BASTONI BATONS 8 BASTOS

Remember those baguette bombs that were headed your way? The promise — or perhaps the threat — that something big was about to happen? Well, forget it. The reversal means there's been a flight delay, and now there's no ETA for that *something.* The baguettes aren't even falling to earth anymore. They're flying skyward. Everything's up in the air — literally. Of course, what goes up must come down, but now there's no way of knowing where or when — or on who.

Miss Chance, *Infinite Roads to Knowing*

"I'm Victor."

"I'm GW."

The two men shook hands.

I wanted to bury my face in mine.

"What are you doing here?" I said instead. I didn't address it to one of them in particular. The question applied equally to both.

Victor spoke first.

"I did a lot of thinking last night. And I realized that you were just doing what you could — what you know how to do — to help a friend. And even if I don't like how you go about it, if *I* want to be a friend, I should be helping, too."

GW nodded, impressed, and jerked a thumb at Victor's broad chest. "What he said."

I gritted my teeth and glared at him. Obviously, a courtroom wasn't the best place to throttle somebody. An assistant DA was twenty feet behind me, so I'd have to resist the urge for the time being.

"Shouldn't you be at school?" I asked Victor.

"I took the day off."

I turned to GW. "Shouldn't you be committing a felony somewhere?"

"I took the day off, too."

And he smiled his Lando Calrissian "I'm a charming scoundrel" smile.

Screw the assistant DA. I was gonna kill him.

GW saw the murderous fury in my eyes and dialed his smile down accordingly.

"I put the you-know-what back," he whispered.

"You *what*?" I said.

"The you-know-what. I went back to you-know-where and put it back where you-know-who found it."

I narrowed my eyes. "With the you-know-what still inside?"

He didn't know what.

"Wait . . . we're talking about a different you-know-what now?" GW said.

"I am *so* confused," said Victor.

"The money," I spat at GW. "It's still in the backpack?"

GW looked around, alarmed. "Could we not talk details in here?" he said under his breath. "I have a lot of bad memories of this place — and I don't want more."

"Fine. Outside. Come on, Victor."

I took Victor by the arm and marched out of the courtroom and through the lobby without ever glancing back to see if GW was coming with us.

He was.

"No offense, Vic," he said once we were out on the sidewalk, "but could you stick your fingers in your ears and go 'la la la laaaa' for a minute?"

"No," Victor said firmly.

GW shrugged. "Suit yourself. Just trying to keep you out of an accessory rap if this goes sideways."

"Just talk," Victor said, though I noticed his voice was about half an octave higher than usual.

"Fine." GW focused on me. "When I saw all that cash Riggs had stashed, I assumed you'd been playing me somehow — that there was an angle you hadn't told me about because you didn't want to cut me in. So I double-crossed you before you could double-cross me. It was just a knee-jerk re-action."

"You got the jerk part right," I grumbled.

"I said I was sorry, Alanis. And by the way — I knew there was a vent filter down in that crawl space that you'd be able to get out through. I was trying to delay you, not trap you."

"My god," Victor said. "What did I miss?"

I just squinted at GW skeptically.

"Anyway," he said, "I gave it some more thought later, checked out what you were saying about Marsha, then decided to take the backpack back — with the money. It's right where we found it. When the time comes, you can use it as evidence of . . . whatever it's evidence of. As for what you want to do next . . ." GW straightened up and saluted me. "Reporting for duty."

Victor looked tempted to snap a salute, too. Instead he just nodded at GW.

"What *he* said."

I took a moment to look them both over. They were actually a pretty good-looking duo as accomplices go.

I leaned in close to Victor and gave him a peck on the cheek. "You're on standby. If I can't wrap this up in the next two hours, I'm going to need you."

"You could 'wrap this up' in two hours?" Victor asked, looking both confused and disappointed.

"If we're lucky." I turned to GW. "All right — you're coming with me."

GW swiveled his head to offer me his right cheek. "Don't I get a kiss?"

"No," I said.

Victor still looked confused, but he looked slightly less disappointed.

I already had the Fixer's down payment in the Cadillac: two twenty-dollar bills, forty-eight pieces of identically sized paper, and a yellow wrapper with "$1,000" printed on it to hold them all together. All I needed now was a bag for it.

We went to McDonald's.

"You want something?" I asked GW as we pulled into the drive-thru line.

"Nah."

"Me neither."

"Then why are we here?"

I told him: Fixer's orders.

"Does that seem like the guy's standard MO?" I asked.

GW shrugged. "It's hard to say."

"That doesn't exactly fill me with confidence. I chose you for this because you said you'd heard of the guy."

"And because your friend Mr. Muscles isn't used to taking walks on the wild side, am I right?"

"What makes you say that?"

"Oh, come on. Like I don't know how to spot a civilian. That dude's so squeaky clean you could use him to brush your teeth."

"And there's nothing wrong with that," I said. "Back to the Fixer. Do you think you could spot him?"

GW started to shrug again but caught himself. "I only know him by reputation, but that might be enough. He's not gonna be toothbrush material, that's for sure. So what's our plan?"

"I talk to him, try to feel him out on Marsha, and you follow him to his car and get the license plate number so we can give Burby an anonymous tip on the guy."

GW nodded his approval. "Not bad."

"Or," I said, "the Fixer smells a rat, decides to off me, and you jump in to save my bacon."

GW stopped nodding.

There was a crackle of static and what sounded like someone saying "Can I help you?" through a megaphone filled with bees.

It was our turn to order.

I looked at GW. He didn't seem like the kind of person to pass up free food.

"Well, as long as we're here," he said, "how about a Happy Meal?"

Red Rock Factory Outlets was uncrowded by both consumers and, more surprisingly, factory outlets. Half the storefronts were vacant, and what stores were open were quiet and still.

The Fixer's choice made a little more sense now.

Cops like to swarm. If this were a trap — the official law enforcement kind, anyway — it would be easy to spot.

Being the unofficial kind, though, all I had to do was tell GW to wait in front of the L'eggs Hanes Bali Outlet Store for five minutes before following me to the outdoor fountain at the center of the mall.

"Will do," he said. "And be careful. Don't forget this guy's a killer."

"Oh, it's on my mind. Trust me."

I moved on alone.

A dozen or so concrete benches ringed the fountain. On one sat a little old lady clutching a Lane Bryant bag. A four-year-old was dancing on another bench while singing "Let It Go" for her mother. Neither looked like the Fixer.

I picked an empty bench, sat, and put my McDonald's bag down beside me.

After a moment, there was a flurry of movement to my right. I looked over.

The little old lady had left her bench and come to join me on mine.

"Beautiful day, isn't it?" she said.

Great. I'm trying to rendezvous with an

assassin and one of the Golden Girls decides she's lonely.

"It sure is." I picked up the McDonald's bag and stood. "Enjoy it."

The old woman looked disappointed that she wouldn't have the chance to share more observations about the weather.

I walked halfway around the fountain, found another empty bench, and sat again.

It was high noon now. The Fixer would be showing up any second — if he wasn't there already. He might be the tattooed UPS guy pushing the dolly loaded with brown boxes. Or he might be the older, outdoorsy-looking man striding out of the Timberland store.

Or he might be slipping up on my left and sitting beside me. *Somebody* was.

I looked over.

The old woman had followed me.

"Such a perfect day," she said. "Nothing to fix about it."

I stared at her.

"Too bad things need fixing sometimes," she went on. "But that's why we have people to fix them. You know. Fixers."

I was still staring.

She was a tiny woman in a pink pantsuit and pearls. Her hair was a halo of perfectly styled white. She looked like she should be in her room at the rest home watching

Lawrence Welk, not setting up a hit.

"Well, say something," she said. "I'm not here to get a suntan, sugar."

"Okay. Did the Fixer send you to meet me?"

The old woman sighed. "Ageism. It's an epidemic nowadays. Don't let my looks fool you, hon. I get things done."

And she gave me a big wink.

Oh.

My.

God.

"*You're* the Fixer?"

She nodded proudly. "A gal's gotta do what a gal's gotta do. Those social security checks only get you so far."

"How long have you been . . . in business?"

"Long enough." She stretched a liver-spotted claw toward the McDonald's bag. "So hand over the dough and we'll talk turkey."

I snatched the bag up and held it tight.

"Just hold on a second," I said. "How do I know you'll follow through?"

The old woman looked hurt. "Oh, honey. You don't trust me?"

"Give me a reason to," I said. "Name a job you've done recently."

"Hmm?"

"Tell me about your latest 'fix.' "

"Oh, I shouldn't do that. Wouldn't be very smart."

I gave the bag a little shake so she could hear the cash (and paper) inside slide around. "Prove to me you fix things or no down payment."

The old woman hmphed. Really actually truly said "hmph" out loud. I didn't think anyone did that in real life.

"All right, then," she said. "Take a look at this."

She leaned closer to me. The smell of White Diamonds was so overpowering I almost swooned.

She opened her Lane Bryant bag and nodded down at it.

Inside, nestled atop a pink cardigan with the price tag still on, was an Uzi.

"So that's how you do it?" I asked.

"You betcha."

"You don't have an assistant Fixer you farm things out to?"

"Nope, it's just me. It's safer that way — you don't want other people knowing the details. Loose lips and all that."

"I understand," I said.

And I did. About her, anyway.

Bill Riggs had been beaten to death with a baseball bat. This woman had had nothing to do with it. She was just a lonely old fraud.

"Time to piss or get off the pot, shug," she said. "I've got another client lined up for today, so it's not like I've got nothing else to do."

"Tell you what . . ." I said.

I started moving my hand toward the Lane Bryant bag. The plan: grab it, get the Uzi out of reach, then call Burby and tell him to come pick up "the Fixer" — and let Marsha out while he was at it.

"Looks like he's a no-show," someone said.

GW was standing in front of us.

"Check your email," he told me. "Sometimes people will change the meet at the last second as a precaution."

"Umm . . . are you talking to me, sir?" I said.

It didn't work.

The old woman plunged her hand into the Lane Bryant bag. "I swear — you can't trust anybody these days," she snarled. "I said come *alone.*"

"Wait," GW said. "Is this — ?"

"Yes," I said. "And she's got a gun."

"Not just a gun," the old woman corrected me. "A mini Uzi submachine gun capable of firing 600 rounds per minute with an effective range of 100 meters. Just because

I'm old doesn't mean I don't know a thing or two." She smiled wickedly. "One squeeze of the trigger and you two are going to look like Swiss cheese."

"Those things are hard to control, grandma," I said. "You start shooting, you're just as likely to fill yourself full of holes."

"I know — and everyone around me, too." The old woman shrugged. "It's a risk I'm willing to take. How about you?"

On the other side of the fountain, the four-year-old was still singing "Let It Go." A gaggle of giggling teenagers walked past us with smoothies and cell phones in their hands. "Oh, for Pete's sake, Carla — there's nothing in Williams-Sonoma we need that we don't already have," I heard someone say.

The place wasn't busy, but it wasn't deserted.

The old woman had us.

She saw my resignation on my face.

"Give me the money," she said. "Then don't leave here for fifteen minutes. If I see either one of you — bang bang *bang.*"

I nodded and handed her the McDonald's bag. She took it with her left hand, keeping her right on the Uzi. Then she dropped the Happy Meal into the Lane Bryant bag, stood, and began backing away.

"Are we really gonna let her go?" GW whispered.

"Absolutely."

I'd already stirred up enough trouble trying to help. I wasn't going to get a bunch of innocent bystanders shot while I was at it.

The old woman turned and began walking away — but she made a point of glancing back at us every three or four steps. Eventually she stepped around a corner and disappeared.

"What now?" GW said.

"This, for starters."

I stood up and punched him in the face.

You think defending yourself against marauding bread sticks was tough in the past? That was nothing. Now not only do you have to fight off the enemy, you have to do it upside down. That takes some skill and balance — and probably anti-gravity boots. In other words, things aren't going to get any easier, but you've got to keep on fighting. If you don't, you're about to find out what a piñata feels like.

Miss Chance, *Infinite Roads to Knowing*

"Ow!" said GW.

"Ow!" I said, too.

He was holding his nose. I was shaking my hand.

It was a good reminder of why I'm nonviolent: punching people *hurts.*

I knew people around the fountain were stopping to stare, but I didn't care.

"Twice," I spat. "*Twice* I let you fool me. No one fools me twice."

"You just contradicted yourself," GW said.

Maybe he felt safe because he had his hands over his nose. He shouldn't have.

"You'd never heard of the Fixer, had you?" I said. "You were just bullshitting me."

"I wanted to seem helpful — so I could stay close to you. Protect you."

"So you lied."

"I exaggerated."

I balled my aching hand back into a fist.

"You go, girl!" a passerby shouted.

"Okay, I lied! I lied!" GW said.

I relaxed my hand.

"Nothing to see here," I said to the shoppers watching us. "Show's over."

The shoppers started going on their way. A few of them groaned in disappointment.

"Look, I'm sorry," GW said to me. "I know I screwed up."

"Do you? Do you really know what you've done? I was *this close* to proving Marsha didn't hire a hit man — and then, thanks to you, I had to let the proof just toddle on out of here. She said she'd be seeing another new client later. For all we know, that was Burby moving in on her. And now she might not show for their meeting because she's already had a trap sprung on her today. No, you didn't just screw up. You screwed Marsha."

As I spoke, GW wilted more and more. By the time I was done, he looked half a foot shorter.

At least he had the decency to be ashamed — or the decency to look ashamed, anyway.

"I am sorry," he said. "I really was trying to help."

Maybe it was the truth. Maybe it was a lie. It didn't matter.

"You're not fooling me again, Fletcher. About anything," I said. "We're through.

For good."

I turned to go.

"Alanis . . ."

I looked back at GW.

He opened his mouth. I think he was going to ask for a ride back to Berdache.

He saw the look on my face and thought better of it.

"Good luck," he said.

I left him there.

I drove back to the five and dime to change clothes and pick up supplies. When I was ready, I called Victor.

"You still up for this?"

"I'm still up for it," he said, with all the enthusiasm of a man bending over for his proctologist.

Which was fine. I didn't need enthusiasm. I needed backup.

"I'll pick you up in ten minutes," I said. "Dress casual."

My cell phone started playing music as I walked to the door: "The Jean Genie."

I stopped and pulled the phone from the oversized purse I'd just scrounged out of the closet.

"How is she?"

"In shock," Eugene said. "Being denied

bail . . . she's devastated."

"Were you able to ask my questions?"

"I asked, but I didn't get any answers. She doesn't know why Jack Schramm would be bringing money to the house, doesn't know why Bill's boss would be spooked when he hears Schramm and Bill mentioned together, and doesn't know anything about pottery in the crawl space or red skulls."

"Great," I sighed.

"Do you really think any of that means anything?"

"I don't know." I started toward the door again. "But it better."

"Nice new look," Victor said as he climbed into the Caddy. "I thought you said 'dress casual'?"

He was wearing sandals, cargo shorts, and a purple Polo shirt.

I was wearing a long white peasant dress with a tie-dyed scarf around my waist.

"I'm in character," I said.

"As Stevie Nicks?"

I laughed. It was good knowing that Victor actually had a sense of humor. I'd been starting to wonder.

I pulled away from the curb.

"All right, no keeping you in the dark this time. I'm telling you everything up front," I said. "We're crashing a picnic."

"We're what?"

"Oak Creek Golf Resorts and Estates is having a staff/member mixer picnic this afternoon. I saw it in Harry Kyle's day planner when we were in his office yesterday."

"So why are we going? Not for the free burgers and lemonade, I'm assuming."

"I want an excuse to talk to Kyle again — and hopefully meet Jack Schramm, too."

"Jack Schramm? I remember you mentioning that name yesterday. It seemed to give Kyle the heebie-jeebies. Who is he?"

"A construction guy out at Oak Creek — and the person who found Bill Riggs's body. Or pretended to find it, maybe. He and Riggs were cooking something up together, but I can't figure out what."

Victor gave my clothes another up-and-down look. "So why the gypsy outfit?"

"I'm the entertainment for the mixer. I'll be doing free readings. Bill Riggs set it up with me before he was fired."

"Really?"

I took my eyes off the road just long enough to throw Victor a look.

"Oh, right," he said. "Lies."

"You'll get the hang of 'em one day."

"I hope not," Victor said. "So how'd it go with that other guy — GW? You two weren't able to 'wrap it up'?"

I shook my head. "It was a close call, but no. This is the backup plan."

I didn't add what some people might have called it: "clutching at straws."

"The ILF strikes again," I said as we drove through Oak Creek.

The unfinished house that had been covered in graffiti the day before had been spray-painted again. Instead of saying INDIAN LAND FOR INDIANS, this time the message was KEEP THE RED ROCKS RED — WHITES GO HOME. Once again it was signed Indian Liberation Front.

"You sure there isn't a tribe that claims this area?" I asked Victor.

"Well, I'm sure *somebody* got kicked off the land at some point. I don't know of any dispute now, though."

"What would happen if a tribe did have a beef with building out here?"

Victor shrugged. "A legal mess, I guess." He sniffed the air and sat up a little straighter in his seat. "Hey . . . you smell that?"

Up ahead was a clearing with tents and tables and balloons. Thirty or forty people were milling about, most of them dressed like Victor. Off to one side were two grills, both of them smoking.

Victor's stomach growled.

"Let me guess," I said as I pulled into the nearest parking spot. "You haven't had lunch."

"It's been a weird day."

"Tell you what — while I do my thing, you can get yourself something to eat and work the crowd."

"What do you mean?"

"See if Jack Schramm's here. He's supposed to be a big bald guy. Rocks the Brawny man's lumberjack look. You can ask around about Riggs, too. And that graffiti, while you're at it."

Victor looked dubious. "I'd rather just grab myself a hot dog and stay out of the way."

"And how many murderers do you think have been caught because people grabbed themselves a hot dog and stayed out of the way?"

"Uhhh . . . not many?"

"That's right."

"Fine," Victor sighed. "I'll work the crowd."

"At least you still get the hot dog," I said.

Victor made a beeline for the grills and the cluster of casually dressed people milling around them. I headed for a picnic table in the shade of the clearing's one tree — a tall, twisting juniper.

Victor blended right in. I didn't. Which was just how I wanted it.

Harry Kyle approached as I seated myself and pulled my tarot deck from my purse. From the waist down, he was dressed the same as the day before — pressed slacks, shiny brown shoes. But from the waist up he was all pineapples and flowers and crashing waves.

The Hawaiian shirt: one-stop shopping for the middle-aged man who wants to say *hey, I can be fun!*

"Jennifer, isn't it?" he said, grinning at me in a stiff, unnatural way — a taxidermist's idea of a smile.

"Hi, Harry! Are you gonna be first?"

"First for what?"

I put the deck on the picnic table. "A reading."

"A what?"

I slapped a palm to my forehead. "I should have known! Bill never told you, did he? I do tarot cards, and he said I should come read at the picnic. It'd be fun for you guys, and maybe I'd pick up a new customer or two."

"Tarot cards?" Kyle threw a nervous

glance over his shoulder. "That's not satanic or anything, is it?"

"Not in the slightest. Sit down; I'll show you how it works."

"I don't have time right now. It's my job to be the life of the party."

Kyle tried to shoot me a hearty smile. He managed the smile — barely — but not the hearty.

"Oh, come on, Harry. Aren't you curious about your future?"

Kyle looked over his shoulder again. This time something caught his eye.

I followed his gaze.

By the nearest grill, Victor was chatting with a muscular bald man in a flannel shirt.

Jack Schramm, I presume.

When Kyle turned my way again, the polyester pineapples over his armpits were starting to look darker.

He was sweating.

"Sure, why not?" he said. He forced out a laugh as he sat across from me. "I'd love to know if my golf game is ever going to improve."

I held out the deck. "Think of your question as you shuffle."

Kyle took the cards and fumbled with them awkwardly for a moment.

It didn't look to me like he was thinking

about golf.

I held out a hand, and Kyle gave the deck back. I spread the cards in an arc across the table.

"Pull out five cards, but don't turn them over yet."

Kyle thought carefully before selecting each card, as if some might be booby-trapped. Once he'd picked five, I arranged them facedown in front of me.

"All right," I said, "let's see what's going to happen to that handicap of yours."

I flipped over the top card.

"The Three of Pentacles. This card indi-
cates a group project, generally work related.
But in your case — given what you were
just thinking about — it might mean you've
been playing golf with some new people.
Like there's an ongoing game you've become a part of. Does that sound right?"

"Wow, yeah," Kyle said with a jerky nod.
"There has been something like that — a

new game."

I flipped over the next card.

"Oh, man. That is some golf game!" I said. "That poor woman's been up all night thinking about it. See the swords? Those are worries about how it's gonna turn out."

"Who is she?" Kyle asked.

"Well, *you,* I assume."

Kyle swallowed hard. His armpit pineapples were growing darker by the second.

"This ongoing game you're in," I said. "You've been letting it get to you."

"Oh, well, maybe a bit." Kyle reached out and tapped the next card impatiently. "What else do you see?"

For a man who barely knew what the tarot was, he was taking this reading pretty seriously, which told me how good a reading it was.

I moved on to the next card.

"What's that?" Kyle asked. "An angel?"

"Yes."

Kyle smiled. "So this is a good card."

"Not really. It's reversed."

Kyle's smile wilted. He was the quickest convert I'd ever seen. Underneath the pineapples and flowers, the guy was desperate.

"What do you mean 'reversed'?" he said.

"Flipped. See how it's not turned the same way as the others?"

"Yeah?"

"Well, Temperance — that's this card — is usually pretty positive. It's about mixing different energies to create something new. But reversed . . . it might mean the mix isn't working. Like maybe your new golf buddies are throwing off your game."

"Oh, yeah — they are. Definitely," Kyle said. "Let's see what's next."

I flipped the fourth card.

"Justice," Kyle said, reading off the corner of the card. "Like the statues on old courthouses."

The thought seemed to haunt him.

"It's sort of like that," I said. "But she's not blindfolded like the traditional symbol for Justice; she sees clearly. And her sword points straight in the air; it doesn't lean to one side or the other. She's not biased. It's all about the facts. Same with the scale in her other hand; it's perfectly balanced. The outcome is going to be fair."

"What outcome?"

I shrugged. "The end of your game, I guess."

I remembered something I'd read in *Infinite Roads to Knowing* and decided to see how Kyle would like hearing it.

"Some people call this the karma card," I told him. "You know the old saying 'what goes around, comes around'? That's what this is all about. You've put something in motion — and it's not going to stop until it comes back to you."

As I suspected, Kyle didn't like that at all. He'd seemed so controlling and commanding the first time I'd seen him working the floor in the sales office. But now he looked anxious, confused, lost.

It wasn't that the cards had broken him. He was broken already — inside. The cards had merely parted the curtains.

He reached out and flipped over the last card himself.

"Well, that doesn't look good," he said with a joyless laugh.

"The Five of Pentacles is about loss — usually financial. But since you asked about your golf game, the loss would relate to that. Maybe golf isn't the game for you. Ever think about taking up tennis?"

Kyle barked out another bitter laugh. "Tennis . . . if only."

"Harry," I said, "the cards just show a moment in time: what you're facing now, where you could be headed if things don't change. You have the power to change everything. If these new golf partners of yours are causing you problems, you need to stop playing with them. Turn to someone else. Talk about what's been going on. Get help."

Kyle finally tore his gaze away from the Five of Pentacles and looked me in the eye.

You know we're not talking about golf, don't you? his expression said.

Kyle opened his mouth.

"Whatcha playin'?" a woman said. "If it's poker, deal me in!"

"Me, too!" another woman chimed in. "But can we make it blackjack? Poker's got too many rules."

Kyle winced. He looked like he really, *really* didn't want to turn around to see who was talking, but he forced himself to anyway.

Five people were headed toward us: Victor, Jack Schramm, a wiry thirtyish man with the deep brown tan you get from working outside all day, and two women, a long-haired blond and a long-haired brunette. The women were both slightly stocky and extremely drunk. Each carried a large plastic cup with a straw poking from the top, and with every other step they sloshed slushy red liquid out onto the sun-bleached grass. The brunette was wearing a baseball glove on her other hand. The blond was using a softball bat as a cane.

Kyle stood up.

"I'd better go make sure no one's burning the burgers," he said to me. "Thanks for the help with my golf."

He turned and walked away.

"Awww, Harry — don't go," the brunette said. "Stay and play cards with us."

"Please please please," the blond begged.

They both spoke with slurred, mush-mouthed words. The party had started early for these two.

"Sorry, ladies," Harry said as he passed them. "No rest for the wicked."

"Oh, I don't know about that. *I'm* feelin' pretty rested!" the brunette said.

The blond cackled so hard she lost her balance and stumbled sideways into the tan man. He gave her a look of such raw, un-hidden contempt it could only mean one thing: they were married.

"Hey, Jennifer," Victor said to me. (I was impressed that he remembered my fake name.) "I found some more customers for you."

The brunette squinted at me. "You said she's a fortuneteller. Where's her crystal ball?"

"Maybe she's a palm reader," the blond said. She tossed aside the softball bat and held up her hand. "What do you see?"

The correct answer, of course, would have been "a drunk."

What I said was, "Not much from over here. Come have a seat."

The blond and the brunette stumbled toward the picnic table.

"Jennifer, this is Cathy Schramm and Debbie Luchetti," Victor said. "And their husbands, Jack and Carl."

"Hell —" the tan man — Carl Luchetti — started to say. Before he could get to the "-o," Debbie thrust her cup out toward him and said, "More."

He took the cup and turned back toward the grills.

"Strawberry!" Debbie said as he left. "Not that mango shit!" She looked at me and grinned. "I hate mango."

"Uhhh . . . Jack and Carl both work for the company that's putting up the houses here," Victor said. "They were telling me something interesting about that graffiti

386

we've been seeing."

"Oh?"

I turned to Schramm, who was watching as his wife took a seat across from me. He looked worried that she might not be able to sit down without hurting herself somehow.

"Yeah. It's been going on for weeks," he said, distracted. "The Indian Liberation Front keeps hitting the new houses we're putting up on the north side of the development."

"Any idea what they're mad about?" I asked.

Schramm shrugged. "The usual stuff, I assume. We stole their land, yada yada."

His wife squinted at me from the other side of the picnic table. "Hey . . . do I know you?"

"I don't think so." I turned back to Schramm. "Has anyone tried talking to the local tribes about it?"

"Harry got in touch with some group in Sedona — Indians for Community Empowerment or something like that — but they weren't any help," Schramm said. "Looking out for their own, I guess. I just hope it doesn't escalate."

"Escalate how?"

"The redskins are going on the warpath,"

Debbie Luchetti said. She'd stumbled off toward her softball bat and was bending down toward it very, very slowly. She patted her right hand over her mouth and did an old-fashioned imitation of an Indian war whoop: "Woo woo woo woo!"

"Debbie," Schramm said. He widened his eyes and jerked his head at Victor.

"Oh, he's not an Indian," Debbie said. She picked up the softball bat, tried to twirl it like a baton, and immediately dropped it again. "He's Mexican. He doesn't care."

Victor's face turned a shade darker.

Across the table from me, Cathy Schramm tried to snap her fingers.

"The Black Magic Savings and Loan!" she said.

I looked at her. "Excuse me?"

"It's where you work — in Berdache," she said. "I was in there a few weeks ago looking for gag gifts for a bachelorette party. Everything was too expensive, so I ended up ordering it all online. But yeah — I remember you. And wasn't the store in the news, too? Someone was murdered in there, right?"

Debbie gasped, but she looked more amused than horrified. "Murdered? Really?"

"I'm afraid you've mistaken me for someone else," I said coldly. "And by the way, my full maiden name is Jennifer Spotted Bear and I am a proud member of the Cherokee Nation. I am deeply offended by what I've just seen and heard, and I plan on letting the National Congress of American Indians know about the racial hatred I encountered at the Oak Creek Golf Resort."

"Look, I apologize if —" Schramm began.

Cathy cut him off.

"You go, girl!" she said to me, pumping a fist in the air. "Get Geronimo after us!"

Debbie did another war whoop.

"Come on, Jonathan," I said, scooping up my cards and jamming them into my purse. "We're leaving — and we're not coming back."

I stalked off, Victor at my side.

"I assume you're not really a proud member of the Cherokee Nation," Victor said once we had the picnic table a safe distance behind us.

"I might be, for all I know. I have no idea who my father is."

"Oh," Victor said.

He gave me a quizzical look, seemingly thinking (for probably the one-hundredth time) *who* is *this woman?*

"But you're right — I was just looking for an excuse to get out of there," I said. "If we're going to be poking our noses into a murder, I prefer to do it around people who don't know my name and address."

"Did you find out anything useful before our cover got blown?"

I smiled to myself. I had to practically blackmail Victor into helping me in the beginning, and now here he was talking about blown covers. Next thing you know, he'd be asking which possible perp I liked for the 187.

"Maybe," I said. "I'll know more after we make our next stop."

"Our next stop? Where are we going now?"

I pulled my phone from my purse and called up Google. I had an address to find.

"We're going into Sedona," I said, "to pay a call on the fine folks at Indians for Community Empowerment."

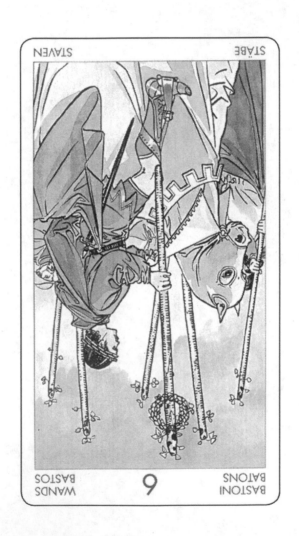

STÄBE STAVEN

BASTONI BATONS 9 WANDS BASTOS

Right-side up, this is a premature victory parade; reversed, it's a premature pity party. You've gone from overconfidence to resignation, but neither will get you what you want. So turn that frown upside down — or at least sideways. That horse could still take you *somewhere,* and you're going to need all your strength to stay in the saddle.

Miss Chance, *Infinite Roads to Knowing*

There was no Indians for Community Empowerment in Sedona. But there was a Native Americans for Empowered Communities.

Close enough. That's where we went.

During the day, Sedona's all primary colors — red soil, green brush, white mountaintops, blue sky — and brown buildings. Lots and lots of brown buildings. It's as if the local Home Depot only stocks paint in two colors.

"Over here you've got your Autumn Bronze," the guy in the orange vest would tell you. "And over here you've got your Dog Shit. Which'll it be today?"

Whoever called the shots at Native Americans for Empowered Communities had gone with Autumn Bronze. The building was last and largest in a row of low brown offices not far from the rinky-dink airport on the southwest side of town.

Inside was a reception desk and a surprisingly large, bustling waiting room. NAEC ran a family health clinic and a daycare center and a job training program, and all three seemed to be practically spilling out the doors. It felt like a YMCA, only with no pool and with dreamcatchers instead of basketball trophies.

We went up to the front desk, and I asked the smiling, bespectacled woman stationed there if we could talk to whoever was in charge.

"That would be Mr. Smith," she said. "I can call back and see if he's available. May I say what this is regarding?"

"Sure," I said. "We've come from Oak Creek Golf Resort and Estates. We have some questions about the development's relationship with the local Native American community."

The woman's smile didn't waver.

"Ooo — I'll see if I can remember all that," she said cheerfully. "Why don't you have a seat . . . if you can find one!"

We ended up sitting next to a woman who was busily texting while her two young sons wrestled on the floor, seemingly to the death to judge by their cries and curses. Whenever one or the other howled too loudly, she'd nudge him with her toe and say, "Indoor voice."

"I have to admit, Alanis," Victor said. "This feels a little like a wild goose chase. I mean, what connection could a place like this have to Bill Riggs's" — he dropped his voice and looked around furtively — "death?"

"I have a hunch this place isn't connected at all," I said. "Which is why we're here."

"Wait. We're here *because* it might have nothing to do with the" — again he dropped his voice and glanced this way and that — "murder?"

"You don't have to bother whispering, Victor. I don't think anyone but me can hear you anyway."

"*Ahhhh!* Not in the nuts, Kenny! Not in the nuts!" one of the boys screamed.

"Indoor voice," his mother said.

A burly man with short-cropped black hair and dark skin appeared before us. He was wearing a tan work shirt, a green tie, and jeans.

"Fight fair, Kenny," he said.

"Yes, Mr. Smith," the younger of the boys said sulkily.

His older brother took the opportunity to bite him on the leg. The man ignored the resulting scream and turned to me and Victor.

"Hello. I'm Rick Smith. I'm in charge around here — as much as anyone is. You wanted to speak with me?"

"That's right. Thank you for seeing us," I said. "Do you mind if we go somewhere a little more private?"

"Not at all."

I thought he'd lead us back to his office. Instead, he headed to the parking lot.

"Quieter out here than anywhere in there," he explained. "Now — what can I do for you?"

I stepped closer to Victor and snaked an arm around his waist. He stiffened in surprise, but fortunately Smith didn't seem to notice.

"My fiancé and I are thinking of buying a home in the area," I said. "Specifically, we were looking at the Oak Creek Golf Resort. Do you know it?"

Smith didn't frown, didn't flinch, didn't hesitate.

"Sure," he said, nodding.

"Do you know of any reason why someone *shouldn't* buy a home there?"

Smith furrowed his brow. It was an impressive brow, too. He had a large blocky head and thick black eyebrows.

"No," he said. "Well, maybe one."

"Yes?"

"For the price they're asking, you could buy two houses in Sedona or three in Berdache," Smith said. "But then again, I'm not much of a golfer."

I pulled Victor to me more tightly.

"Perhaps I should mention that my fiancé is one-sixty-fourth Choctaw on his mother's side," I said.

Smith blinked at me a moment.

"Okay," he eventually said.

"That makes us very sensitive to Native American issues," I said.

Smith nodded blankly.

"That's nice," he said.

"So if the tribes around here had any kind of issue with the Oak Creek development, we'd want to know."

Smith was still nodding.

"Sure," he said.

He stopped nodding, and a grin slowly spread across his broad face.

"Ohhh . . . the spray-painting thing, right?"

I nodded along. "The spray-painting thing."

Smith swiped a big hand at me. "Ignore it."

"What do you mean?" Victor asked.

Smith gave him a sly sideways glance, then looked at me. "I was starting to wonder about him. Never saw a Choctaw go so long without talking."

"Oh, he's usually quite the chatterbox," I said. "I think he's just a little upset about what we saw at Oak Creek today. Isn't that right, hon?"

I gave him an affectionate squeeze.

"That's right," he said. He wrapped an arm around me and squeezed me back — hard. "Sweetie."

"What did you see out at Oak Creek?" Smith asked.

"Another message from the Indian Liberation Front," I told him. " 'Keep the Red Rocks red — whites go home.' "

Smith shook his head and clucked his tongue. "Oh, that's not nice — not nice at all. But I'll let you in on a little secret about the Indian Liberation Front."

He milked the moment with a dramatic pause.

Victor gave in and said "Yes?" first.

"It doesn't exist," Smith said. "Or if it does, the entire membership is three teen-agers and a case of Coors."

"You're saying you've heard of the Indian Liberation Front?" I said.

"Not until I got a call from someone at

Oak Creek the other day. I told him the same thing I'm telling you. If there was an Indian Liberation Front in Yavapai or Coconino County — heck, in *Arizona* — I would have heard of it. And I haven't. So I'd say this 'Front' is nothing but a bunch of bored kids . . . and they're probably not even Indian."

I froze. Suddenly, I was in a *Brady Bunch* echo chamber.

Mom always says don't play ball in the
    house . . .
            . . . ball in the house . . .
                    . . . ball in the house . . .

Except the echo was this:

They're probably not even Indian . . .
            . . . not even Indian . . .
                    . . . not even Indian . . .

"Is she all right?" I heard Smith say.
Victor bent down to look into my eyes. He probably saw pinwheels spinning there.
"Um . . . sweetie?" he said.
"Sorry. I've got a little touch of narcolepsy," I said. "I probably should've told you before we got engaged. Still love me?"
"With all my heart," Victor said through

clenched teeth.

Smith cleared his throat. "Well . . . if I've answered all your questions, maybe I'll just scoot off back to work."

He started to walk away.

"What makes you say they're not Native American?" I said to him.

He stopped. And perhaps sighed.

"When our boys get into mischief, it's usually a lot closer to home. Most of them don't have their own cars, and the ones that do aren't going to bother driving out to some gated community in the middle of nowhere when they can take a baseball bat to a bunch of mailboxes right on their own road."

"So there's nothing special about Oak Creek Golf Resort and Estates so far as the Native American community is concerned?"

"Nope."

Smith looked behind us where the sun was setting, turning the sky behind the mountains a brilliant orange-pink. I didn't get the feeling Smith was pausing to appreciate the splendor, though. He was just thinking about how much work he still had to do that day.

"What if artifacts were found at Oak Creek?" I said before he could start walking away again. "Or even bones?"

"Oh, that would change everything. Then the developers would have to deal with ARPA — that's the Archaeological Resources Protection Act of 1979. Federal law — big-time stuff. And if there are human skeletal remains, that could mean the land is sacred — a burial ground. Then you'd get the state and the tribes jumping in to try to figure out what the story is and what to do."

"And what would happen to the Oak Creek resort?"

"Well, that would depend," Smith said. "But I don't think the Yavapai-Apache Nation would like the idea of white folks playing golf on top of their great-great-great-great-grandfathers. I know I sure don't."

"Rick!" a woman called out.

We turned to see the friendly woman from the front desk leaning out the front door of the NAEC building.

"Rick, Darlene and Mrs. Rubio are going at it again. It's starting to get ugly."

"Oh, that's too bad," Smith said. "I guess I'll have to come in and see what I can do."

Despite the "too bad," Smith looked profoundly relieved to have an excuse to escape us.

"Thank you for your time," I said as he walked away. "You've been a huge help."

"My pleasure — and congratulations."

"Congratulations?" Victor said.

"On your wedding," said Smith. "When is it?"

"Oh! Right! April 1!"

"Well, good luck!"

Smith gave us a last wave as he hustled inside.

"April 1, huh?" I said to Victor. I still had one arm wrapped around his back. "A romantic spring wedding?"

Victor shook his head.

"April Fool's Day," he said. "If I've got to start telling lies, it seemed like the place to start."

"I'm confused," Victor said as I pulled the car onto the highway and gunned the motor. "You look — I don't know — excited, I guess. Like that conversation we just had was actually helpful. But I don't see how it ties in with your friend at all."

"That's because I know something you don't know." And I told him about the money, the pottery, and the skull I'd seen in the crawl space under the Riggs's house.

"Ahhh," Victor said, nodding.

Then he stopped nodding and shook his head.

"I'm still confused," he said.

"Look," I said, "it would be a disaster for

Harry Kyle and the parent company if the Oak Creek development turned out to be on land that was sacred to the local Indians. So much so that if the construction crew accidentally dug up artifacts from an Indian village or whatever, Kyle might want to hush it up."

"Ahhh," Victor said, nodding again. "And you think that's what happened."

"No."

Again, Victor's nod stopped.

"No?"

"No. Riggs's neighbor says he saw him painting the skull. I'm guessing he was trying to distress it somehow — make it look older than it really is. I don't think that skull came from Oak Creek. For all I know, Riggs bought it on eBay. The same with the pottery."

Victor mulled that over.

"Because," he said slowly, "he just wanted Kyle to *think* Indian stuff had been found at Oak Creek."

It was my turn to nod.

"It was a scam," I said. "I'd been wondering how Riggs could afford the most notorious criminal defense lawyer in the state; now I know. He was putting the squeeze on Kyle — probably through that Jack Schramm guy. He'd need an accomplice on the construction crew. There are just two things I still don't know."

"Yeah?"

"Yeah. First, there's that bogus Indian Liberation Front graffiti. It must be part of the plan. But why? What's the point?"

"And the second thing?"

I took my eyes off the dusk-darkened road ahead just long enough to throw Victor a *hell-lllllooooo?* look.

"Oh. Right," he said. "Who killed Bill Riggs?"

"Yeah, that. I have a hunch, but there's only one way to follow it up. You still game?"

"I've come this far."

"Well, this is going farther, Victor," I said. "You're getting a little more comfortable with lying. How do you think you're going to do with trespassing?"

Welcome back to Fight Club. We've made a little adjustment to the rules now that everything's flipped over. As of now, the first rule of Fight Club is *there are no rules.* The gloves are off, the brass knuckles are on, and things are about to get nasty. The second rule of Fight Club is *see rule #1,* the third rule of Fight Club is *see rule #2,* etc. And good luck.

Miss Chance, *Infinite Roads to Knowing*

I called Clarice as Victor and I continued our drive up the highway. Instead of picking up with a "Hello" or a "Hi, how are you?" the first thing she said was, "Where the hell have you been? I've been worried sick."

"Sorry I didn't check in, Mom. I've been busy. Am I grounded?"

"Just tell me if you met with you-know-who today."

Clarice was savvy enough to know not to start talking about a hit man on a cell phone call.

"I did," I said. "It didn't go well, which is why I've got more errands to run tonight. Just grab some more money from the till and pick up whatever you want for dinner."

"Your errands — are you going to need any help?"

"Yes, and I've got some."

"More couldn't hurt."

"Yes, it could."

"Come on, Alanis! It's driving me crazy sitting here doing homework when I could be out there helping Marsha with you."

"And it makes me feel much, much better knowing you're sitting there doing homework," I said. "I'm the grownup. I win."

Clarice said something to me that seventeen-year-olds aren't ever supposed to say to adults (or anyone).

I said it back to her with a voice full of sisterly love. Then I hung up.

I looked over at Victor.

He was watching me wide-eyed.

"That's . . . um . . . an interesting family dynamic you've got going there," he said.

I shrugged.

"We're an interesting family."

I didn't feel like driving all the way back to Berdache for supplies (or dealing with Clarice when we got there), so I pulled off the road the first time I spotted a dollar store. I told Victor to wait for me, then came out a couple minutes later with a package of batteries and the only flashlights the store had in stock.

"You get your pick," I said as I handed everything to Victor. "Spider-Man or Batman."

"I guess I'll take Batman," Victor sighed.

"My mom always tells me I look like George Clooney."

He opened all the packages and began putting batteries in the flashlights as I drove us back to Oak Creek Golf Resort and Estates.

During the day, the little guard house at the entrance to the Oak Creek development was empty and the gate was up. At night, we discovered, there was a uniformed guard and the gate was down.

Fortunately, I had the magic key: I was a well-dressed white woman in a Cadillac.

"Mr. Kyle said he'd wait in the office for us if we couldn't get here in time for the last presentation," I told the guard. I smiled and crossed my fingers. "If we can work out the financing, you might be looking at Oak Creek's newest residents."

"I'm sure Mr. Kyle can make it happen," the guard said, smiling back. "Congratulations."

He put up the gate, and we cruised through and headed to the sales office — which we cruised past on our way to our true destination.

We stopped on a street that was half homes, half empty lots. One of the houses still had nothing but reddish dirt for a lawn, plastic instead of glass in some of the windows, and a Huggins Construction sign out front.

It also still had *KEEP THE RED ROCKS RED — WHITES GO HOME* spray-painted on one side.

I was guessing that this was Oak Creek lot #235. Harry Kyle had a note about a late-night meeting at #235 with a "J.S." a few days before. And the Indian Liberation Front kept targeting the house — an impressive feat considering they didn't exist.

There was something special about this place — some key role it had played in Riggs's extortion plan. But what?

Victor and I sat and waited for the world to get darker. When there was no light left at all, we would make our move.

Victor passed the time talking. I passed the time listening.

Not that Victor was being a bore. I just didn't have a lot I wanted to add.

It had started with me jokingly asking what his mother would think of our second "date."

"She'd be thrilled if our second date was a bank heist," Victor said. "I have three sisters and eleven cousins and I'm the old-

411

est and I'm the only one who's not married."

"Tell me about them," I said. "Your family."

And Victor had obliged. It lit him up in a way I'd never seen before. Stolid, straight Victor had a spark inside him after all.

He told me about sibling rivalries, family vacations, holidays, weddings, funerals, births. It obviously made him happy to talk about it, and I guess it just as obviously made me sad.

Victor stopped himself in the middle of a story about the way his father used to tease his mother.

"You all right?" he asked, peering at me in the darkness. "You got really quiet there."

"I'm fine. It's just . . . your life sounds nice."

"It is. I know I'm lucky to —"

Victor stopped himself again.

"I'm sorry, Alanis. I just realized. You said earlier you didn't even know your father, and here I am going on and on about my dad."

"It's okay. I like hearing about happy families. It's like listening to a fairy tale, except it's real."

"Did you know any of your extended family at all?"

"Nope. The only family I knew when I was kid was my mother and her boyfriend Biddle."

"How long was the boyfriend around?"

"Years. My whole childhood, pretty much."

"How do you know he wasn't your father?"

"Because he was black, and whatever I am . . . well, it ain't black."

"I guess that is a bit of a giveaway," Victor said. "Hey — how about Clarice? She's half black, isn't she? Is Biddle her father?"

I shook my head. "Biddle died a long, long time before she was born. He crossed the wrong people, and . . ."

My words trailed off. If they'd kept going, they would've dredged up memories I didn't feel like reliving just then.

Victor got it.

"When you're ready to tell *your* stories," he said, "I'd like to hear them."

He reached out and put one of his hands over mine.

"Thanks, Victor. You're a good man," I said. "Now let's go break into that house, shall we?"

I thought of GW Fletcher as we walked around the house. I didn't have him or his tool kit with me for this B&E. The man was a liar, a cheat, and a thief, but I was going to end up missing him in a minute if we couldn't find a way inside.

"Can you pick a lock?" Victor whispered as we slinked up to the sliding glass door at the back of the house.

"I've managed it once or twice, but it's not a specialty," I whispered back. I reached out for the door handle. "Hopefully we'll get insanely lucky, and — well, I'll be damned."

We'd gotten insanely lucky. The back door slid aside easily. It had been left unlocked.

We went inside and closed the door behind us. I turned on my Spider-Man flashlight, and Victor turned on Batman.

The house had a large open interior with a high steepled ceiling. We were standing in what would probably be the dining room. The kitchen was to our left: the countertops were in place, but there were just blank spaces for the stove, refrigerator, and sink. Ahead of us was what would be the living room. At the far end of it was the front door and the stairs leading up to the second floor. Here and there along the floorboards were rectangular holes where outlets would presumably go, but there was no wiring in sight.

"I thought it was going to feel more finished than this," Victor said.

"I know what you mean. The outside looks pretty much done."

We did a slow tour of the first floor, hoping Spider-Man and Batman would reveal something to justify our being there. But the house was just a shell; there was nothing inside.

"I hate to say it —" Victor began.

"Then don't bother," I cut in sharply.

I knew what he was going to say already because I was thinking it, too. The house was a dead end, which wasn't Victor's fault.

"Sorry," I said to him.

"It's okay. I understand," he said. "Why don't we check out the second floor before we decide what to do next?"

"Good idea."

We started up the stairs, which creaked alarmingly with our every footfall.

"I might take back that good idea," I said. "I feel like I'm about to fall right through the staircase."

"I know what you mean."

Victor reached out to steady himself with the banister. It wobbled so badly that he quickly snatched his hand back.

"This place is a death trap," he grumbled.

"Please don't use that phrase right now."

"Sorry," Victor said. "But you know what I mean. I would've thought the houses out here would be built better than this. This place feels like it's made out of papier-mâché."

I paused a few steps from the top of the staircase.

"Maybe *that's* what makes this house special,"

I said. "It's especially crappy?"

"Yeah. Exactly."

"What would be the point of that?"

"The point would be — *shit.*"

I turned off Spider-Man. Victor quickly did the same with Batman. He'd heard it, too.

Something moving. Inside the house.

We stood there on the stairs and listened. Then there it was again: a rattling, scratching, banging somewhere off in the darkness.

"I think it's coming from the second floor," Victor whispered.

"I agree."

"What should we do?"

"Well, *I'm* not leaving till I know what it is," I said.

There was a pause while Victor let that sink in. If we'd been in a Scooby-Doo cartoon, I would've heard him gulp.

"Me neither," he eventually said. "So . . .

lights or no lights?"

"No lights. For now."

"Right. Lead on."

Slowly, cringing with every creak of the floorboards, I moved to the top of the staircase. When there were no more steps, I reached out to my right, found the wall, and followed it by touch.

I was moving down a hallway I couldn't see. But I knew that at the end of it would be a door.

A door that was still rattling.

I came to a doorway, but it wasn't the right one. The noise was still ahead of me. I kept going, still blind.

I reached another doorway. The rattling seemed slightly to my left now, and the noise echoed slightly in a way that told me the door I was looking for was in a small room.

I turned on Spider-Man.

I'd been right. I was facing a bedroom — the not particularly big kind the youngest kid in the family might get stuck with. On the far wall was a closet door.

The door rattled again. Something was trying to get out.

"You ready for this?" I whispered to Victor.

He was still right behind me.

"No," he whispered back. "But let's do it

anyway."

We crept toward the closet. When we were about ten feet from it, Victor motioned for me to stop. He was going to take the last few steps alone.

I pointed Spider-Man at my face so Victor could see that I was shaking my head. I mouthed one word.

Together.

Victor nodded.

We reached the closet door. It was clattering in a wild, frantic way now, as if whatever was on the other side knew we were there.

I put a hand on the doorknob and started to turn it.

The door burst open, knocking me in the nose, and I heard something go scrambling past us and shoot out of the room.

"Ow!" I said.

"Jesus!" said Victor.

And then all was quiet again. Whatever it was had startled us so badly, it had gotten away before we could even see what it was. The smell told me, though.

The stench came pouring out of the closet like an invisible wave of *yuck.*

Ammonia and feces.

I shined my flashlight into the closet. The floor was one big yellow puddle pocked here and there with large brown lumps.

"It doesn't make any sense," Victor said, "but I think that was a cat."

"Not just any cat," I said. "That was Son of Kong."

"Uhhh . . . huh?"

"He belonged to one of the Riggs's neighbors. Bill Riggs hated him, apparently. The neighbor thought Riggs had killed him, but obviously not. He brought him here."

"And stuck it in a closet? Why would he do that? Just to starve the poor thing to death?"

"To kill him, yes. But not to starve him. Riggs knew what was going to happen to this house. And I finally do, too."

Son of Kong let out a *"mrow!"* as he went skittering down the stairs.

"Come on," I said. "We need to get out of here before —"

I froze.

It was too late for *before.* Downstairs, someone was sliding open the back door.

Son of Kong cut loose another mighty *"mrow!"* and I could hear him scrambling across the floorboards.

"Yah!" a man said.

"What the hell?" said another.

Then they both laughed.

"It was that damn cat," I heard the first man say. "He must've clawed his way through the door."

"I'm not surprised, the way this piece of shit is built," said the second man. "Well, good for him. I was going to let him out before we did this anyway."

There was a shushing sound as the men closed the sliding door behind them.

Son of Kong had escaped.

It wouldn't be so easy for me and Victor.

I turned off my Spidey light and moved as quietly as I could — which wasn't as quietly as I would've liked — to the room's one window. I tried to open it, but it wouldn't budge. Either it hadn't been installed properly or it had been painted shut.

"Dumb idea anyway," I muttered.

We would've had to drop all the way to the ground, and it's not easy to make a clean getaway on broken ankles.

There was no avoiding it. We were going to have to go downstairs.

"What are they doing down there?" Victor whispered.

We could hear the men walking around the first floor. Every now and then there would be a slosh or a splash.

I moved to the doorway and sucked in a long, deep breath through my nose. I smelled what I expected — and dreaded.

Gasoline.

"We've gotta go," I said.

Then Victor smelled it, too. "Oh my god. They're about to burn the place down."

"With us in it, if we don't leave *now*. The front door is at the bottom of the steps. Hopefully, it's unlocked. If it's not —"

Victor finished my sentence for me.

"We're going to have to fight our way out of here," he said.

Actually, I'd been thinking *we're screwed*. I didn't correct him.

We tiptoed up the hall to the top of the stairs. Then the time for tiptoeing was over.

The men had brought a flashlight with them. It was lying on the floor near the back door. In the low light it threw across the room, we could see what we were up against: big, bald, beflanneled Jack Schramm and the other Huggins Construction worker we'd met at the picnic that day, leathery-brown Carl Luchetti. They were hunched over, walking backwards. Each had a plastic canister that was gurgling gasoline out onto the floor.

If we came down the stairs, they'd see us for sure. But if we *didn't* come down the stairs, we'd be trapped on the second floor when they lit up the gas.

So down the stairs we came, quickly and not quietly.

"Whoa!" one of the men said, startled.

"Hey!" said the other.

I reached the front door just before Victor. I grabbed the knob and turned — or tried to, anyway.

It was locked.

We looked at each other. The grim determination on Victor's face made it plain what he was thinking.

So we fight.

I could only hope what was going through my mind wasn't so obvious.

Because I still figured we were screwed.

They say a man's home is his castle, and you thought you'd built a solid one for yourself — a place to feel safe and secure once the drawbridge is up. But look at it from another angle — upside down, maybe — and you can see how flimsy it really is. It's not strong walls that keep you safe; it's who you have inside those walls with you. So don't be fooled by spiffy towers and turrets and the best moat money can buy. Maybe all you've really built for yourself is one hell of a mausoleum.

Miss Chance, *Infinite Roads to Knowing*

Victor and I turned to face Jack Schramm and Carl Luchetti.

Schramm was on the left side of the living room, near a half-finished chimney. Luchetti was on the right side of the room, closer to the kitchen. Here and there, puddles of gasoline shimmered in the dim light.

"It's those people from the picnic," Schramm said. He was a foot taller and fifty pounds heavier than Luchetti and had a deeper voice to go with the extra heft. "The girls were right about them."

"So what'll we do?" Luchetti said.

I was thinking the same thing. And I hoped I had an answer.

When the going gets tough, the tough get going — out the back door, Biddle used to say.

I could see the sliding glass door at the back of the house, thirty feet beyond Schramm and Luchetti. The gap between the two men was all of twenty-five-feet wide.

It would have to be enough.

"Run!" I shouted.

I took my own advice, of course, bolting across the living room. Victor had been ready to make Castellanos's Last Stand, but I could hear him follow me half a second later. We splashed through the gasoline as we went, and I could feel the hem of my dress growing more soaked with every pounding step. The fumes were so strong, they made my head swim. But I didn't stop.

I was three steps from the back door, already reaching out for the handle, when someone grabbed my wrist and jerked me to a halt.

"Where do you think you're going?" Schramm growled.

"Out," I said, and I went for the classic move in such situations: I tried to knee the guy in the balls.

Unfortunately, I was out of practice, and Schramm was so much taller than me I couldn't get my leg up high enough to do any real damage. Instead of doubling over in pain, Schramm just glared at me in rage.

"Mistake," he spat — just before Victor's fist flew in from the side and slammed into his jaw.

Schramm let go of me and stumbled into

the wall.

"Keep going!" Victor yelled. Only he wasn't going anywhere.

Luchetti had already thrown himself onto his back.

I knew Victor coached the high school wrestling team, but I didn't know till that moment how good he must be at it. He went with Luchetti's momentum, moving forward but falling to his knees and hunching his back at the same time. As his knees hit the floor, he reached around with one arm, grabbed Luchetti by the shirt, and threw him off his back.

Luchetti flew forward and hit the floor hard.

Victor popped back up to his feet — just in time for Schramm to lunge forward with a punch that caught him in the side of the head. It looked like Victor had been clobbered by a bald Paul Bunyon. He staggered sideways a few steps, and before he could recover, Schramm had wrapped his big arms around him.

"Carl, I've got him!" Schramm said. "Get up and cold cock the son of a bitch! Quick!"

Victor started squirming, searching for a way to break Schramm's hold, as Luchetti pushed himself to his feet. It looked like Victor had about five seconds to get away before Luchetti clocked him.

I meant to clock Luchetti first. I bent down to pick up the long metal flashlight on the floor by the door, thinking I'd use it as a makeshift billy club. It looked a lot heftier than my plastic Spidey model.

When I saw what was lying beside the flashlight, I changed my mind.

Luchetti stepped toward Victor, balling his hand into a fist.

"Don't do it," I said.

Luchetti leaned back and brought his fist up for a haymaker.

"I said *don't do it*!"

It was the little flicker of light that finally got his attention. His eyes darted my way — then went wide with terror.

"Okay, okay! I'm not gonna hit him!" he said, stepping away from Victor.

"Good," I said.

I didn't lower the lighter, though, or put out its flame. Or move it away from the rags I was holding in my other hand.

"Let go of him," I told Schramm.

"Or what?" he said. "You're gonna burn your boyfriend alive — and probably yourself, too?"

"What's my alternative? Give in to you two and get burned alive anyway? Nah. I'd rather take you with us."

Victor gaped at me. He looked deeply unhappy with our options.

"Listen, lady," said Luchetti, his deeply tanned skin glistening with sweat. "I don't want to burn anybody. I didn't even want to burn a cat."

"I believe you. That must have been Bill Riggs's idea."

Luchetti and Schramm shared a quick rattled look.

"I know what you're thinking," I said. "*How much does she know?* Well, all you have to do to find out is let my friend go."

My arms were getting tired from holding up the rags and lighter, but I didn't dare lower them or let them tremble.

"Talk first," Schramm said. "Then we'll see."

"Okay, I will," I said. "To start with, this beautiful home has been nothing but kindling from the get-go. The plan was to burn it down and blame it on a nonexistent Indian radical group. On paper it would look like a big loss for the development company, but you've been skimping on materials and labor. There's a lot to be skimmed from even just one house; you could clear a couple hundred thousand easy. You'd just need to cover two bases: the construction crew and the head office. You two handled the construction end; Harry Kyle took care of the paperwork. How am I doing so far?"

Schramm just glared at me over Victor's shoulder.

Luchetti gave me a shaky nod. "No one was gonna get hurt. We'd just transfer some money from the company's pocket into ours. They'd never even miss it. Then you showed up this afternoon asking questions and spooking Kyle, and we figured we needed to speed up the schedule and torch the place tonight."

"Shut up, Carl," Schramm snapped. "We don't know who she is."

"Oh, lighten up, Jack," I said. "Carl's not telling me anything I haven't already guessed. And I think I've got the next part worked out, too — the part with Bill Riggs."

Luchetti's eyes went wide again.

Schramm clenched his jaw. "Oh, yeah?" he grunted.

"Yeah. Riggs got wind of the scam, so he knew Kyle had a bunch of off-the-books money lying around. When he got into legal trouble and Kyle fired him, he decided to kill two birds with one stone. He was going to get the money to hire the best defense attorney in Arizona and get his revenge on Kyle at the same time. All he had to do was convince you two to put the squeeze on Kyle with some phony Indian artifacts. You'd tell him you needed cash to — what's the matter?"

Luchetti had gone about as pale as a man can when he looks like he's spent the last twenty-four hours napping on a tanning bed. He jabbed a finger at the rag in my hand.

"Be careful!"

As my arm tired, it had lowered the rags closer and closer to the lighter, until now they were less than inch from the tip of the flickering flame.

I quickly raised the rags up again.

"See why you should have let my friend go?" I said to Schramm. "We almost had our own private Burning Man — with three burning men and a burning woman."

"Just finish," Schramm said.

"Fine. Where was I? Oh, yeah. You'd supposedly need money to hush up the crew. Kyle probably suspected it was bullshit, but calling you on it would be risky. He was already in too deep with you two. So a lot of cash changed hands — and Bill Riggs got the last part of his split from you, Jack. On Sunday. In a blue backpack."

The resentment on Schramm's face told me how good my guesses had been. But even if I'd still had some doubts, Luchetti would have dispelled them.

"Goddamn, Jack," he said hoarsely. "She knows everything."

"Oh, no. Not everything. There's still a big ol' loose end to tie up," I said. "Who killed Riggs?"

I'd have thought Luchetti would have seen the question coming, yet it still seemed to catch him off guard.

"Don't ask us!" he squeaked, eyes bulging wide again. "We got no idea! I swear!"

Schramm didn't look so surprised. In fact, he seemed chagrined to be giving an answer he knew was going to sound like bullshit.

"It's true. We don't know," he said. "Maybe it was Kyle. He could've figured out that the scam with the Indian skull was Bill's idea . . . somehow. Other than that . . . ? Not a clue."

He shrugged miserably. He knew how it looked — and knew he'd only make it look worse if he tried to pull more suspects out of his butt.

Which was part of the reason I believed him. That and the fact that if Luchetti was play-acting the role of panicky, hapless would-be criminal, the man was a bronze-colored Brando.

I'd come so far and learned so much. Yet

the one thing I really needed to know remained a complete and utter mystery.

I thought I'd been zeroing in on the killer — and I'd been fooling myself.

"Uhhh . . . Alanis?" Victor said.

He was staring at my hand with a distressed expression on his face. I glanced down, expecting to see that I was letting the rags get too close to the flame again — perhaps even that they were already on fire. But that wasn't the problem at all.

There was no flame anymore.

The lighter had finally run out of fluid.

There you stand, watching for the fleet you launched, hoping to make your fortune. Remember how you prodded the ships away from shore with your long carrot sticks, already counting the money they'd bring back to you in your head? Well, you forgot to do one thing. Check. The. Weather. You were so overconfident, you sent your fleet out smack-dab in the middle of monsoon season . . . with no insurance! Let me tell you, it's worth the extra eighty bucks a month. Now you know. Too bad it's too late.

Miss Chance, *Infinite Roads to Knowing*

I looked at the dead lighter.

I looked at Schramm.

I looked at Luchetti.

I looked at Victor.

"It doesn't matter," I said.

"What?" said Victor.

"It doesn't matter that the lighter's dead. I'm not a killer, and neither are they." I looked at Schramm again. "So we can all stop pretending. Right, Jack?"

Schramm looked at *me.*

And looked at me.

And looked at me.

"Goddamn it," he muttered.

And he let Victor go.

As Victor walked over to stand beside me, I finally lowered the lighter and rags.

"Owwwwww," I moaned. I began flapping my arms to get the blood flowing again. "You have no idea how much that hurt."

"Oh, what a shame," Victor said. "And all

this time you were suffering, I was having *so* much fun thinking you were about to *set me on fire.*"

"Yeah," I said. "Good times."

"Who are you people anyway?" Schramm asked us. "No way you're cops."

I shook my head. "I'm a friend of Riggs's wife, Marsha. She's being charged with his murder. She didn't do it."

Schramm narrowed his eyes. "How can you be so sure?"

"Like I said: she's my friend."

Schramm looked like he was *this* close to scoffing. I guess he didn't think so highly of his friends.

"So are we gonna cut some kinda deal?" Luchetti said. "You keep quiet about what we've been doing, and we . . . you know . . . we . . . um . . ."

He turned to Schramm. Schramm just shrugged.

I said the obvious out loud.

"You two have nothing to bargain with, but that's all right. We'll make a deal with you anyway."

"We will?" Victor said under his breath.

"Yes. We will," I said. "All we care about is who killed Riggs. If it turns out his death had nothing to do with what's been going on out here, we'll have no reason to talk to the cops about it. So we won't. All we ask is that you clean up your mess and don't draw any attention to yourselves. Where there's smoke, there's fire. So no smoke. You understand me?"

Luchetti nodded tentatively — so tentatively that the nod turned into a shake of the head. "Not really."

"She means don't burn the house down," Schramm explained.

"Oh," Luchetti said. "Right."

"So, do we have a deal?" I asked.

Luchetti nodded with a lot more confidence this time. "Yes. Absolutely. Thank you."

I looked at Schramm.

"Deal," he said.

"Good. Let's go, Victor."

I spun on my heel and started walking quickly — but not *too* quickly — toward the back door. Victor fell in beside me. When we were still half a dozen steps from the door, I noticed him shifting his weight, turning his head.

"Don't look back," I whispered.

"What if they change their minds and jump us?" Victor whispered back.

"Exactly. I don't want to give them ideas."

We kept our gazes pointed straight ahead at the darkness outside as I slid the back door open. Then we were outside in the cool desert night, marching robotically away from the house.

"Can I look back now?" Victor said.

"No. But you can run if you want."

He wanted to. So I did, too.

"That," Victor said as I hit the gas and gunned us away from the house, "was the worst experience of my life."

"The night is young," I said.

Victor shot me a glare that said *not for me; this night is over.*

And it was for me, too, I had to admit. Where was there to go? What was there to do?

We'd solved the wrong crime — and used up all our leads in the process. My day was done. And so was my crusade.

I'd set out to help Marsha Riggs, and now there was a good chance she'd be going to prison.

I'd told myself I could be a do-gooder, yet I'd done bad bad *bad.*

I drove Victor to his apartment building on the west side of Berdache.

"What will you do next?" he asked as we sat out front in the Cadillac.

"For now, sleep. Tomorrow . . . we'll see.

That man I told you about — my mother's boyfriend Biddle — he used to have an expression: 'It's not just the bees you have to watch out for when you knock down their nest. It's the bears that come for the honey.' "

Victor blinked at me blankly for a moment.

"I think that might be a little too folksy for me after the day I just had," he eventually said. "What does it mean?"

"That you can't know what you're gonna get when you start stirring things up. Biddle meant it as a warning. But right now it's about the only hope I have to cling to."

"Your hope is . . . bears?"

I nodded.

Victor sighed.

"I still don't get it," he said.

He started to get out of the car.

"Hey," I said.

He stopped to look back at me.

"Thank you for your help, Victor."

"My pl—"

Victor stopped himself. He'd started to say "my pleasure," but even as exhausted as he was, he'd realized how untrue that would have been.

"You're welcome, Alanis," he said instead. "Let's talk tomorrow."

"Sure. Good night."

Victor nodded and got out of the car. I sat and watched him trudge slowly away.

He never looked back. I got the feeling he never would.

I'm a woman. I've been around a while. I know what "let's talk" means.

I put the car in gear and drove home alone.

I parked in the little lot behind the White Magic Five and Dime and cracked all the windows before getting out of the car. My dress still reeked of gasoline, and if the Cadillac didn't air out it was going to smell like a Texaco station for the next three weeks.

I stood in the lot a moment, gazing up at the stars and appreciating the fresh air and trying — and failing — not to think about the mess I'd made of things.

As has been the case so often in my life, it was the thinking that got me in trouble.

If I hadn't been lost in thought, I might have noticed movement in the shadows by the building. Might have sensed that I was being watched. Might have turned and run instead of simply standing there awaiting my fate. Might not have been surprised when someone stepped out of the darkness holding a gun.

Might have remembered, in other words, to be ready for the bears.

STABE · STAVEN

2

BASTONI · BATONS · WANDS · BASTOS

You thought and thought and thought about making a change; you agonized about stepping out into the world on a new adventure. For too long you hid behind the wall, gazing into your beloved bowling ball, but then you finally made the change — and your world flipped on its head. The walls crumbled down around you, and the bowling ball broke your nose. Looks like you forgot that "adventure" means "danger." No doubt you'll keep that in mind next time . . . if there is a next time.

Miss Chance, *Infinite Roads to Knowing*

The woman had a Glock in one hand — pointed at me.

In her other hand was a bottle — pointed at her lips. She was throwing down a long swallow of Bartles and Jaymes strawberry daiquiri.

"Betcha didn't see this coming, Joan Dixon," she said to me when she was through.

"Who's Joan Dixon?" someone else said.

Another woman — a stocky blond — lurched from the shadows by the White Magic Five and Dime. She was also holding a Bartles and Jaymes bottle.

No gun for her, though. She'd brought a softball bat.

"Some psychic," the first woman said, slurring the words into *thumb thigh-kick*. "Used to see her in the tabloids at the grocery store when I was a kid."

"Never heard of her," the blond said.

So these were my bears — Debbie Luchetti and Cathy Schramm. They were still dressed for a company picnic, in khaki shorts and colorful, loose-fitting blouses and sandals. Cathy should have had a Frisbee in her hand, not a semi-automatic pistol.

Which was still pointed at me. Cathy was swaying slightly, unsteady, yet her aim never wavered. Not that it mattered that much.

She was less than twenty yards away. With a Glock, even a drunk would get off enough shots to hit me if I tried to run. My only consolation: she hadn't started shooting yet, which meant they weren't just there to cover their husbands' tracks.

I looked beyond them at the back door of the building. It was closed, and there were no lights on upstairs.

I had to hope that Clarice was safe. And I had to make sure she stayed that way.

"You want me for something?" I said. "Whatever it is, I'll give it to you."

"Cool!" Cathy said with a lopsided grin. She jerked the gun to the side. "Let's go, then! That way!"

I started walking out of the lot.

"Girls' night out!" Debbie hooted, jabbing at the air with her bat.

As she and Cathy fell in behind me, I remembered how Bill Riggs had died. *Brains bashed out with a baseball bat,* Burby had said.

That was one more thing the twerp had got wrong.

I knew now it had been a softball bat.

They led me to a minivan parked on a darkened street around the corner. Cathy got in the back with me, her gun still levelled at my gut.

I had to sweep popcorn and cookie crumbs and a couple beaten Betty and Veronica comics off my seat before I could sit.

"Sorry about the mess," Cathy said. "Kids!"

Debbie climbed in behind the wheel. She put her Bartles and Jaymes in a cup holder. Her bat got the passenger seat. When she turned on the engine, the radio began blasting "Highway to Hell."

"KISS!" Debbie roared. "Yeah!"

She looked back at us, stuck out her tongue Gene Simmons–style, and made the sign of the horns with both hands.

Cathy gave her a "woo-hoo!" and started singing along with the song.

I didn't bother saying that the band was AC/DC and the psychic was *Jeane* Dixon. They wouldn't have heard me anyway.

Cathy and Debbie were rocking out. And they kept rocking out all the way across town.

Within half a mile, I knew where we were going. Cathy told Debbie to turn the radio off two blocks before we got there.

"Aww," Debbie groaned. "I love the Rolling Stones."

The song had been "Won't Get Fooled Again" by the Who.

Cathy shushed her.

"Sneaky time," she said.

Half a minute later, Debbie was parking the minivan in front of 1703 O'Hara Drive. The Riggs residence. I guess not pulling into the driveway qualified as being "sneaky."

"Be quiet," Cathy told me. She waggled the Glock. "Or I'll be loud."

"Good one! Bang!" Debbie giggled. "Ooo, speaking of which . . . gotta reload before we go."

She bent down and fiddled with something on the floor by her feet. When she straightened up again, she was holding two more bottles of Bartles and Jaymes. She handed one to Cathy, then took a long pull from the other.

"None for me?" I said.

"Maybe later," said Debbie.

Cathy snorted. "Yeah. Later."

They gave each other a smirky look that told me there wouldn't be any "later." Not for me.

Debbie reached out for her softball bat.

"All right," she said. "Let's get this party started."

I stayed quiet as the three of us walked around the side of the house. I didn't want Cathy getting loud — especially not with the Glock shoved into the small of my back.

I watched the neighboring houses out of the corners of my eyes but saw nothing. No light, no movement, no hope of a quick call to 911. Not that I necessarily wanted the cops showing up anyway. Given Debbie and Cathy's condition, there was no telling how they might react.

Thanks a million, Bartles and Jaymes.

"I was the one who picked this the other day," Debbie said proudly as we walked in the back door. "Seems like every time I sneak into the garage for a smoke, my three-year-old locks me out of the house. Speaking of which — you bring your American Spirits, Cathy?"

"Stay focused, Deb," Cathy said as she closed the door behind us and turned on the light in the kitchen. "We can stop at the 7-Eleven when we're done here."

"Ooo, yeah!" said Debbie. "Buffalo chicken rollers!"

She took a glugging, gulping pull on her bottled daiquiri that emptied half the bottle. Then she stretched out the softball bat and prodded me in the side with it.

"All right — where is it?" she said.

"Where is what?"

The prod turned into a jab. A hard one.

"I played ball in college, you know," Debbie said. "My senior year I batted .366 and hit 13 home runs."

"Sun Devils!" Cathy whooped.

"Sun Devils!" said Debbie.

They reached out their bottles and clinked them.

"I don't know what you're asking me to do," I said.

This time, Debbie used her bat to tap me on the top of the head.

It hurt.

"The backpack, biatch. We want it," Debbie said. "We know you were Riggs's girl-friend. That's why you were sniffing around Oak —"

"*Wife's* girlfriend," Cathy cut in.

"What?"

"Jack said she was Riggs's wife's girl-friend."

"Really? And all this time I thought you said 'Riggs's girlfriend.' "

"Maybe I did," Cathy said.

She belched. It smelled like strawberry Kool-Aid and hot dogs.

I decided not to breathe for a while.

"So Jack called you from Oak Creek," I said. "He told you what we talked about tonight."

"Our husbands called us," Debbie snarled, "to tell us about their latest screw-up."

"Which is why, yet again, the wives have to step in and bat cleanup," said Cathy.

Debbie cackled. "Good one!"

"They really don't know what you did here, do they?" I said.

"It's going to be a surprise," Cathy said.

"We're going to Cancun!" Debbie blurted out.

"Cancun, baby!" Cathy said.

They clinked bottles again.

"Let me guess," I said. "You knew about the scam your husbands were pulling with Riggs — and you thought they should cut Riggs out."

"Wimps," spat Cathy.

"Pussies," said Debbie.

"So — maybe over a couple daiquiris —

you decided to do it yourselves."

"Margaritas," said Debbie.

Cathy shook her head. "Whiskey sours."

"Oh, yeah," said Debbie.

"Only you couldn't find the money."

"We tried persuading Riggs to tell us," Cathy said. "But Debbie doesn't know her own strength."

"Thirteen home runs," Debbie said. "I've still got it."

"Fortunately, I recognized you at the picnic today," Cathy went on. "So we know where to go to get a second chance at that —"

"Blah blah blah!" Debbie cried. She poked my shoulder with the bat. "Show me the money!"

Cathy dug the gun into my back.

"Right!" she said. "Show us the money!"

Just my luck: I was about to die and everyone was doing their Cuba Gooding Jr. imitation.

I didn't have any choice. I was going to have to show them the money.

The most amazing thing about these two, I realized, was that their plan, such as it was, was actually going to work.

"All right. I *do* know where the backpack is," I said. "If I show you, you'll let me go?"

I had to ask, right?

"Of course," said Cathy.

"Absolutely," said Debbie.

They looked at each other and all but winked.

"This way," I said.

I led them into the living room, then up the hall to the closet.

"We looked in there," Cathy snapped as I opened the door.

"Not good enough," I said.

I bent down and lifted up the carpet, uncovering the trapdoor in the floor.

"Cool!" said Cathy.

"Open it," Debbie ordered me.

I didn't like kneeling anywhere near her while she had that bat in her hands, but I didn't think arguing would get me anywhere. And I could picture myself opening the trapdoor, then diving through it and hightailing it to the busted air vent I'd squirmed through a few days before.

"Sure," I said.

I unlatched the trapdoor and pulled it up.

The second it was open all the way, Debbie used her bat to shove me back out into the hallway.

She leaned forward and peeked down into the crawl space.

"It's too dark," she said. "I can't see anything."

"It's there," I said — and as soon as the words left my lips, I realized they might not be true.

Fletcher *said* he had returned the backpack. What kind of fool had I been to believe him?

Cathy walked over to the trapdoor and took a quick — *very* quick — look down. She might have a few four-packs of B&J in her, but that damn gun stayed steady as steel.

"Told you we should bring a flashlight," she said.

"No, you didn't," said Debbie.

Cathy thought about it a moment.

"Well, I meant to," she said.

"One of us is going to have to go down there," Debbie said.

Cathy jerked her head at me. "I need to guard her."

"I could guard her."

"With a bat?"

"You could give me the gun."

"It's my husband's gun."

"So?"

Cathy took yet another drink.

"I don't like cellars," she said.

"*I* don't like cellars," said Debbie.

"I could go," I offered.

Both women snorted.

"Fine. I'll go," Debbie said sourly. "But you owe me."

She lowered herself so she was sitting with her meaty legs dangling into the darkness. Then she reached down as far as she could with the bat.

There was a dull thud. She'd found the ground beneath her — which gave her the courage to drop down to it.

She disappeared into the black square of the trapdoor.

I got set to scramble to my feet and bolt for the back door. But Cathy was still watching me even as she called into the abyss.

"You okay, Deb?"

"I'm fine. It's just that — *ahhh*!"

"What?"

Debbie let out a nervous laugh.

"I think that dumb skull must be down here," she said. "I'm pretty sure I'm touch-ing it right now."

Cathy smiled. "That means that *is* Riggs's hiding place down there."

"Hey, you're right! So it's just a matter of —"

Debbie suddenly fell silent.

"What is it?" Cathy said.

There was another moment of silence. Then, more quietly than before, voice trembling, Debbie said, "There's something down here with me."

"Oh, come on."

"*Really,* Cathy. I heard something move."

"The dark's got you spooked, that's all. Don't freak out."

"Don't tell *me* not to freak out!" Debbie shouted. "I'm not freaking out! I'm — *ah-hhh! Ohhhhh! Eeeeeeee!*"

Debbie was freaking out. Which gave me the chance I'd been waiting for.

"Debbie, what's happening?" Cathy called down into the crawl space. *"Debbie!"*

At last she was distracted.

I launched myself at her and managed to get a grip on her wrist before she saw me coming. I pushed her gun hand up, and she squeezed off three rounds into the ceiling. Plaster rained down onto us as we struggled for control of the gun; Cathy was so intent on ripping her hand free from me, she finally dropped her daiquiri.

Even as Cathy and I struggled in the hallway, I could hear another fight down below in the crawl space. There were screams, curses, and the sounds of scuffling and body blows with blunt objects.

"Let go!" Cathy shrieked at me, giving me another sickening whiff of artificial straw-berry and Oscar Meyer. "Get your hands off me, bitch!"

Then she was suddenly flying backward and hitting the floor with a thud.

She'd slipped on the Bartles and Jaymes bottle.

Before she could get her bearings, I kicked her in the face — fortunately for me I'd decided to wear boots instead of sandals that afternoon — and her head snapped back and the Glock dropped from her hand.

I bent down and snatched up the gun just as someone clambered up through the trapdoor, softball bat in hand.

I whirled around and aimed.

"Whoa whoa whoa! I hope you're not still *that* mad at me!"

I stared in shock — but lowered the gun.

"Jesus," I said. "Fletcher."

He grinned at me.

"I keep telling you, Alanis," he said. "My friends call me GW."

STABE   STAVEN

BASTONI   1   BASTOS
BATONS   WANDS

Here it is again: the magic cucumber, aka the Ace of Wands. Once upon a time, it helped launch you on a bold quest — but now the situation is reversed. Is the hand of Fate snatching it back or telling you, "Hey, dummy! You've been using this thing upside down"? Either way, you've come to an ending, which is just another way of saying a new beginning.

Miss Chance, *Infinite Roads to Knowing*

"So . . . what now?" Fletcher asked me.

It took me a moment to process that.

We'd just finished a fight for our lives. I hadn't even caught my breath yet, and my ears were still ringing from the gunshots. What did Fletcher expect me to say? "Let's bake cookies"? He should have known what was next.

I listened for the sirens.

I didn't hear them yet.

"It'll be a few minutes before the cops get here," Fletcher said.

"Yeah?"

"So how about . . . ?" Fletcher nodded at the darkened pit he'd just crawled from. "You know."

"What? The backpack? That's evidence. It's what these two killed Bill Riggs for."

"Yeah, but —"

"Oh my god! Is *that* why you're here? You're still angling for the money?"

"No! I was worried about you! I knew I blew it with that Fixer thing, and I didn't want you poking around on your own."

The conversation woke Debbie up. She tried to lift her head, failed, and settled for staring into the carpet, groaning.

"How's the one down there?" I asked Fletcher.

I got an answer before he spoke.

Down in the crawl space, Cathy was throwing up.

"She'll live," Fletcher said.

"So were you watching this place or my place?"

"Your place."

Fletcher cocked his head, listening again for distant sirens.

"You know, the police won't need all that cash to wrap this up," he said.

"No."

"A few g's should be enough."

"No."

"Who knows? The cops might take a taste themselves. It happens all the time. So why shouldn't we — ?"

"Goddammit, Fletcher, don't make me say no again."

I looked from him to my right hand and back again. A little reminder for him: he was talking to a pissed-off woman holding a gun.

"Okay, okay," he said. "I could've taken the whole thing, you know. And I do believe I just saved your life. So a *little* gratitude would be appropriate."

"You're right. Thank you, Fletcher."

"Oh, come on, Alanis. You can do better than that."

"What do you want? Flowers?"

"I was thinking more like . . ." Fletcher rubbed his chin, then flashed me a grin. "Dinner."

His smile didn't last long.

We finally heard what we'd been waiting for.

Sirens.

The cops weren't Fletcher's favorite people, and he wasn't one of theirs. Yet he stayed there on the floor by the trapdoor, waiting for what was to come next, sticking by me when he could just grab the backpack and run.

He'd already fooled me not once but twice. But who was keeping score? Well, other than me?

GW Fletcher had just proved he wasn't *all* bad. Just 50 percent. Maybe even 49. And that was enough.

"You like Mexican?" I said.

■ ■ ■ ■

Fletcher and I were split up. We were thrown in separate police cars, then separate cells. Detective Burby showed up, and I was yelled at and threatened. I could only assume Fletcher was yelled at and threatened, too. But eventually someone — Debbie or Cathy or one of their husbands — cracked, and the evidence backed us up anyway.

The next morning, Burby had to let us go.

"I'm gonna be keeping my eye on you," he warned me the last time we were in the interview room together.

"You aren't going to be seeing much," I told him.

He scowled, probably thinking I was gloating, telling him I was too slick to get up to anything he could catch me at. But that wasn't what I'd meant at all.

I was ready for some peace and quiet.

I wasn't just a retired criminal now. I was a retired crime fighter.

Eugene and Clarice and Ceecee were waiting for me when I walked out into the little lobby.

The girls pressed in on either side and

wrapped their arms around me.

Eugene just stood there and smiled, which was the equivalent of a bear hug from him.

"Oh my god! I've been so worried!" Clarice said. "I can't believe someone tried to kill you *again*!"

"Is this going to happen all the time?" Ceecee asked me.

"No," I told her. "That's done."

The door behind me opened again, and Fletcher came out into the lobby. He walked around us, keeping his distance, moving fast.

Group hugs were definitely not his thing.

"I'll see you later for that Mexican," he said to me with a wink.

Then he was out the door and gone.

"Ooo," Ceecee said. "You hooked up with a hottie *in jail*?"

Clarice shook her head at me. "Some role model you are."

"I'm going to get better. I promise." I turned to Eugene. "Is everything set over at the county jail?"

He nodded and gave me another smile.

"Excellent," I said. "Come on, girls. I'll tell you the whole story on the way."

I remembered the role model thing as we headed toward the door.

"Well," I said, "maybe not the *whole*

story . . ."

Marsha was crying when they let her out of the county lockup — the good kind of crying. They were tears of joy, relief, gratitude.

Clarice and Ceecee didn't know Marsha well, but they joined in the second they saw her.

Me, though — I'm a hard-bitten, world-weary cynic. It took me two seconds.

Eugene just stood to the side with a strained smile on his face. There was weeping and hugging and lots and lots of emotion, so he looked like he should be wearing one of those corny old bumper stickers.

I'D RATHER BE GOLFING.

Still, he put up with all the blubbering as he drove us back to Berdache.

Marsha finally started wiping away the tears as we pulled up in front of the White Magic Five and Dime. I'd already told her she was welcome to stay there as long as she wanted.

"Is it really over, then?" she asked me. "It's all done?"

"Yes," I said. "It's all done."

But that wasn't entirely true.

There was one more loose end to tie up.

Victor and I walked around the charred

ruins of the house we'd almost gone up in smoke in the night before.

"We had a deal," Victor said. "I can't believe they burned it down anyway."

"I can. Their wives probably told them to — to cover their tracks on the building scam." I shrugged. "Or they just decided it was too much of a pain in the ass to mop up all that gasoline."

"Oh, well. It was a piece-of-junk house anyway. Hopefully they'll build something better here now. A *real* home."

"Yeah. Maybe sometimes a little fire does the world a favor. Come on."

I headed toward the next lot over. It was empty except for a few low, spiky cactuses and a large, thick patch of dull green bushes.

"How are you holding up, Alanis?" Victor asked as he tagged along. "I'm surprised you're out here after everything that happened last night."

"Oh, I'm fine. Ready for a break from the trouble business, though."

"I'd say you've earned it."

We reached the bushes, and I squatted down and peered into the dark tangle of overlapping branches.

"So . . . last night you said we should talk. Was there something you wanted to say to me?"

"That can wait till later."

"I think I'd rather hear it now," I said, without looking up at Victor. "As long as we're taking care of unfinished business."

"All right."

Victor crouched down beside me. He kept his eyes on the bushes, too.

"You know I've had doubts about you, Alanis. I didn't think you were someone my mother and I could trust. And, well . . . you *do* tend to lie a lot."

I kept looking straight ahead.

Something shifted in the shadows far back in the bushes.

"But," Victor said, "I have never seen anyone stick their neck out for a friend the way you did for Marsha Riggs. You are an amazingly loyal and brave and tenacious person. And, yes — you still scare me. But I like you, Alanis. I like you a lot. And I'm going to try to work on the being scared part."

I didn't — couldn't — say anything for a moment.

"That's . . . not what I was expecting," I finally said.

"What *were* you expecting?" Victor asked.

I shushed him.

The movement in the shadows was coming closer.

"Mew," it said.

A few seconds later, a tabby as big and blocky as a microwave oven came trotting out of the bushes. It began rubbing itself against our knees and thighs, purring so loudly it sounded like an outboard motor.

"My god, that's a big cat," Victor said.

"And a lucky one. Come on, buddy. You're going home."

I picked up Son of Kong, and we headed back to Berdache.

Life was quiet. I actually managed to keep the store open for eight hours at a time. It helped that I wasn't running around chasing murderers. Plus I had a new assistant manager backing me up: Marsha Kurland. (Marsha had gone back to her maiden name. It was time, she decided, to leave the Riggs part of her life behind.)

I was still helping my mother's former clients/victims, but in small ways now. A discount here, a free reading there, advice, a smile. I stayed out of Burby's way as much as I could, I tried not to think about the Grandis, and I started paying more attention to when Clarice went to bed and whether her homework was done or not.

"Bored yet?" I asked my mother.

An air bubble escaped from the little

pirate ship that housed her ashes at the bottom of the fish tank.

I took that as a yes.

"Good," I said.

The front door opened, and I turned to face the White Magic Five and Dime's final customer of the day. It was almost time to turn the sign off and head upstairs and make dinner for Clarice and continue boring my mother's restless spirit to ghostly tears.

"And what might you be looking for this evening?" I asked.

I was looking at a seventyish black man with a beard and glasses and a wry smile on his handsome, weathered face.

"You, actually," he said.

The voice. The smile.

It was impossible — yet instantly I knew it was true.

It took all my old training to stay calm, keep breathing, not faint, not scream.

I smiled back.

"Hello, Biddle," I said.

ACKNOWLEDGMENTS

This book would not have been possible without the able assistance (and ample patience) of Toni LoTempio, Mar Ortmann, Christian Falco, Danielle Burby, Josh Getzler, Rebecca Zins, and Terri Bischoff. Thank you!

ABOUT THE AUTHORS

Steve Hockensmith (California) is the author of the Pride and Prejudice and Zombies novels *Dawn of the Dreadfuls* (Quirk Classics, 2010) and *Dreadfully Ever After* (Quirk Classics, 2011). His book *Holmes on the Range* (Minotaur Books, 2006) was a finalist for the Edgar, Shamus, and Anthony Awards for Best First Novel. He also writes a series of middle-grade mysteries with "Science Bob" Pflugfelder. For more information, visit his website at stevehockensmith.com.

Lisa Falco (Los Angeles) received her first tarot deck at the age of eight years old. She holds degrees from both Northwestern University and Cal State University Northridge, and is the author of *A Mother's Promise* (Illumination Arts, 2004).